Sarah Conley

Sarah Conley

A NOVEL BY

ELLEN GILCHRIST

LITTLE, BROWN AND COMPANY
Boston   New York   Toronto   London

First Edition

The characters and events in this book are fictitious.
Any similarity to real persons, living or dead,
is coincidental and not intended by the author.

Library of Congress Cataloging-in-Publication Data

Gilchrist, Ellen
    Sarah Conley : a novel / Ellen Gilchrist. — 1st ed.
        p.   cm.
    ISBN 0-316-31477-3
    I. Title.
PS3557.I34258S27   1997
813'.54—dc21   97-8207

            10 9 8 7 6 5 4 3 2 1

                    MV-NY

        Published simultaneously in Canada
    by Little, Brown & Company (Canada) Limited

    Printed in the United States of America

For Roger Donald

The crisis consists precisely in the fact
that the old is dying and the new cannot
be born; in this interregnum a great
variety of morbid symptoms appears.

Antonio Gramsi

NURTURE, F, Mf, norreture, norriture; the sum of the
influences modifying the genetic potentialities of the organism.

Sarah Conley

CHAPTER I

It was a warm spring day. All the windows were open in the room where the editors of the *Tyler Favorite* sat. Mrs. Becker sat at her desk with her cocker spaniel at her feet and two fans blowing on her shoulders. The papers on the desk were held down with an assortment of paperweights. A rock, a bronze spaniel on point, a heavy glass ashtray full of half-smoked cigarettes. One was burning in the ashtray now and Mrs. Becker adjusted the fan so that it blew farther up into the air. She was reading the column Sarah Conley had written that morning and she was laughing.

Mr. Becker sat five feet away at a matching desk. His fans were on the floor and papers were stacked haphazardly on his desk. In the midst of the papers he was adding up figures in an account book. He had inherited the *Favorite* from his father and he had kept it alive for twenty years and he was going to keep it alive if he had to set the print himself. The people of Tyler, Kentucky, loved their newspaper and he loved giving it to them and was going to keep on doing it. Witness the publicity they had been getting from the column the young girl sitting at the third desk was giving them. She was the daughter of a widowed friend, and she could write like a dream. She had only been writing the column for a few months and already the mail was full of praise for her work. "No one believes she writes them," Mrs. Becker said, and got up and took the paper she was holding and laid it down in front of him. "Read this. I wouldn't change a word, would you?"

At the third desk Sarah was drinking a Coke and smoking a cigarette she had borrowed from Mrs. Becker. She was fourteen years old and already she was making fifteen dollars a week for two afternoons' work. She would not always be poor. That much was clear. All she had to do was keep on going the way she was going and she would never, never, never be poor.

Sarah was not poor now but she was worried about it because her father had died six months before and her mother was worrying about money. All her mother talked about was money. Her father had died suddenly of a heart attack and there was a mortgage on their house and all her mother talked about *to anyone who would listen* was money, money, money.

"I don't know what we'll do about the house payments," she told people who came by to visit. "I don't know what we'll do about the car," she told Sarah's grandparents when they phoned from Tennessee. "I don't know what I'll do about Sarah's college," she told Mr. and Mrs. Becker when they came to call.

"Let Sarah come down to the *Favorite* and work for us in the afternoons," Mrs. Becker had suggested. "She's a big, strong girl. She'll be able to help." She reached out her hand and drew Sarah to her side. "I was younger than Sarah when my father died and there were five of us. At least you only have one child. It will be all right, Sally. Anyone in town will give you a job. There's an opening for a secretary at the high school. Go apply for that. George Minette would hire you in a minute. It would be good for you to get out of the house." Mrs. Becker was a distant cousin of Sally Conley's. She took over Sally's transition from a married lady to a widow. The job at the high school was duly applied for and won. And fourteen-year-old Sarah was hired to come to the *Favorite* office two afternoons a week to help out and clean up ashtrays and walk the dog and write want ads. Less than a week later she wrote her first column and turned it in and the typesetter set it in print and put it in the paper. By the second week they had thought of a name for the column and added a photograph of Sarah to the byline. The fourth week a radio station in Nashville picked up the piece and read it aloud on a morning show. The station mailed Sarah a check for ten dollars.

Mr. Becker read the column Mrs. Becker had handed him. When he was finished he called Sarah over to his desk. "This is very good, Sarah. Now I think you should take the rest of the afternoon and go over to the swimming pool and do a catch-up piece on how the pool is going. Here." He wrote a note on a piece of stationery. "Take this over there and tell them I sent you to write a story about the pool. How long has it been open now?"

"Two weekends and a week."

"Have you been there yet?"

"No. I haven't had time."

"Well, go on. Your first columns helped raise the money. They should give you a lifetime pass. Wait a minute." He reached in his pocket and brought out a twenty-dollar bill. "Buy a season ticket for the newspaper. A summer's pass. I want several more columns about the pool."

Sarah took the money and the piece of paper and put them in the pocket of her shirt. Ever since she had begun the job at the *Favorite* she had been wearing shirts with pockets. Her father had worn shirts with pockets when he went to work in the mornings. He was an engineer who had worked for the government inspecting road jobs. Every morning he had dressed in clean khaki pants and a white shirt with two pockets. One for his papers and one for his pens. He had worn work boots and a wide-brimmed hat and had been a handsome, laughing man. It seemed impossible to believe that he was dead. One minute he was alive and the world was safe. The next day he was dead and her mother couldn't stop crying and saying they were poor.

"Where did you go?" Mr. Becker asked.

"I'm sorry. I was just thinking about something."

"Take a notebook with you and think about writing another piece as good as this one on my desk." Mr. Becker tried to look businesslike. He had known Sarah's father all his life. It made him sad too. It made the whole town sad.

"La, la, la," Mrs. Becker said, and took Sarah's arm and led her to the door. "Out you go. Enough of being in this stuffy office on a beautiful May afternoon. We'll see you next Wednesday."

Sarah walked down the wooden stairs of the building and across a vacant lot to Cherry Street. She had a notebook in her hand and two pencils clipped to it. She had gotten out of school early to go to her job and she was hoping that her mother wouldn't be home yet. It was too nice an afternoon to watch her mother look sad or to answer her questions. She hurried to her house and went in the unlocked kitchen door and found a bathing suit and cap and put them in a bag and stopped in the kitchen to eat an apple and a piece of bread with cheese. She left a note on the kitchen table. "Mr. Becker sent me to the swimming pool to write a story. I'll be home when I'm finished. Don't Worry!"

Then she went out the back door. She felt wonderful as she left the house. She felt as if her heart was expanding, getting fuller and fuller until it would burst like a balloon. No, her heart would not stop. Her heart would go on forever. Mr. and Mrs. Becker loved her column about the trees. She had another one to write and she was going swimming.

Sarah's father had taught her to swim when she was four years old. She was a fast, strong swimmer who had done her swimming in rivers and lakes. Only a few times in her life had she been in a swimming pool. A swimming pool was a wonderful new addition to the town and her column had helped raise the money to finish it. She had been wanting to ask her mother if she could go, but she hated to ask for money for anything. Asking for money, even for lunch at school, could set off a burst of crying and things she didn't want to hear. "We have to be so careful. They could cut our lights off. I know you want to have more than fifty cents but I have to watch every cent. When the lights go out you would hate me for not being careful." Things like that. Well, now I'm going and not just as a person going swimming. I'm a reporter on my way to get a story.

She walked down Main Street to where it turned into the new street that led to the pool. It was in an undeveloped section. The only house nearby was a white two-story mansion at the top of Main Street. A house no one had been living in for several years. Sarah glanced at the house and noticed a car in the driveway. Also, there was a woman standing on the lawn. Maybe someone moved in, Sarah thought. Someone rich will have that house. They'll never have to worry about money.

The office of the pool was a window behind which Stephanie Marks was sitting on a stool selling tickets. Through the fence Sarah could see there were about ten people in the pool and several more sitting around the edge taking sunbaths.

"I'd like to have a season ticket for the newspaper office," Sarah said to Stephanie. "Mr. Becker wants me to write some more columns about the pool."

"You ought to get a discount for that," Stephanie said. "Let me find the manager. Mr. and Mrs. Becker aren't going swimming, are they?" She laughed. "They're a little old for that."

"I don't know. Here's the money and a letter. That's all I know about it. May I go in?"

"Sure, go in. There's a footbath you have to step in. It's chlorine. Be sure and step in it. We're worried about athlete's foot."

"Where is it?"

"At the door from the dressing room to the pool. Wait a minute. I'll show you. No one's coming for another hour anyway. They never get here until four-thirty." Stephanie left her post and led Sarah to the girls' dressing room. It was a large concrete square with curtained dressing booths and wooden benches. The curtains were bright green shower curtains on rods. The whole place smelled divinely of chlorine.

"This is wonderful," Sarah said. "This is so nice."

"Wait till you're in the water. I'll come swimming in a while if I can. I have a bathing suit under this playsuit." Stephanie held up her skirt, and Sarah could see the suit.

Sarah changed into her blue wool bathing suit. It was a Catalina. Her mother had bought it for her right before her father died. It was sort of tight now but Sarah loved it. It was a two-piece so it didn't matter if it was a little tight. She'd never buy me a Catalina now, Sarah thought. Well, I just won't gain any weight.

She walked out the open door that led to the pool. At the corner she dutifully stepped into the little pool with its slippery Clorox mixture. She looked down at her feet, watched the edges turning white, then stepped out and walked onto the concrete deck surrounding the pool. There was a girl she had never seen before sitting on the edge of the pool near the diving boards. She was sitting on the concrete edge with her feet dangling in the water. She was tall and blond and pretty and happy looking. She had on a white one-piece suit with the little Catalina swimmer on the hip. Her hair was wet and slicked down behind her ears and she was holding a kickboard. She's waiting for something to happen, Sarah decided. I know that look.

Sarah went to the deep end and climbed up on the low diving board. Her father had taught her dives on a pier in the river. He had made a springboard out of two-by-fours and practiced with her until she was perfect. She tested the board on the pool several times, then dove in with a beautiful clean dive. She swam to the end of the pool and back. Then she pulled herself out of the pool and did a back dive off the diving board. Then she swam twenty laps without stopping, doing a perfect Australian crawl. She and her father had swum miles together in the lake or when they went to the river near her grandfather's house in Tennessee.

Sarah pulled herself up the ladder and sat down on the edge of the pool about three feet away from the new girl.

"That was great swimming," the girl said. "I'm Eugenie Moore. We just moved here, which is why I'm not in school. I live up there." She pointed to the white house on the hill. "We just moved in. I've been working all day trying to get my room fixed up. What's your name? How old are you?" She smiled a beautiful wide smile at Sarah, then looked down and giggled.

"I'm Sarah Conley," Sarah said. "I'm fourteen. How old are you?"

"Fourteen. I'll be in the ninth grade. What are the schools like here? My mother's going crazy. She thinks the schools won't be any good."

"They're wonderful schools. I write for the newspaper here and I'm fourteen. That's how good the English teachers are. My cousin's the English teacher in the high school. We'll have her next year. So why did you have to move here?"

"Because of him." She pointed to a tall man in khaki pants standing behind the chain-link fence looking at them. "That's my father. He makes us follow him to the ends of the earth. He's got coal mines in Tennessee so we had to move here so he won't have to drive so much. My mother will probably not recover. We've moved six times in ten years. This move is the last straw." He was watching them, but Eugenie didn't turn around to look at him. "I'm mad at him."

"Why? Because you moved?"

"No. Because he wants me to be fat. Well, let's go talk to him." She stood up. Sarah couldn't believe how developed she was for fourteen. She had breasts and little hips and a stomach. Her stomach stuck out of the white bathing suit but she didn't seem to care. She was so sure of herself. Sarah had never met a girl who was so sure of herself.

Eugenie's father stood watching them, a big grin on his face. Whatever was going on between them was a joke. Later, Sarah would know, the Moores made a joke of everything, but for now she just knew something interesting was happening. Something terribly, very, very interesting. The most interesting thing that had happened to her in years, perhaps forever.

"This is my new friend, Sarah Conley," Eugenie said. "This is Douglas Moore, my father. He said I'd meet someone but I didn't believe it. I thought I'd be alone the rest of my life."

"Hello, Sarah," he said. "Are you the girl who has the column in the paper?"

"Yes. I am. That's why I'm here, to write another column about the pool. I think it's great. I love the water. The water's wonderful."

"My construction company built it. I'm glad you approve. There wasn't as much money as we needed. I wish we could have made it longer."

"It's long enough. I've only been in a pool three times in my life. It's funny to have to turn around." Sarah liked this man named

Douglas Moore. The khaki pants, the white shirt. It was as though her father were standing there.

"Well, don't keep watching us," Eugenie said. "I'm fine. See, I have a friend with me now. I'll be home after a while."

"Bring Sarah with you," Douglas said. "Come home with her, Sarah. We'll feed you supper. The cook is frying chicken and we'll make ice cream." He smiled and let go of the chain-link fence and smiled again and turned and left.

"Well," Eugenie said. "Do you want to swim some more or sunbathe?"

"My father died last year. He wore khakis like that. If you knew what that was like you'd be nice to him."

"I'm nice to him. I just don't let him rule me. That's all he thinks about, is dying. He has more life insurance than God. We have so much life insurance we can hardly buy clothes or furniture for the houses he keeps buying. All he does is worry about life insurance."

"I wish my father had had some. We were left with debts. He's right about that, Eugenie. You can't know what it's like."

They were very near each other. Eugenie squinted her eyes together. She looked deep into Sarah's face. She looked as if she was terribly, deadly sorry, either for Sarah's loss or for the direction the conversation had been taking.

"Let's swim," she said. "I used to be on a swim team. I heard they were going to have one here this summer. If they don't, Dad's going to start one and be the coach. Come on, let's swim laps."

They swam until six o'clock. They went together into the dressing room and took showers and fooled around getting dressed. Stephanie Marks came in and told Sarah her mother was on the phone. Sarah went into the office and picked up the receiver. She held it away from her ear, sighed, then listened. "I'm sorry. I'm writing something for Mr. Becker. I have to finish it. And I met a new girl, she lives in the old Harrison house. They just moved here from Illinois. Well, I'm going by her house first. They asked me to have supper with them. I'll be home by seven-thirty or eight. I swear I will. Okay, goodbye."

She handed the receiver back to Stephanie. "She's so nervous about me it's unbelievable. She hovers over me."

"Your dad died," Stephanie said. "No wonder she acts that way."

Sarah went back to the dressing room. Eugenie was sitting on a wooden bench waiting for her. "I heard you talking to her," she said. "You talk to your mother as bad as I talk to my dad."

"Let's go," Sarah said. "I think you're right, Eugenie. Either you let them rule you or you fight back. That's it. I wish I could write about that for the paper but Mr. Becker would never put it in."

"Write it anyway." Eugenie was very close to Sarah. She looked deep into her eyes. "To hell with all of them."

They walked up the hill by a path that was a hundred years old. The Harrison house sat on a site that had been one of the first homesteads in the county. The path had been worn by goats and horses and carts long before it had become a shortcut to town. They walked along with the scrub land beside them blooming with bluebells and Queen Anne's lace and small yellow waxy flowers of several varieties. Sarah led the way, carrying her bag over her shoulder. Eugenie followed. "Pretend we're in the Pyrenees," Sarah said. "I did a report last year on the Pyrenees. This is probably about what it looks like there." They were huffing by the time they reached Eugenie's lawn. They stopped for a minute to rest. "Where are the Pyrenees?" Eugenie asked. "What country are they in?"

"In the south of France where it meets Spain. I'm going there someday. When I can, I'm going all over the world. But I wish I could go this summer."

"I don't like to go anywhere," Eugenie said. "I'd just like to stay in one place long enough to get my clothes put away."

They walked across the lawn to a side porch with a swing and a covered latticework arbor. Eugenie's mother came out the door to meet them. Her name was Janet. She was a sweet-looking woman with a worried face. Her hair was soft and blond and her eyes were a deep liquid blue. She took Sarah's hand and held it and drew her down onto the swing. They talked for a few minutes and then Janet insisted on calling Sarah's mother and introducing herself. "After dinner we'll drive you home and meet your mother," Janet said when she returned to the swing. "Now I have to go and see about dinner. You can help Douglas with the ice cream if you like. He's turning it on the back stairs."

They walked through the house. Furniture was still sitting in corners. Rugs were still rolled up and tied with rags. The house looked like a stage set. "This looks like backstage last year when we did a play at the high school auditorium," Sarah said. "As if anything could happen. As though everything is not already fixed."

"You wouldn't like it if you had to be the one to help put everything away. Which is my fate for the weekend."

"I'll help," Sarah said. "I'll come over and help all weekend."

"Eugenie." It was Douglas Moore calling from the back porch. "Come and turn this ice cream. Bring Sarah back here. I want to talk to her some more."

They had dinner together in the dining room. There was fried chicken and corn on the cob and fresh green beans cooked with small white potatoes. There was cornbread, dripping with butter, and iced tea and the homemade peach ice cream for dessert. It was after eight o'clock when they finished eating. Then they all got into the Moores' car and drove over to Sarah's house to ask her mother if she could spend the night.

"Eugenie has to start school here in the morning," Mr. Moore explained to Sally Conley. "It would mean so much to her if Sarah could go with her. I know you don't know us but I promise you your child will be as safe as though she were in your arms." He was a charming man and he charmed Sally into agreeing. The Moores sat on the porch talking to Sally and hearing about her husband's death, and Eugenie and Sarah went into Sarah's room and collected her clothes for school the next day. Suddenly, with Eugenie sitting on her bed, Sarah was ashamed of her possessions. Her home seemed so small, so old, so usual and uninteresting. "My mom and dad have lived here since they got married," she said, pulling open drawers to find clothes to wear. "We would have bought a larger house if Daddy hadn't died. We were talking about it all the time. We wanted a new house that we would build. Well, that didn't happen."

"This house is perfect," Eugenie said. "I feel good here. Come on. Get some clothes and let's go home. I have an idea."

"What is that?"

"I think we can sleep out on the roof of the garage. I went out there last night and it's almost flat. It's right outside my bedroom window. I love to sleep outside. I like to feel the universe raining down on me when I sleep. It's good to stay near the stars."

"I've never slept outside," Sarah said. "I don't think I've ever slept beneath the stars."

"You have to keep remembering where you are in space and time," Eugenie said. "Dad taught me that. Otherwise you'll spend your life being afraid to die."

At ten-thirty they went to bed. At eleven they heard Douglas walking around the house turning off the lights. At eleven-fifteen they climbed out the bedroom window onto the garage roof. Eugenie climbed out first and Sarah handed her things through the window. Two blankets, two pillows, a radio attached to an extension cord.

They fixed pallets on the flattest part of the roof. They put the radio between their pillows. Sarah tuned it in to station WWL New Orleans and the soothing voice of Dick Martin came on talking about jazz. "I write to him and ask him to play songs," Sarah said. "So far he hasn't played one but I think it's because I can't listen to it every night."

"What are you going to do when you grow up?" Eugenie asked.

"I'm already doing it," Sarah said. "I'm going to be a reporter and write for newspapers. I never wanted to do a thing but that. What do you want to do?"

"I'm going to be a doctor. I'll marry another doctor and then we might go overseas and save people in Africa or maybe just stay here or live in Illinois where we used to live. I'm not sure about that. But I'm not going to have children. I've made up my mind to that. You should have seen my cousin when she was going to have her baby. She looked like a freak in the circus."

"I don't want any either," Sarah agreed. "I don't want them growing inside of me. It might kill me. My mother almost died when she had me. It's a miracle she didn't die. I don't think we have the right kind of bodies for having children. I think you need big hips."

"It's disgusting to think about it." Eugenie moved nearer to Sarah and put her hand upon her waist. "Talk about something else. Say you are so glad you met me. The minute I saw you I wanted to be your friend."

"I always get lucky about meeting people I need to know," Sarah said. "Oh, God, look at those stars. They seem so near to us. It's wonderful to look at them."

"It's a funny thing. If I sleep outside and look at the stars I am not afraid. But if I'm inside a dark room I can barely sleep for being so afraid. I have to have a light on to go to sleep."

"Maybe you have a scientific mind," Sarah said. "And need to see what's going on. The dark stands for ignorance. My editor, Mr. Becker, told me that. I think about it all the time. See, you probably want the light so you can see things, not because you're afraid."

"I'm afraid all right," Eugenie laughed. "You ought to be here when it happens. I think things are in the room."

"Then turn on the lights," Sarah decreed. "Sleep with them on. Who gives a damn?"

"What the hell," Eugenie agreed. "Who gives a damn."

CHAPTER 2

In the morning they woke in Eugenie's double bed. They had come back inside the room around two in the morning. It was six-thirty when Sarah woke. She slipped out of the bed and went into the hall and found the bathroom and washed her face and hands and combed her hair. Then she slipped back into Eugenie's room and dressed and went downstairs, meaning to sit on the porch until the household woke. Mr. Moore was in the kitchen making coffee and boiling water in a skillet for poaching eggs. "Sit down, Sarah," he said to her. "Join me for breakfast. I can't do a thing with the people in this house. They'd sleep all day if no one woke them. Do you like poached eggs?"

"I've never had one. We scramble ours. My father used to like them fried."

"I'm sorry you lost him." He was quiet for a long while. Long enough so that Sarah knew it was not just something he was saying. He was thinking about it. He was suffering it for her. "I'm going to have some bacon done here in a minute. Get the orange juice out of the refrigerator and pour yourself a glass. There we go, now we're railroading." He lifted two strips of bacon from a pan and put them on a piece of paper sack he had waiting. He broke two more eggs into the skillet of boiling water and pulled open the oven door and brought out a pan of toast that looked like a child's painting. Each piece of toast had four pats of butter arranged in a square. The toast was dripping with butter.

"What's the cheerleading situation around here?" he asked, when he had put the toast on a plate and added the bacon and eggs and handed it to Sarah. He took his own plate and sat down beside her. "We have to find Eugenie a spot on the cheerleading team or she'll probably end up being an ax murderer." He laughed hilariously at the thought and then looked very seriously at Sarah. "We had to move here. I had to get closer to the place where I'm making money but I can't get any of them to understand that. When do they try out for the cheerleading squad? Who's in charge of that? Is there anyone I can talk to?"

"We try out in the fall. I was a junior high cheerleader. I can let her try out with me. We can practice this summer. The cheers are easy. You just have to be popular and pretty. She's so pretty, I bet she won't have any problem if she wants it."

"How many do they have on the squad?"

"I don't know. I think they have as many girls as they want to. I never thought about it much. I just always got to do it if I wanted to. I used to take dance classes from Miss Kay and that sort of helps."

"Who is Miss Kay?"

"This friend of my mother's. Her dance school is by the bakery. Eugenie could take lessons there this summer. I would take them if we could afford them but we can't afford it now."

"We'll see about that. How is that poached egg? How do you like it?" He watched as Sarah cut into the egg and let it run onto the buttered toast. She cut off a piece and ate it.

"It's delicious," she said. "It's wonderful."

Eugenie and her mother appeared sleepily in the kitchen and ate a piece of toast and had some orange juice and then everyone got dressed and Mrs. Moore took the girls to their school.

Two weeks later Sarah and Eugenie were enrolled in Kay's School of Dance for the summer session in tap, ballet, acrobatics, and cheerleading. Sarah knew the Moores were paying for the lessons but she felt she was earning them by making sure Eugenie was elected cheerleader in the fall. It was the beginning of Douglas Moore's paying for things for her. She never bothered about it. She never felt bad about it. She worked hard and made good grades and the universe provided for her needs. By the time he paid her tuition to Vanderbilt she took his largesse for granted. As she did the summer trips they took to Washington, D.C., and Mammoth Cave and even once to Colorado to see the mountains. "You're over there more than you're here," her mother complained down through the next four years. "You spend more nights with them than you do with me."

"I have to," Sarah would reply. "I have to have something to write about in my column."

CHAPTER 3

Ten-fifteen in the morning, January 10, 1996.

Sarah came into the office ten minutes late. The offices of *Time* magazine occupy four floors of the Time-Life building on the Avenue of the Americas at 51st Street. In the three years Sarah had been at *Time* she had had three offices. She had been in the large corner office for six months. "I put out fires," she told her friends. "I come in and clean up other people's messes. I go to meetings and talk on the phone and try not to get mad at anyone. It's a waste of energy. I meant to go to Pakistan to write about child labor factories. But instead I got caught up in meetings about the cover. We spent two weeks trying to redesign the cover. Meanwhile, *Life* magazine got to Pakistan first and did the story."

Sarah complained constantly about her job, but it was more an affectation than a considered complaint. She wasn't sure how she felt about being an editor. Sometimes she hated the idea and other times she secretly liked thinking she had to wear better shoes to the office. Several mornings lately she had woken up thinking about what shoes to wear. That's bad, she would chide herself. That's not what I came here to do.

Worrying about shoes, however, was not the reason she was late this morning. She was late because her thirty-two-year-old boyfriend was having a crisis and she had stayed to calm him down. "A writer is someone who writes," she told him. "So either do that or don't do it. Write about your little crisis. Satirize the letter she wrote you. Not that it needs any help. Obviously the editor is a chain-smoker who's never had an orgasm. It's a classic anal-retentive epistle. She just got a divorce. I heard that recently." Sarah was dressing as she talked. The young lover had been up all night in a rage because the *New Yorker* had turned down his story. "The *New Yorker* turns down everyone," Sarah continued. "That's what they do. Take the woman out to lunch and pick her brain or better yet, send it somewhere else and go to work to write another one. I have to go, Robert. I'm already late." She pulled on gloves and touched him on the cheek and turned to leave.

"It's easy for you to say," he said, but he was cheering up, she could tell. "You're successful."

"Well, I didn't get this way by letting sixty-year-old women at the *New Yorker* jerk my string. Write a satire about her, then take her out to lunch and see if you knew who she was from the letter."

"What a shrink you would have been, Sarah. Did you ever think of going to medical school?"

"I'm leaving. Write something. It will cure you. I'll read it when I get home." She was out the door and down the elevator and out onto the street and found a taxi and looked at her watch and wondered for a minute if she shouldn't get rid of Robert and then she put him out of her mind and went to work.

"Sorry I'm late," she told her secretary. "What's up?"

"Someone called you from Nashville," the secretary said. "A Doctor McAllen. He said it was important. He said he was a friend."

"When?"

"The call was here when I came in. Then he called back a few minutes ago. I told him you were on your way in. He sounded . . . well . . ."

"What?"

"Worried. Nice. I don't know." She picked up a yellow slip from a stack of them on the desk and handed it to Sarah. Sarah took it and slipped off the shoes she had worn and sat down behind her desk.

"Would you get me some coffee, Jane? With milk, no sugar. I

need to call him. They were my best friends, years ago, at Vanderbilt. He married my childhood friend."

"Sure." Jane disappeared and Sarah picked up the phone and called the number. The phone rang three times, then he answered.

"Jack, is that you?"

"I'm sorry to have called your office. I got the number from Jimmy. He's fine, by the way. He said to tell you hello. Are you well? Is everything all right with you?"

"Yes. I have a new job actually. I'm an editor, did Jimmy tell you that?" She laughed. It had been fifteen years since she had heard his voice and it was as if no time had passed. She pulled off her glasses and, carrying the phone, walked to a window. "What can I do for you?" she asked. She laughed again. "Or did you just call me?"

"It's bad news, Sarah. Eugenie is dying. She's very ill. She wants to see you. I wanted her to call but she made me do it. Because of the letter she wrote you after the book came out. I'm making a mess of this."

"No, you aren't. How sick? What kind of dying?"

"Cancer. Acute lymphoma. It's been almost a year. We didn't think it would go so fast. She's fine mentally. Will you come to see her? We can send you a ticket. If you could come."

"I don't need an airline ticket. Of course I'll come. I'm stunned, immobilized. I can't believe this."

Jane appeared in the door with Sarah's coffee. She was followed by a second girl, carrying a file of papers. "I will call you back in two minutes," Sarah said. "Can you let me call you back? I need to clear this room. I don't want to talk with all these people here."

"Of course. I'll be here all morning. They'll put you through. Thank you, Sarah. It was hard for me to call."

"Don't say that. It's just us, Jack. Nothing could make us strangers."

Sarah stood up, pushed the phone to off, shook her head from side to side. She kept shaking her head, very small tight movements.

"What is it?" Jane asked. "What happened?"

"The worst thing," Sarah told her. "The thing we don't believe. The thing we hate. The thing we dread. A friend is dying. Going to be dead." She walked back to the desk, picked up the coffee cup Jane had put there and drank of it. " 'This. This set down. Were we led all this way for a Birth or Death. This Birth was hard and bitter agony for us, like Death, our Death.' I never need that poem unless I am near Jack or Eugenie." The young women were stunned. They were in awe of Sarah Conley to begin with and this was no way to start a morning in an office. "I'm babbling," Sarah said. "Leave me alone for a while. Hold the calls. It's just bad news. There's always bad news, isn't there? Everyone gets it all the time." She smiled and the younger women left the room and closed the door.

Sarah picked up the telephone and walked back to the window holding it. "We were so wonderful," she said out loud. "We fulfilled our dreams, Jack and Eugenie and Timothy and I. We did it. We were strong and beautiful and brave and now the dying starts. We were wonderful. I'm not imagining that, and we were brave. Except it should have been Jack and me. We weren't brave enough for that." Then she began to cry. Holding the phone and thinking of their strong young bodies, the energy, power, strength, and beauty that had been theirs to waste and hold.

CHAPTER 4

Sarah and Eugenie had been at Vanderbilt two weeks. It was eleven o'clock at night. "His name is Jack McAllen." Eugenie had come bursting into their dorm room. "And I'm going to marry him."

Sarah put her books away and went to Eugenie's bed and sat on it while Eugenie removed her dress and shoes and hose. It was her best new dress, a navy blue silk shirtwaist with a white collar and cuffs. "He's the son of Dad's old friend. He's the best-looking man I've ever seen. Well, not best-looking exactly. I don't know. He's so mature or something, hard to describe. Intense. He's a freshman but he had to stay home a year because he broke his arm in two places. He has a brother who's a freshman too. I mean it, Sarah. I'm in love. He asked me to the Kappa Sigma house to a pledge party."

"Well, I finished my paper for English. I guess that's not much news."

"This is it." Eugenie went to the bed and sat beside Sarah and took her hands. "This is the moment you live for. This is the day you don't forget."

A few days later Sarah was introduced to Jack when he came to pick up Eugenie for the party. They met at the desk and then walked out together and stood on the steps outside the residence house that was their dorm. It was still light, the afternoon sun making brilliant red shadows on the lawn and steps and trees. They stood in a triangle. Eugenie had on a new blue sweater set. She was very manicured and exact, not a hair out of place. In contrast Sarah was a deliberate mess. She had on a cotton dirndl skirt and an off-the-shoulder white blouse, her uncombed hair tied back with a ribbon. She was wearing her oldest sandals, a pair of red Capezios so worn they barely stayed on her feet.

She had not expected to like Jack, perhaps was jealous of Eugenie's interest in him. She had been prepared to criticize, protect her friend, engage him in banter and best him.

She was not prepared for the way he moved in, took up space, took over. She wiggled her toes in the Capezios as he charmed her, threw her off guard, captured her imagination. He was wearing a blue oxford cloth shirt with the collar buttons unbuttoned and the back of the collar turned up. Not some affectation but as though he had dressed in a hurry. It suited him, that imperfection. It caught Sarah's eye, drew her attention to his neck and shoulders, which were wide and strong, not like a boy's but like a man's. "My brother's in a class with both of you," he said to Sarah. "He's fascinated by you both. He wants to meet you."

"We would rather have him fall in love with us," Sarah said. "A cobra can fascinate someone. Would he be willing to fall in love, do you think?" She pulled the cotton skirt around her body and held it so the ruffled hem fell like a Spanish dancer's across her thigh. Eugenie was laughing. She had seen Sarah pull this before. It had worked very well on boys in Tyler.

"I'm sure that could be arranged," Jack answered. "He'll be glad to fall in love. I'm sure he'll fall right in line."

"Good." Sarah let the skirt drop and moved up the steps until she stood on a level with Jack. "Then bring him over. We'll give him some tests."

"Next weekend then. If you're free."

"We are always free, aren't we, Eugenie? It's our credo, we don't get entangled." Sarah laughed and climbed another step to the top of the stairs. She let her hand slip down into the long skirt, which moved with the motion of her legs. It was very Spanish, very silly and unusual, sexy, in contrast to Eugenie's expensive wool skirt and cashmere sweater set. Sarah was aware of her bare shoulders, of Jack's watching her. She looked down, filled with the acute awareness of the moment that is the province of the young, constantly aware of each new possibility, change of mood or atmosphere, of any moment's offering to the feast of self.

Jack looked at his watch. His hands were tanned and strong, elegant and wide. He pulled Eugenie to his side. "We'll see about all that," he said, and laughed his father's careful, warning laugh. They walked away. Sarah stood looking after them. This is what we came here for, she decided. To meet people we could not have imagined knowing.

Six days later Sarah was introduced to Jack McAllen's brother, Timothy. By the end of another week the four of them had become an item, a fortress, a subject of envy, a shield. Timothy was taller than Jack, less intense, more open and predictable and forgiving. He had been watching the two girls for several weeks before he met them. He knew which one he wanted. If Jack was the pick of the two men, Sarah was the pick of the two women. It was nothing obvious. In many ways Eugenie was prettier, more vivacious, surer of herself. But Sarah had something else, a haughtiness or disdain, a definition, perhaps a genius, perhaps only a deeper need.

The sorority and fraternity system on the Vanderbilt campus had suffered setbacks in the early sixties but was still healthy enough to have captured the four of them. Jack and Timothy had pledged Kappa Sigma, their father's fraternity, and Sarah and Eugenie had been pledged by the Chi Omegas, thanks to much politicking and letter writing by Eugenie's mother, grandmother, and several aunts in New Orleans and Mobile. The Chi Omegas were still new on the campus, by Vanderbilt standards, and were on the lookout for girls who were good students, trying to make their mark in categories other than looks and cheerleading skills. Vanderbilt had wisely always put off allowing freshmen even to talk to fraternities until after Christmas of their freshman year, but the year the girls matriculated the university had relaxed the rule to see if it would be better to get rush week out of the way before the school year started.

So the four young people were pledged to fraternities and somewhat cordoned off before they met. Sarah and Eugenie now were cordoned off more. They became Kappa Sigma girls, eating at the fraternity house for lunch on Wednesday and dinner on Friday night, when the cook made chocolate fudge pie with ice cream for dessert.

Sarah had expected Vanderbilt to be difficult, she had expected to have to study for hours every night, but it was not so. The stimulation of the classes and the teachers and the ancient old trees and buildings and the feeling of learning turned her mind into a dynamo. She stayed so far ahead of her classes that she began to teach seminars in the Kappa Sigma basement. She taught freshman English, Shakespeare, and history. She would read the assignments and then give lectures with a blackboard. Pledges from other fraternities started coming by, especially to the Shakespeare "help sessions."

"They aren't even reading the plays," Jack told her. "They're just memorizing your notes."

"Well, so what? It helps me learn it to teach them. I want to know these plays by heart. He's the best writer who ever lived. If I write I will write in the light of that."

"I thought you said W. H. Auden was the best writer who ever lived."

"I said 'Sir, No Man's Enemy' was the best poem I ever read. I can't believe that poem. 'Look shining at,/New styles of architecture, a change of heart.' That's what we're here for, Jack. To help make the future. I want to tell people about the beautiful things I find. That's how I am. I don't care if they aren't listening. It's hard to believe how dumb they are though, isn't it? It's hard to believe they don't want to read the plays, don't want to learn anything."

"Maybe they're shy."

"No, they're dumb. I thought people at Vanderbilt would be different from kids in high school. Well, I was in a good mood. Now you've ruined it. Thanks for that." She smiled at him. She and Jack were sitting on the back stairs of the Kappa Sigma house waiting for Timothy to bring the car around. It was almost eleven, when she had to be back at the dorm.

"You just like being the teacher. And you're so good at it, Sarah. I wouldn't be teasing you if you weren't good. I was really proud of you tonight. Proud to know you." Jack let his hand rest for a moment on Sarah's leg. They were very quiet. It had happened before, these moments when what they felt for each other would bleed into the status quo and make them quiet. Usually Sarah shook it off. Now she left his hand on her thigh and leaned back on the stairs. "Are you happy?" she asked, without looking at him.

"I'm busy," he said. "I'm the oldest son, Sarah. We stay busy. They're doing some very interesting research into how our place in family forms who we become. I sometimes wish I could be as light-hearted as Timothy, but all I think about is doing well."

"I'm that way too," she answered. "I can't stand for anyone to be ahead of me. Well, who cares? That's how we are, isn't it?"

The lights of Timothy's borrowed car appeared in the driveway. Sarah got up and gathered her books and went down the stairs without telling Jack goodbye. She was not yet to the point where guilt could make her sad or make her slow. If she knew that she and Jack had more in common than she and Timothy, it didn't matter. That was how it was. It was an imperfect world and all she knew for sure was that she was going to have her share of all those imperfections.

For four years the four of them were together every day if they were on the campus. They became a legend, for their accomplishments, their gaiety, their united front. Sarah and Eugenie and Jack and Timothy.

At the end of their freshman year the four of them went to Florida together in Jack and Timothy's mother's Pontiac. It was a fairly new car and roomy and they had packed it full of sleeping bags and a tent and drinks and food. There were twenty Kappa Sigmas and their dates traveling in half that many cars. They were going to Fort Lauderdale, all the way to the southern tip of Florida, a twenty-three-hour drive. Jack and Timothy and Sarah and Eugenie decided to drive it without stopping.

It was three in the morning when they came to the Atlantic Ocean. Jack was driving. Eugenie and Timothy were asleep in the backseat. Jack and Sarah got out and walked from the road to the water's edge. "It's the first time I've seen the ocean," Sarah said. "It's so wide, so alive. I'm glad it's night. I want to watch the light come to it."

"I've only seen it once. And that was the Gulf." He was walking beside her, very close to her.

"Listen to it. It's so loud. I didn't know it would be so loud. The air has a taste to it. Oh, this is just what I thought would happen, but not this much, not that it would envelop me this way. Should we wake them up? Eugenie will die if she misses this."

"We have a week to watch the ocean. Let's walk in." He reached down and took off his shoes and socks and began to roll up his khaki pants. Sarah sat her shoes beside his and walked before him into the water. She was wearing a blue and green print skirt she had made Easter vacation on her mother's sewing machine. It had heavy rick-rack around the hem. She gathered it around her waist and walked into the water up to her thighs. Jack came up behind her and put his hands around her waist. The waves lapped at their legs. It was very sexual, very tight, the moment strung like a violin. Suddenly, there was light all around them in the water. Part of Sarah's skirt fell into the waves. It caught the light and moved it. She had no idea what she was seeing. She pulled away and began to run back to the beach, struggling against the water.

"It's all right," Jack called out, running after her. "It's phosphorescence. It's microorganisms. It's very rare. It won't hurt you. I've read about it, but I've never seen it."

She bent down and put her hand into the water. When she raised her hand, light fell with the water. Cascades of water, cascades of light. She waved it toward him, her free hand still holding her skirt. "We should wake them. Get our bathing suits. I want to swim in it."

They walked back to the car and woke Eugenie and Timothy. They got their suitcases out of the trunk and found their bathing suits. They dressed in the shadow of the car. Then they went into the water and swam in the phosphorescence. They stood in a circle throwing it to one another, throwing light and water into each other's hands and arms and hair.

"Let's swim out and see how far it goes," Timothy said. Sarah swam out with him, to show off for Jack, to show him she was fearless, braver and better than Eugenie in every way. She was nineteen years old. Guilt did not invade every thought. Eugenie was wealthy and her father was alive. She had seen Jack first and staked her claim. Still, Sarah thought she had a right to challenge that claim, as long as it only happened in their minds. Or else, she was so full of life and unused sexual energy that she had to lay claim to any alpha male who crossed her path. So she flirted with Jack by swimming out into the sea with Timothy.

"I'm floating," she told Timothy, when they stopped to breathe.

"It's salt," he replied. "You can't sink."

Jack swam up beside them. They floated on their backs beneath the stars. When they turned to swim back, Jack moved his body next to hers for a moment in the water. He moved near to her, then let her swim in front of them to the shore.

It was always that way between them. Whatever unspoken things moved between them, the main thing was the four of them together. The main thing was that they were envied. Other young women envied Sarah and Eugenie their security and promised bright futures. Young men envied Jack and Timothy what they imagined was constant sexual access. They were right to envy Jack. Eugenie gave in to him sexually on the second date and continued to do so whenever they could find a way to be discreet. She insisted on its being kept a secret. Even with Sarah she never discussed it. She went to a doctor in Nashville and was fitted for a diaphragm. She wore it religiously and hoped for the best. If she got pregnant, Jack would marry her. He told her that and she believed it. She had met him, wanted him, and done what it took to get him. She liked making love to Jack, was orgasmic most of the time, even under complicated circumstances, but her real interest in him was Oedipal. He reminded her of her father. She understood that and took it for granted that that was the best life had to offer.

Sarah was not so generous with Timothy. She wanted her degree and a good job in journalism. Her mother seemed to grow weaker and more ineffectual each year. It was up to her to make her way and she was not going to let anything stand in that way. She desired Timothy and enjoyed necking with him on beds at house parties or in the backseat of his car, but she was taking no chances on getting pregnant. It was the status of the four of them together that she needed, not to be bedded by a man she wasn't even sure she loved.

Timothy actually loved Sarah. She was the pick of the two women and he was sure Jack knew it. Nineteen years of sibling rivalry had culminated on the day Sarah took his pledge pin and put it on her sweater.

And what of Jack? Dutiful, oldest son of a powerful man? He had been paired up with Eugenie by his father. That was that. If he longed to have Sarah also, that was life, wasn't it? Most of all he wanted to graduate at the top of his class and have the university pay for medical school. His father had done it and his grandfather had done it. He could do it because he had the genes. Sarah could wait. Eugenie Moore was his fate.

Then, in the last month they were at Vanderbilt, something happened that changed things forever. It was the twenty-third of April, Shakespeare's birthday, a day they celebrated, thanks to an idea Sarah had found in a novel by Lawrence Durrell. Jack and Eugenie were formally engaged now, with a ring and a date. Sarah and Timothy were expected to follow within the year.

For three years the four of them had owned a small houseboat on the Cumberland River. It had bunk beds and a thirty-horsepower motor and they would take it out in the late spring evenings and motor up and down the river, wearing French peasant shirts Eugenie had made for them and talking about the future and the war.

Jack and Timothy and Eugenie were all accepted to Vanderbilt Medical School for the fall. Sarah had a job on the *Atlanta Constitution* and would come back and forth on the weekends. Their lives were planned, set.

Then it was Shakespeare's birthday, a day they usually spent on the river with champagne, only this year Timothy and Eugenie couldn't get away. They settled for breakfast at the Waffle House. "It's going to rain later this afternoon anyway," Jack said. "Still, I'd like to take the boat out for at least an hour or two. Will you go, Sarah, so I won't be completely alone on your favorite writer's natal day?"

"Why not," she said. "It's the last year."

Later, when she remembered that day, it always began with the boat. The smell of the gasoline they were bringing for the motor, the smell of the river, Jack's faded polo shirt, the old scar on his forearm, the muddy lines they threw aboard, the warm, clear air. He held her arm while she stepped onto the deck. "Thanks for coming," he said. "I had to get away from that place. I'm worn out. Nothing bothers Eugenie. She just does the work, but I get crazy from studying. I feel like I've turned into an old man from staying bent over books. It's an obstacle course and this is only the beginning. Everyone says next year will be really bad. The teachers already treat us differently, the ones who got in medical school. Why make it so hard on us? How does that make us better doctors?"

"It's what you wanted. A year ago you were all afraid you wouldn't get in. Now you're in. Nothing can stop you now. I'm jealous. I wish I had a life before me as clear as the one you have."

"God sells all things at the price of labor? Isn't that what you used to tell the pledges? It used to crack me up when you'd start preaching to them."

"Well, it's true. I'm only going to be making four hundred dollars a month. I'll barely be able to afford a place to live. You'll all still be here, lap of luxury, running our boat."

Sarah had thrown her bag on one of the bunk beds and was on the deck untying a line. "Let's go. Slip the surly bonds et cetera."

Jack took the pole they used for that purpose and pushed the boat out into deeper water. It was moored on a small industrial pier that belonged to a friend of his father's. For the years they had owned the boat they had expected to be kicked off the pier but their free anchorage had continued.

The inside of the boat was painted sky blue. The outside was white with dark blue trim. They had painted the boat the week they bought it. It was named *Refuge*.

They drifted into deeper water. Jack stood by the motor while Sarah steered. Soon they were thirty feet from shore and going downstream in a nice current. Going out was always fun. Chugging back in with the small motor was sometimes difficult but they were young and could live in the present.

When he was sure the motor was running smoothly Jack came and stood beside her. The mud-covered embankments slid by, piers and a few fishing boats. The Cumberland River was an industrial waterway that was near to Nashville. Only students would have thought of using it for recreation. But neither Jack nor Sarah thought of it as ugly; they were away from school, and oddly, strangely, alone together.

"Does Eugenie really want medical school?" Sarah asked. "Sometimes I think it's to prove something. She doesn't talk about it to me. She used to talk to me about her plans." She passed the wheel to him. As he took it he let his hands stay on hers for a moment. They were very quiet. "It could have been you and me," he said. "Someday one of us has to say that."

"No. We don't have to say it. That isn't what happened, is it?" She started to pull her hands away and then she left them beneath his. He was behind her now, the power and energy of his body covered her. They were very still. The boat moved down the water.

"Don't let this happen," Sarah began. In front of them a boat pulling a water skier moved in a circle.

"That fool," Jack said. "Who would ski out here? That's nuts." A man was steering the boat and a woman and a child were in the bow. It was a Boston whaler with a huge motor on the back. The skier was holding on with one hand now and waving with the other one.

"Drunk fraternity boys," Sarah said. "What are they doing?"

She moved her hands from under Jack's and stood by his side. The whaler had swerved to avoid a barge and was headed right at them. It swerved again and the skier dropped the lines and sank into the water. The whaler went on in a circle at full speed and hit a sandbar. The woman and child were in the water.

"Get up front," Jack said. "Grab the lines." He was trying to steer the boat in the direction of the woman and the child but the current was too strong and he couldn't get near.

"I'll get them," Sarah said. "I'm going in." She pulled the life ring off the wall of the cabin and threw it in the direction of the woman. Then she pulled off her sweatshirt and dove into the river wearing her shorts and a small brassiere, which the force of the water tore from her body. She retrieved the life ring and swam toward the woman. When the woman had hold of the ring, Sarah took the child and kept him aloft until help came. Help was coming from two directions. The barge had thrown out an anchor and was launching a lifeboat. Also, Jack had managed to steer the houseboat to a pier and tied it up and was swimming in their direction. The crew from the barge arrived first. Sarah handed up the child, then the woman was taken aboard, then a tall man pulled Sarah up onto the boat. He took off his plaid shirt and handed it to her. She buttoned the first button and tied the tails around her waist.

They were taken to the deck of the barge, then the lifeboat was sent ashore to rescue the young man who had been steering the whaler. Whatever he had been drinking was dissipated now. He was cold sober by the time he reached the barge and found his passengers were still alive.

The coast guard arrived and took over. Then the tall man took Jack and Sarah back to their houseboat in a dinghy. Sarah was still wearing the long plaid shirt. Her breasts were loose and full beneath the worn plaid material. "Keep that shirt," the sailor said, as he helped her onto the pier. "My mother sent it to me. It might be good luck for you."

"Thank you," Sarah said. "It might be. I will."

*   *   *

Jack held her arm as she climbed back onto the houseboat. They stood on the deck together until the coast guard boat and the barge had left that part of the river and only their boat disturbed the peace of the scene.

They poured glasses of Scotch whiskey and drank it. Then they went into the cabin and Jack pulled her into his arms and kissed her and did not let go. They lay down on the bottom bunk bed and held each other for a long moment without speaking. Then they began to make love and they kept on making love without talking of it and without remorse and without sadness. They made love with passion and hunger and will and when it was over they still did not feel remorse.

"It was always us," Jack said. "You know that, Sarah. It has always been us. We're alike. It isn't them. I have no business marrying her. I should not have let her talk me into it. Sometimes I think I did it just to keep on being near you. We have to do something about this. We have to act on it."

"Why did you ask her?"

"For her money. That's it. There's nothing noble or high in it. I couldn't resist. Her father's going to be one of the richest men in Kentucky. His company's going public in a month. I couldn't resist it, but now I can. She doesn't need me. I make her nervous. If it wasn't for me she'd quit this notion of going to medical school. She isn't bright enough. I'm not even sure she can do the work."

"She's doing it for him, for her father. And she is bright. She's as smart as you are." Sarah pushed him away and got up from the bed. It was hot in the cabin and she was wet with sweat and the sweet, dark smell of the river water. "Come on. Let's take this boat back. I want to take a bath."

He pulled her into his arms and kissed her again and they lay back down on the bed and held each other long enough so that it would never be over now, never, never, never.

There were jugs of water on the houseboat. After she got up from the bed Sarah washed her body with water she poured into a bowl.

She put her shorts back on and the shirt she had thrown down on the deck when she went into the water. He lay on the bunk bed watching her as she dressed. Neither of them was ashamed of their bodies or their nakedness. "We won't do anything about this," Sarah said. "We will forget it ever happened. I'm indebted to her family, Jack. Her father pays my tuition. I could never repay her family for what they've done for me. That's it. I wouldn't do this."

"We've already done it. We've been doing it for years."

"It doesn't matter. That's how life is. Life's hard. We do what we can. Besides, I don't want to be married. I want to go to Atlanta and begin my work. I want to be a foreign correspondent. This war in Southeast Asia is going to last a long time. I want to be there."

"They'll never send women to that war." He sat up on the edge of the bed. "Thank God. Do you have any idea of the mosquito-borne diseases over there? I wouldn't take the inoculations they give those soldiers. There was a report the other day that was circulating around the biology department." He stood up, went to her, pulled her back into his arms. "Oh, Sarah, my God, do you know how I feel about you? We don't need Eugenie and Tim. They'll be better without us. Already our lives shadow theirs. You know that."

But she pushed him away. She was getting scared. And already she was thinking about getting pregnant. "I've never made love to Timothy," she said. "Or anyone. I should have told you that, shouldn't I?"

"Eugenie told me. I guess I didn't believe it."

"We shouldn't have done this. This was wrong, it was stupid."

"Don't say that, Sarah. Don't be afraid. Nothing is going to happen."

That night, in a rented motel room, she did make love to Timothy, because what Sarah most exquisitely was in the world was a survivor. Nothing was going to ruin her life or shame her or harm her in any way if she could prevent it. Eight days later, when she should have started menstruating, she did not start. Eighteen days later, she still had not started. It made no difference to Sarah whether the father of the baby was Jack or Timothy. All that mattered to her was surviving. There was not a fleeting sentimental thought to slow her down as she assessed the situation and made her plans.

Four weeks later, in a dress she had bought that afternoon, she and Timothy were married by a justice of the peace in a small town in the Kentucky hills. Jack and Eugenie went with them. The four of them drove there in Timothy's car and Eugenie wept and held the flowers while the ugly sheriff read the vows.

The next month Jack and Eugenie were married in a formal wedding in Tyler, Kentucky, and Sarah was Eugenie's matron of honor and Timothy was the best man. At the reception Sarah danced with Jack four times.

"You know it's my baby," he told her. "Why have you done this to us? Why have you made this happen?"

"It's not your baby. It's his. I know that for sure. Wait and you will see."

"How will I see? He's my brother. I love you, Sarah. You know I do."

"Yes, you do." She stopped on the dance floor, pulled him with her out onto a porch, stood leaning on a rail, then stood up, wanting him to see the little pouchy stomach she was developing. She was proud of it, proud and scared and elated. The baby had not moved yet but she was as sure of its presence as she was of sun and air. It seemed a great secret, luminous, full of loveliness and meaning, past words and past all their suffering and happiness and the marriages and even the terrible desire she felt to have Jack touch the pouch and acknowledge it. Once more, she told herself, only once more.

She took his hand and put it on her stomach and held it there.

"Oh, God," he said. "You have to stop this. I won't live with this. How can we face them? You know goddamn well it's mine."

"Only because I want it to be." She gave him that. Then she put his hand back on the rail and turned and faced him. "We have done it and we have married them and they would kill us if they knew and I don't care anymore about any of it. I want to have this child and I want to have a life and forget the rest. It doesn't matter. The child has to be protected. We have to be. They have to be."

"No. You're wrong. You're the one who loves truth so much. You're the one who quotes Kant and Santayana. This isn't truth or ethical or a single thing you say you believe. This is fear and selfishness, Sarah, and you'll pay for it and make me pay. I can't stand it."

"We have to stand it. It's done. I don't want to ever have this conversation again, Jack. I have to move on and bring this child into the world and find myself again. Months will go by and it will be all right."

"I know you love me, Sarah. You can't say that isn't true."

"I don't know what I think or feel anymore. It's just this day to be lived. I love Timothy too. He's been wonderful, Jack. We get along. We really do." He turned and wouldn't look at her. "We have to go back in," she added. "Yes, I love you. There, is that what you wanted, to make me say that?"

"I want you to act upon it."

"I can't. I'm trapped. I trapped myself. If I try to get out I'll lose a foot."

"You won't lose anything. I won't let you lose anything. I could protect you forever. If I had to start over without a cent and work my way through med school, I would make it. If they all quit speaking to us, I could take care of us. You know I can do that, Sarah. There's no reason to go on with this."

"Then why did you marry her? Why did we have that ceremony two hours ago? Where is the bride, Jack? I think we had better go and find her." Sarah left him then and went back into the reception hall and found Timothy and told him she was tired and wanted to go home. She had become angry at Jack as she talked to him. Really angry for the first time since the afternoon on the boat. It had not occurred to her that what they had done had been anyone's fault but her own. She had never blamed him in any way and now she began to blame him too. He had gone on and married Eugenie. Perhaps he wanted us both all along, Sarah began to think. What if it were true? Men are herd animals. No one wants to believe it, but it's true.

*　　　*　　　*

The months of her pregnancy went by like a dream. She was in perfect health and the birth was not as terrible as she had thought it would be. The oxytocin kicked in and erased her negative short-term memory, as it is programmed to do, and Sarah held the small male child in her arms and named him James and called him Jimmy and loved him. Then for six years she and Timothy maintained a cordial, sometimes happy marriage while Timothy finished medical school and did his internship in Knoxville. When Timothy moved back to Nashville to begin his practice, Sarah refused to go with him, not angrily, not meanly, just unmovable once she made the decision and told him. She had applied to the Atlanta newspaper and they had offered her the job again and when it was settled she told Timothy and then she took Jimmy and left. There was no rancor on Sarah's part but it infuriated Timothy as nothing had ever done. It bruised his pride for his wife to leave him and run off with his son. He was sad for a few weeks and very angry. Then he began to date everyone he met. In six months' time he married a sweet, malleable nurse and began a long legal struggle to take Jimmy away from Sarah. For five years Sarah managed to fight off his superior lawyers and keep her son. When Jimmy was eleven, Timothy and his wife finally won a judgment and Jimmy was awarded to them as primary custodians. The judge decreed it would be best for him to stay in Nashville with his father and go to school.

Sarah was exhausted and broke by the time it was over. She had had to borrow money for the legal battles and she was in debt. Also, Timothy and his wife, Jennifer, had won Jimmy over to their side. They had a richer life to offer him and he was pragmatic enough to realize it. Never had Sarah known how much he resembled her and resembled Jack than on the day he testified in the judge's chambers about his wishes.

"I want to stay with Daddy," he told his mother and the lawyers and the judge. "I'll go see Momma on vacations."

"Why do you want to stay with him?" the judge asked.

"Because he doesn't move around," Jimmy said. "And he doesn't leave me with the maid. And Jennifer stays home at the house and I can see Granddaddy and Uncle Jack and Aunt Eugenie. And Daddy takes me fishing with him and he's going to teach me to drive the Jeep." He was eleven years old, sitting in the judge's chambers looking Sarah in the eye while he broke her heart. "I'll come and see you every Christmas and summer like I do Daddy now," he told her. "But I want to stay here and go to school."

So that was that and Sarah's child was gone. I never told anyone he might be Jack's, she consoled herself. In my darkest moment, in my worst distress, his happiness was paramount. I know that and Jack knows that and someday Jimmy will know or sense it. I did not tell and I can live on that until something better comes along.

When the judge finished laying down his decree, Sarah had gone to her son and held him in her arms and told him it was all right. Then she had spent the night with him in a hotel and the next day she had taken him by the hand and gone with Timothy and Jennifer to enroll him in his new school.

She had flown back to Atlanta that afternoon and gone straight to the newspaper office and written a piece about crime in the ghettos. At one in the morning, when the piece was done, she put a clean piece of paper into her typewriter and began to write a novel to pay Timothy and Jennifer and Jack and Eugenie and Nashville back for what they had done. She typed the title. INVASIONS, INCURSIONS, ACTS OF LOVE.

It began,

Linda Lee was a good wife to Doctor Matthews. She wasn't like his crazy first wife who didn't even cook or like to make herself sexy for her husband. She took her marriage vows at face value. She had been proud to promise to obey such a good man from such a fine family with such a fine career and so much money coming in every single day and week and month. She didn't marry him for the money, or for his career, and certainly not for the little boy they had stolen from his mother. The little boy was spoiled rotten. He was a mess. He did exactly what he wanted to and everyone was just supposed to get out of his way.

No, Linda Lee had married David Matthews because she

loved him. He fit all her bills. He was above her socially. He was contemptuous of her taste in clothes and books and movies and he was embarrassed by her lack of sophistication. He did not treat her as badly as her father had treated her but that was only because he had such elegant manners. Underneath the manners he was meaner than her daddy had ever been. Underneath the manners he had bought just what he needed while he developed his career. A housekeeper, a willing piece of ass, a nanny for his son, someone to indulge his aging parents, an extra nurse for the office in case of emergencies, and a woman who would tremble if he got in a bad mood and needed a reaction. Linda Lee's dreams had all come true. She had this good job *for the rest of her life.* When the time came she would even go out and find out from salesladies how a successful doctor's wife ought to dress.

It had not been easy to take the little boy away from his mother and there were times when Linda Lee even regretted helping David do it. At other times she was afraid if they didn't get the boy she would lose her wonderful job as second wife. So she said what she was told to say and did what she was told to do and even let the judge put his arm around her several times at cocktail parties. He was a drunken judge who should have recused himself from the case because he knew them, only luckily the mother never found out about all that.

Linda Lee and David had plenty of help getting the little boy. They had David's brother and his sister-in-law and lots of people the men had known at Vanderbilt. There were plenty of people who were glad to help keep the boy's mother from getting what she wanted in the world. They didn't like her because she had come to Vanderbilt from nowhere and taken a lot of honors away from people who should have had them. . . .

It took Sarah three months to finish the book. Two months to write it and another month to take out a lot of the meanest stuff and anything really libelous or actionable.

It was almost a good novel. It was not as good as it should have been because she took out too much of the meanness and also all the parts based on her relationship with Jack. She took that out to protect Jimmy and substituted an implausible love affair with a professor.

It was good enough to be nominated for a National Book Award, however, and won her a job on the *Boston Globe*, which led to the job at *Time* magazine.

Jimmy sensed Nashville's rage at Sarah's book. It confirmed his teenage idea that his mother was a crazy person and he was better off without her. By the time he was seventeen he would not return her phone calls. When he was eighteen he stopped cashing her checks. The more he hurt and ignored Sarah, the more powerful he felt in the world in which he lived.

While he was in college he began to have a friendship with her again but he never really let her be his mother. His stepmother, Jennifer, let him do anything he wanted to do. He didn't want anyone thinking they could direct or control him.

"Everyone has things they can't fix," Sarah's boyfriend, Robert, would say, when Sarah was sad over her son. It was a piece of wisdom he had stumbled on in his desire to soothe and heal her. "Maybe Jimmy's not something you can fix. He may be having the best life of any kid in the United States. A busy dad, a stepmother he can jack around, and a mother who will do anything to get him to be nice to her. Maybe you don't know the end of this yet, Sarah. You got pregnant when you didn't want to and you changed your life to have him. You gave him your lifeblood. Someday he'll figure that out. If he doesn't, then he's a little shit and you're better off without him."

"Maybe they got him mixed up in the hospital." Sarah laughed and felt better. "If it wasn't for that reddish hair, I'd wonder where he came from. I'm not bad natured. I don't hurt people's feelings. I never was mean to my parents. Well, not very mean. My mother was always in a bad mood. Maybe Jimmy has Mother's disposition. Maybe I gave birth to a male version of my mother. Maybe nature is just as big a bitch as could possibly be imagined."

"Witness the food chain," Robert said. "By the way, Sarah, are you going to write a movie for those people in California? I'd write it if I were you. I think you're nuts to turn down all that money."

"I'm thinking about it. I might do it. I haven't heard from them in a while."

"I'd give anything to have that chance. If you don't want it, tell them I'll write it for them."

"I wish it were that simple. No one tells movie people anything, Robert. Haven't you learned that yet? If they don't pay a hundred thousand dollars for advice they think it's worthless or manipulative."

"Don't turn it down again if they ask you. You don't get many chances like that, Sarah."

"I'm an editor at *Time* magazine. I have all the chances I want just like it is."

CHAPTER 5

Sarah went on crying, holding the phone in one hand and looking out the window at the high white clouds over the city of Manhattan. "Call Jack," she scolded herself. "He's waiting for you to call. And don't let him hear you cry. Don't add to anyone's hysteria." She went back to the desk and drank more of the coffee and called his number. He answered it himself on the first ring.

"Tell her I'm coming," Sarah said. "As fast as I can do it."

"She would have called you herself, but she made me do it. Because of the letter she wrote you. She regrets writing it. She's very clearheaded, Sarah. Her mind is not affected, but I told you that."

"The letter was right. I wrote the book. I've agonized about it. I'm sorry every day that I wrote it. I'm glad to hear your voice, Jack. To talk to you, even with this dreadful, this terrible news."

"When can you come?"

"I think I can leave tomorrow. I'll make reservations and let you know when I'm coming. I hate to keep calling back. I don't know. I can't wrap my mind around this. I didn't think it would happen to any of us, not this soon."

"I'll be here until I make rounds in the afternoon. I can be paged. It would be good if you could come this weekend. There may not be much time." He was silent. Sarah waited. "You always acted fast. I remember how that made sense to me. I used to do it too."

"But not now?"

"Too many mistakes. This means so much to her, Sarah. I can't tell you how much it means. I didn't want to call you. Now I'm glad I did."

"I'll call you again in an hour. And, Jack, find Jimmy and tell him I'm coming there. So I can see him whenever he has time."

"Of course. You're wonderful to do this. It means so much to her. I wouldn't have called you unless it did."

"I want to come. I'm overdue for seeing Jimmy. I'll call you back. Soon, before long."

She hung up the phone and sat back in the chair and shook her head. She opened a drawer and got out a package of cigarettes, and carrying them in her hand, she left the office and went down the hall and got into an elevator and went down to the street floor and out onto the street and stood in the doorway shivering. She had forgotten her coat. She went into the main reception office where she knew a guard and borrowed a coat from him and went out onto 50th Street and stood by the fountain smoking and watching the passersby, the hurrying, busy folk of New York City, tourists and cab drivers, lawyers and shop girls and tramps and out-of-work actors and celebrities and skateboarders and the young of a dozen races, all arrived on the shores of the promised land, passionate and hungry.

She stood watching all that life, thinking of herself and Eugenie the day they arrived on the Vanderbilt campus. Douglas Moore had let them drive themselves to college. They had arrived at the campus and driven up to their residence house and parked in front and walked together into the band of freshman girls. They were the last ones there, as they had planned to be. They were wearing new clothes, Eugenie in a red cotton sweater and Sarah in a white sweater with a plaid skirt. They had gone to Vanderbilt to conquer it, to take territory, and they were starting with their dorm.

Sarah put out the cigarette and disposed of it in a trash can, then she stuffed her hands into the pockets of the borrowed coat and walked to the fountain to watch the half-frozen water falling from the jets. *Now dying, now almost dead.* She clenched her fists inside the pockets as though to pull the past back from the present. The night Eugenie came into their room from meeting Jack. After Eugenie put on her gown and they were in bed, holding hands. When they moved into the room there had been a table separating the single beds. They had moved it so they could touch hands when they talked. In Tyler they had always slept in the same bed, in either of their houses. *The softness of Eugenie's hands and arms, the beautiful symmetry of her rib cage* when they would fall asleep wound up together like spoons. The night she met Jack, Eugenie had talked herself to sleep about him. "He's the dream you dream of," she had said. "He's everything. He was valedictorian at Columbia Military Academy. He has red hair, well, reddish brown, and he has a brother for you. His brother's in one of our classes but you don't know him because it's that big history lecture class. His brother's already in love with you. He told Jack we were the blond twins, the whities. He said one of us was haughty and one was sweet and he was in love with the haughty one. That's you, Sarah. His father is in a real estate deal with Daddy. They're building an office building together to make money."

"I'm not haughty," Sarah had replied, but she had liked the label.

"Timothy McAllen thinks you are. He told Jack you were gorgeous."

"Why are they both freshmen?"

"Because Jack broke his arm and his father wouldn't let him use it even to write with until it got well. He stayed home for a year and read books. His father paid him to read great books. This is it, Sarah, the day my life began." Eugenie had kept on talking until they fell asleep. My oldest friend, Sarah thought. My first and last one true friend. My past lies dying and I must go to her.

CHAPTER 6

Jack and Timothy McAllen had been born a year apart to a fifty-year-old physician and a woman he met when she came into his office complaining of a back ailment. He had diagnosed a kidney infection and put her on a sulfa drug. She returned a week later with a pie to thank him for curing her. The next night he took her to a movie. Then he spent the night in her small apartment.

It was a rebirth for Dr. McAllen. He had never married and had not slept with a woman in a year. He was a tender man, too tender to be a physician in the dark years before antibiotics were in general use. He fell in love with Jack and Timothy's mother for several reasons. For her reddish hair, her country ways, her youth and innocence, her neat apartment with its white sheets and folded towels, but most of all for her recovery from what might have been a serious illness. Her good health seduced him like a siren's song. His diagnosis had been correct and his treatment had worked. He loved Geneva Jones for all these reasons and married her in a month.

It was a happy home. Dr. McAllen doted on his sons. He worried about them and thought about them and spoiled them. He taught them things. He became a scoutmaster and led Jack to become an Eagle Scout at thirteen and Timothy one at fifteen. He tried to make them brothers in their hearts, but even the best parents create envy in their children. No matter how Dr. McAllen tried to even the odds, Jack won every game. He was a year older and ten times meaner. He would not lose. The higher the bar, the harder he fought. Finally, at Vanderbilt, the final game was played out and half the players never even knew they were on the field.

As long as she lived Sarah Conley never understood what had really happened among the four of them. She knew her part and she knew Eugenie's but she forgot to add in the rivalry between the brothers. She thought it was her irresistible charms that had caused the trouble.

She thought she had figured it out. She thought she understood, but she only had part of the information and she would never really have the rest.

"Whatever Giles and I did to Lilian and Daniel, we did it together and we share the blame," Sarah had written, in the part of the roman à clef she threw away and never published.

We were young and we were in a culture that thwarted and controlled us and made it impossible for us to know the truth about how we felt. No, we were too young and scared to know the truth. No, we were too ambitious to let go of Lilian and Daniel. Giles couldn't let go of her because he wanted her money and I couldn't let go of Daniel because I wanted to stay in the group. Tribal instincts. We got what we wanted by sticking together. Giles and I wouldn't have been able to do what we did as a foursome. Neither of us was nice enough to other people. They were the politicians. It's true. It doesn't matter if it's true or not. We believed it and so we acted upon it.

What went on between Giles and me wasn't love or we would have done something about it. It was greed, desire to have it all, all the glory, money, power, love, we could get our hands on. We were young. That's the thing. That's the way it works when you are young. Only once did we act upon it. Because the day demanded it, because it was almost graduation and whatever had gone on between us was about to end. Because nature wanted a child to be conceived and tricked us into it. Because the Boston whaler rammed into the sandbar.

*   *   *

A wind blew around the corner of the forty-story building. It blew across the fountain and stung Sarah's cheeks. She started to go back inside, then changed her mind. She found a kiosk on a corner and bought a cup of coffee and a cold doughnut and sat on the rim of the fountain eating it in large unchewed gulps.

Eugenie dying. Then she began to weep, thinking of the night they lay on the roof and watched the stars, smelling of chlorine from the pool and suntan lotion and the largesse and happiness of fourteen years old, talking of death and knowing they would never die.

She went back inside the building and returned the coat to the guard and thanked him. "You okay?" he asked.

"A friend is dying. I have to go to Nashville."

"You better get on out of here. It's going to snow."

"When did you hear that?"

"It was on the morning news. Didn't you hear it?"

"No. I was arguing with my boyfriend." She laughed and touched his arm and thanked him for the coat. Then she went back up the elevator to the office and went in and asked Jane to get her an afternoon flight to Nashville the following day.

"What time?"

"As soon as I can get away after the one o'clock meeting with Jerry. Get me a car. It's supposed to snow. I'll leave from here."

Why wasn't I watching the news this morning when news is what I do for a living? she was thinking. Well, I had to mother my little broken boyfriend who can't get published because he won't write and who blames me for it and is pouting and now he will really pout. She picked up the phone and called the apartment and let it ring until he answered.

"I have to leave tomorrow for a few days," she said. "It's an emergency. I wanted to tell you now so you could make some plans for the weekend."

"I don't need any plans. I have to write."

"Good. I'm glad. Are you feeling better?"

"It's okay. I'll see you tonight. I'm going to put résumés out in the studios again. I want some movie work. If I had that I'd be better. You're crazy to turn down writing a script if you really get the offer. I wouldn't say that if I didn't mean it from my heart, Sarah. I'm on your side."

"I know you are. Anyway, I need to get to work. I'll see you later." She hung up the phone. I have to get rid of him, she decided. I have to get him out of my apartment but then I'll be alone in the afternoons and I hate the afternoons if I'm not working. To hell with it. I can afford him. At least he's honest and he's talented. Somewhere in there was or is a talent. Or do I tell myself that because I like to fuck him?

It snowed all night and late into the morning. Sarah dressed very carefully and packed two changes of clothes into a carry-on bag and a small cosmetic kit that could fit into her purse. "Where are you going?" Robert kept asking her. "Who are these people?"

"She was my best friend in high school and college. Her father paid my tuition to Vanderbilt. She's dying, Robert. I have to go to her."

"Why haven't you seen her before now?" He was sitting on the bed watching her pack. "You're never going to get out of here in this storm."

"Yes I will. A car's coming to get me in twenty minutes. I'm going to the airport now."

"I thought you had a meeting with Jerry Levin."

"I did. I told him I had to go to a deathbed. He understood. He's a nice man. I'm going to talk to him on the phone."

"I could go with you. I still don't understand why you haven't been to see her before."

Sarah stopped and turned around. She was holding a suit by the hanger. She had spent her life telling the truth and she was going to keep on doing it. It was her religion, her one and only never-to-be-altered faith. If you told the truth the world stayed clear. "Because she married my ex-husband's brother. But that isn't why I don't go there. They are the people I made into characters in *Acts of Love.*

They got mad about it. It's the past, Robert, and I stay away from it when I can. There is plenty of work to be done in the world, real work that can't get done if you live in the past. I wish you knew that. Then you'd go on and write your book."

"I'll make you some toast," Robert said. He had decided to be sweet. She looked so professional, packing her bag. He had suddenly remembered who she was and the power she had in the world and he loved her again and forgave her for not making him smart enough to write a book.

He went to her and began to wrinkle her suit. He ran his hands up and down her hips and kissed her neck. "I won't be gone long," she said, starting to laugh at his youth and craziness and life. The crazy, wild, passionate selfishness of him, the thing she kept him for, the unthinking youthful thing, the beauty of it, the undying of it, the not dying, not thinking of dying.

She put on a long gray coat and her snow boots and kissed him good-bye and went down in the elevator burdened by the bag and the gloves she was trying to pull onto her hands. It was still snowing. The doorman helped her carry her things to the waiting car and she was driven through the heaped-up snowy streets. There was a phone in the limousine but she resisted the urge to use it. She had magazines in her bag and a small book she had had since she was sixteen. It was *The Selected Poems of Emily Dickinson*. On the flyleaf it said, "To Sarah, Love Always, Eugenie." Sarah turned to the poem she wanted. "Elysium is as far as to/the very nearest Room/If in that Room a Friend await/Felicity or Doom." Only it's not about Eugenie, Sarah knew. It's about Jack, as it has always been.

It was five-thirty in the afternoon when the DC-9 finally landed in Nashville. Sarah was the third person off the plane.

Jack was standing there, looking as he had always looked, as powerful, as determined as always. Graying hair and a few wrinkles had not changed him in any way. He was wearing a tweed jacket and wool slacks and a shirt and tie. He took her bag and dropped it on a chair and then embraced her.

"You can't know how much this means to her," he said. "She's so happy that you're coming."

"Did you call Jimmy?"

"He knows. He'll see you tomorrow as soon as he's out of classes. He's back in law school this semester. Did you know?"

"Of course. He doesn't completely ignore me."

Jack picked up her bag and carried it. They walked in a crowd of people, side by side, their bodies linked as if not a day or mile had ever been between them.

"How is she?" Sarah asked.

"She's dying. It's going to get worse. There were more tests made today. Neither of us is expecting to hear anything we didn't know." He stopped and turned to her. "It's good of you to come. She wants to see you." He began to walk again. "Do you have other luggage?"

"No, that's it. Old journalist's trick, learning to travel light."

"You've always done that. So we'll burden you again. She wants to see you while her mind is clear."

"Is her mind clear?"

"I think so. She looks bad. I should warn you about that. She's very thin."

They walked very close together. His physical presence was overwhelming, as she remembered. He was in charge here. This was his town. Sarah found this comforting. It felt as though he were her husband, carrying the bag, shepherding her to some duty. "I want you to know I have agonized over that book. I'm sorry about it. I shouldn't have written it. I should have set it in London or Los Angeles. I needed the money, Jack. I was broke at the time."

"It wasn't about us. I told Eugenie that."

"Yes, it was about us, about all of you. It was vindictive because I envied you your sureties."

"They wanted it to be about them. If they hadn't made a fuss no one would have noticed."

Sarah stopped now. "Oh, you thought because I didn't write about you and me. I never thought of that. Now I know why you weren't angry."

They stood very still, taking each other in. "It's how we were," he said. "We are stuffy and self-important and insular. Everyone we know is that way. It could be anyone in Nashville that we know. I'm going to get the car and bring it around. Can you wait here?" He had brought her to a sidewalk covered with an overhang. It was raining very hard. It was raining as hard in Nashville, Tennessee, as it had been snowing in New York City. Sarah buttoned her heavy gray coat and turned up the collar. "I'll be right here," she answered.

In a few minutes he brought the car around and parked it and put her bag in the backseat. He held the door open for her. He pulled her seat belt across her body and attached it. He got in the other side and started driving. It was a large automobile with pale gray leather seat covers. There was a dashboard with computers. She wanted to ask what kind of car it was but decided against it. I am already altering myself, she thought. Editing my conversation.

He left the airport road and pulled out onto an eight-lane highway. It was still raining very hard. She could barely see out of the passenger side.

"Typical Nashville night," she said. "I remember this weather. Is our houseboat still on the river, do you think?"

"I doubt it. The piers are all rebuilt now. There's a park where we used to moor it. You may want to see it while you're here. Nashville's a big city now. I thought we'd go by the hospital first, if you don't mind. She checked in for two days while they did tests. It's better to see her early. In case she wants something for sleep. You could call her. There's a phone."

"I'll wait. I don't like car phones."

"I talked to her on my way here. She wouldn't tell me about the tests. She's gotten very ethereal these last weeks, Sarah. Spiritual, I suppose you might call it. I've seen that before."

"The Aztecs tried to tap into that, that force before death. It was the reason for a lot of their worst atrocities. Well, that has nothing to do with anything."

"It's interesting. Go on."

"Somehow they knew about the white light before death and

they wanted to tap into it. I don't know. It's terrible to say that. Eugenie isn't about white light, but she was always spiritual, Jack. When we were young, she wanted to have a God. Even if she didn't really believe it, she wanted it. We used to go to early Communion together. She had a white piqué dress. I coveted that dress and her religion. I coveted a lot of things she had."

"Hap Terrebone is her oncologist. He might be there. Do you remember him? He was a Kappa Sig with us."

"Of course I do. I remember everyone."

They arrived at the Vanderbilt Memorial Hospital and parked the car in an underground garage and went up on an elevator to the seventh floor. They went past the nurse's desk, where the nurses all looked up and spoke to him, then into her room, a corner room with two windows. She was in the bed with an IV hooked up to her left arm. An oxygen machine was in a corner. She was very, very thin, her hair pulled back with a ribbon. What was left of her hair. All that gorgeous long blond hair, Sarah thought, and was overtaken by sorrow and friendship and terrible loss, this present loss and all that was past and never to be recovered. She moved to the bed and took Eugenie in her arms and held her there. Eugenie was wearing a soft pink gown and robe that were much too large for her. Her bones stood out on her shoulders and arms. Jack picked up a set of papers from the desk and began to read them. They were the test results.

"Are these all?" he asked. "What about the white cell counts?"

"They wanted to do them over. Some mixup. Give me a kiss. Then go on. I want to be alone with Sarah."

Jack moved to the bed, kissed her on the forehead. "I'm leaving then," he said. He stopped at the door. "I'll be back for you, Sarah, say, in an hour. Is an hour long enough?"

"It's plenty," Eugenie said. "For now."

When he was gone, Eugenie spoke first. "Bring that chair over here. It's so good of you to come to me. I wanted so much for you to come. I have been so proud of you, Sarah. I want you to know that."

"Are you all right. Will you be all right?"

"There's nothing to say about me. I'm finished. Please, I want to talk about you. It was wrong of us, of me, to be angry about the book. If we hadn't made a fuss about it, no one would ever have known it was us. It was your book, about yourself. You had to write it. I know that now."

"I shouldn't have done it. I'm ashamed that I did it. It was cynical. It wasn't even true."

"It's all right. It led to things for you."

"I was angry with Timothy for taking Jimmy. It was to get back at Timothy. I shouldn't have made the men brothers. I could have written it without that. But it wasn't about you and Jack."

"I knew that, in the end. Maybe I wanted you to write about me and make me a great heroine. I wanted one of us to be famous, to fulfill all the promises. I used to pray for you to get what you wanted. When I prayed."

"You've always been religious."

"No more. I'm angry now. At this stupid disease and our inability to stop it. I think the anger is worse than the pain. Because I can't act upon it. There's nothing to do, no revenge."

Sarah moved nearer. "What can I do for you? Is there anything I can do?"

"Take care of Jack. He's going to be lost. I did everything for him, Sarah. I ran our life. He won't know what to do. He doesn't have other women, you know. It isn't his way. He barely has any outside interests. Just his practice and me and the children, but they are gone now. Neither of them is here."

"What could I do for Jack?"

"Keep in touch with him. Talk to him. He adores you. He's so proud of you. He tells people about you. He never was angry about the book. I'm the one who was angry."

"I wish I could undo it, take it back."

"Don't wish that. It wasn't us. It was my jealousy. I wanted to write and be an artist too, but I never had any talent that wasn't practical."

"How could anything equal what you've done with your life?"

"I don't know. Maybe it's why I'm here. Maybe sickness breeds sickness. What if we had gotten it wrong about the germ theory?" She laughed then, and for the first time Sarah could see the friend she had so long ago, riding bicycles through the streets of Tyler, Kentucky.

"Remember the night my cousin was born and we rode bikes and smoked a cigar? It was a June night. Can you believe how powerful and beautiful we were? Wonderful and powerful and alive."

"Let's go out on the balcony," Eugenie said. "Bring the wheelchair over here. We can wheel the IV out. I hate being in this bed. I wish I could go somewhere with you. A road trip. Just start driving. I wish we had a million miles to drive and talk."

"Remember when we borrowed your mother's fur coats and wore them riding in the Oldsmobile? We drove all the way to Russellville. Can you believe she lent them to us? Two sixteen-year-old girls riding around all day in borrowed furs. Me in the mink jacket and you in the cape?"

"Bring the wheelchair over here. We went to Leland Morais's house and honked the horn until he came out. She lent them to us because she did anything we told her to. Good, that's it. I can get in if you can hold the IV."

Sarah brought the wheelchair to the side of the bed and Eugenie slipped into it and they wheeled the IV along beside it. The windows were floor length and opened out onto a small concrete balcony that overlooked the parking lot. It was still raining but there was an overhang and the two women sat under the shelter of that and watched the rain.

"It's hard to believe I'll never have fun again," Eugenie said. "I think I don't believe it, Sarah. I think at least once a day that this is a dream from which I will awake."

"You lived your life. You didn't leave things undone."

"After I met you it was better. After we met each other were the best years of my life. I have never stopped missing you, Sarah. I missed you most of all when I was mad at you. I want you to say you forgive me for that."

"We forgive each other." Sarah kissed her again and could smell the hospital smells, the alcohol and something else, the smell of death, she knew. When Eugenie dies, it is all our deaths, the death of our lives.

"Do you have a man?" Eugenie asked.

"Yes. I wouldn't answer that for anyone but you. He's very young and wild and crazy and he probably likes me because he thinks I will help his career."

"Does he have a career?"

"No, just talent and ambition and anger. It won't last much longer. This may be the end of it. But I liked it for a while. He's so young. It took me out of myself."

"Thank you for telling me that. I like picturing you in New York City with a crazy young man. It makes me happy. I'll be thinking of that tonight. It will be my night's happiness."

The nurse came in then and brought Eugenie back into the room and straightened up the tray table and IV and bedclothes.

"She wants me to go," Sarah said. "I'll be back in the morning."

"Come close." Eugenie beckoned and Sarah went to her and sat beside her on the bed, as close as she could get to her, so close she could hear her breathing. "There," Eugenie said. "My wonderful Sarah, so brave, so smart. I have so much to tell you, but mostly this." She stopped, held on very tight to Sarah's hands. "Remember those stars and we used to say they only seemed to be far away. We were right. They are so close to the earth, all of this is so much closer than it seems. I don't mean to be mystical. This is not a mystical observation. It's something I've found out the last few months. Will you be looking at them for me, even tonight, even through the rain?"

"I will do anything you tell me to."

"Remember that I told you they are very close to us. The energy is still very balled up in the universe. I don't know how to say this."

"Oh, Eugenie." Sarah wanted to ask about her father and her mother, she wanted Eugenie to tell her they had not been angry with her about the book. But she would not ask it. I have no right to keep talking about myself, she decided. Only put whatever I can into her, to strengthen her, for the night ahead.

"What do you want to say?"

"To tell you how beautiful you were in that white Catalina bathing suit. With your breasts the size of rose petals or something so lovely I can't speak of it. That's what I'm thinking of. How much I liked to look at you. And how you used to sass your daddy and then you'd both laugh about it. That's all I'm thinking of."

The nurse was standing by the side of the bed.

"Go on," Eugenie said. "This won't be the end. We've found each other now."

Sarah walked back down through the corridors of the beautiful new wing of the hospital. She was sad and thoughtful and glad to be alive. Too empathetic to be happy but too wise not to value her own life in the light of what she had seen.

Jack met her in the front hall. He was coming in the wide front doors as she approached them. "Should I go up?" he asked.

"They were getting her ready for bed."

"Perhaps not. I'll call in a while." They went back out the doors and found his car and got in and he started driving. "How did she seem to you?" he asked.

"Wonderful. Like she has always been. Clear thinking. I don't know. She's Eugenie."

"The test results were dismal. I think I was still hoping for a miracle, as if I don't know better."

"No one knows better."

"Now I just want it to be easy. It won't be long. There's very little time. I know you're starving. There's a French restaurant near our house. Let's eat dinner, then go home."

"Fine. That's fine."

At dinner he asked her about her work. "It's interesting. Not as good as being in the field. I wanted to go to Pakistan to write about the child labor factories, but *Life* beat us to it. It was a brilliant piece. Did you see it? It was in *Life* several months ago."

"I don't read enough now. Only medical journals. I get caught up in the patients."

"You are doing real work. I am only an observer."

"Reporter. You report on it. Don't deprecate yourself." He laughed. It was the first spark of gaiety since she had gotten off the plane. Maybe it was the wine. "You always did do that, right before you showed us your grades or won an award, you'd start deprecating yourself."

"Someone has to be the editor. That's currently the lie I tell myself. It isn't really fulfilling, though. It's the money, of course. No one can resist that kind of money. It's difficult to live in New York if you aren't well fixed."

"Can't you go on assignments still?"

"Actually, I may go to Paris this summer to write a screenplay. I wish Eugenie could go. I wish the three of us could go somewhere, anywhere. I even wish for Timothy. I wish it was a million years ago and the four of us were on our way to France." She raised her wine glass. "How is Timothy?"

"He's fine. He's happy. He likes Jennifer and she likes him. They get along. She bores Eugenie to death so we don't see much of them but she's good to him."

"Your parents were kind people. Timothy never wanted to argue. If I'd wanted to, I could have lived any life I liked with him, as long as I was kind."

"They were kind. The only cruel thing either of them ever did was wanting us to be surgeons." He was laughing but there was no happiness in his laughter.

"You were made to be a doctor. You love your profession."

"Not this year. This year it's let me down. We work in the dark, Sarah. We are so primitive, compared to what we can imagine; we don't know enough yet. We're only beginning to understand the causes. We treat the symptoms. I'm sorry. Do you want coffee or dessert?"

"No. Let's go home. I want to see where you live."

CHAPTER 7

Coming home from the restaurant, in his car, in the driving rain. He had taken her arm to help her into the car, he had held her coat in the foyer of the restaurant, had helped her put it on, had touched her and touched her coat. It was very sensual, the most sexual thing she had felt in a long time, maybe in years. She was wearing the long gray coat. Underneath it a wool jacket. Through all those barriers and all those years his touch had traveled and he took her arm and put her into the car.

For several blocks neither of them spoke. "Tell me about the children," she said at last. "I have missed seeing them, knowing about them. Jimmy fills me in but not much."

Jack swerved to avoid a puddle, then pulled the car back out into the turning lane. They were in a residential section now but not one Sarah recognized or remembered. Hills, houses on hills. All she could really see was rain. Jack turned on the high beam lights. They were the only car on the street.

"Elise is an interior decorator and an architect. I don't know if you knew that. She lives in Atlanta but has an office here. She's here half the time, which has been a blessing the past year. She's very good at it. We're proud of her."

"What does Johnny do?"

"I don't know. He's always been a problem. He lives in Lexington, near Jimmy, and was going to architecture school but he quit. I think he's working as a gardener at the college. He doesn't call us. We have to call him. I think he calls Eugenie but she never tells me about it. I don't have much patience with him, Sarah. He annoys me."

"I'm sorry."

"It's difficult having physicians for parents. There've been studies done on it. He's very bright, brighter than I am, for sure. He's like Eugenie. Unforgiving when he gets mad at something or other. He's mad at the United States now. He blames other things and other people for his problems. Eugenie's always taken his side. It's going to be devastating for him when she dies, worse because he doesn't come to visit."

Jack drew in a breath, straightened his arms on the wheel of the car. Again, as before, Sarah was filled with a sense of his physical power, his presence. She wanted to bring up the subject of the book she had written about them, to tell him what Eugenie had said to her, but she couldn't summon the courage to begin. It was raining so hard she could barely see out the window on her side. "I'd better be quiet and let you drive," she said. "I remember these rains. Once I went to the Parthenon and sat in the shelter of the overhang and watched one of these storms all night. I wonder if I was drunk."

"We didn't have to be drunk to do things like that," he answered. "We were on the houseboat in worse storms than this." Now they had both said it. Now it was there between them. It had happened and it had mattered and neither of them had forgotten it or decided to act as though it didn't matter.

Sarah sat back in the leather seat of the car and watched the windshield wipers push against the rain. Whatever she had expected to have happen in Nashville, it had not been this. Not this terrible desire to touch him.

He turned into a driveway and went up a hill and parked the car in a garage beside a sports car. He turned off the motor. "I'll bring your bag in later. Let's go in and have a drink."

A covered walkway led to a wide marble porch and a heavy wooden door that was opened by a uniformed maid before Jack could finish hunting for his key. "I stayed," the woman said. "I wanted to be sure Mrs. Conley had everything she needed. Dr. McAllen called from the hospital. She said to tell you she was going to sleep."

She held the door open wider. They came into the hall and the maid disappeared to get the bag. Jack took Sarah's coat. She looked around her. It could have been any wealthy house in Nashville, the antiques, the framed portraits, the bright sofas and chairs, the polished floors and elegant lamps. It was warm and inviting and only a little overdone. Overdone by New York standards, Sarah thought. By Nashville standards it's an A-plus.

"I'll go upstairs and wash up, then I'll be right down," Sarah said. The maid reappeared with her hanging bag and took her up the stairs to her room.

They had put her in a blue and white room with long, sky blue drapes against a bluer wall. There was a white rug on the floor and a small sitting room and bath. It was very pretty, more than pretty, it was a beautiful, tasteful room, elegant and light.

"Miss Elise's room," the maid said. "She decorated it the last time she was here. We think it's very pretty."

"It's perfect."

"Well, I'll leave you then." The maid left and closed the door. Sarah went into the bathroom to wash her hands and comb her hair. She heard the phone ring in another room and was glad she had no reason to answer it. She stayed upstairs for six or seven minutes, repairing her makeup, putting on lipstick, changing shoes.

As she was coming down the stairs to the hall she saw Jack in the den talking on the phone. As she came nearer he looked at her and began to shake his head. He finished his conversation and turned to her. "It's Eugenie, Sarah. She's dead."

"How?"

"Heart. That's what's going on the death certificate. I don't believe it. I think she did it. Goddammit." He sat down on the sofa and put his head in his hands.

"How could she have done it? Wouldn't they know?"

"Potassium. She could have injected it into the IV. Hap found her. She knew he would be making rounds at ten. If he found a syringe he would have thrown it away. I would have done it if I was him."

"Did you ask him?"

"No. A lot of insurance wouldn't apply if it could be proved she killed herself."

"I can't imagine Eugenie caring about insurance money. You don't need it, do you?"

"The children might. She liked money, Sarah. You didn't understand a lot of things about her. She wasn't a saint by any means."

"What do you think happened?"

"I think she injected potassium into the IV. It would stop the heart in fifteen seconds. There would be a syringe, but Hap would never tell me. He may have helped her, but I doubt it. She wouldn't involve anyone else. There'd be no need to."

"Maybe she just died."

"No." He got up and stood three feet away, looking straight into her eyes. His face was steely, hard, passionate, the Jack she had never been able to forget. "That isn't how doctors are, Sarah. Doctors are a law unto themselves. You don't know. You can't imagine."

Sarah moved to him, put her arms around him, embraced him, felt him sob, then stop himself. "She was half my life, Sarah. My enemy and my best friend. She was the nucleus, the idée fixe, the spirit of our life."

"I hope she did kill herself. I wouldn't want to live like that. She said, when I was there tonight, that she wanted us to get in the car and go somewhere. Maybe she went to the only place she had left to go. Should we go to the hospital?"

"They've sent the body to the morgue. There's no reason to go there now. I have to call the children first. Oh, God, what time is it?"

He pulled away from her and she looked at her watch.

"It's after ten. Let's go sit in the den. Let's have a drink. Then you can call. Let's sit down, Jack. Let's just go sit down a minute."

"All right. Come on. There's a fire." They moved into the beautiful, small den and sat down on a blue and white sofa facing the fire. Eugenie was everywhere, in the needlepoint cushions, the photographs, the tasteful sofa and chairs, the beautiful blue and white rug. "Blue and white, they always were her colors," Sarah said. "She planned this, didn't she? So I'd be here with you."

"I don't have many friends now. She was my friend, Sarah. We made this life together. It was a good life, mostly, not what you and I would have had, perhaps, but it was something I understood."

Sarah made drinks. She brought them back to the sofa. They drank them. Then Jack called the children. "Sarah is here with me," he told them. "Aunt Sarah. Your mother asked her to come see her. Yes, she's here now. Elise wants to talk to you." He handed her the phone.

Something was dawning on Sarah as she took the phone and talked to her niece and godchild. I was the last person to see her alive. Except for that nurse. The last words were for me and I can't remember what they were.

"She told me how proud she was of you," Sarah lied. "She said you were such a fine woman. I'm sorry it's been so long since we talked. Sorry it has to be like this."

"Stay until I get there tomorrow," Elise said. "Promise you won't leave."

"I won't leave," Sarah said. "I'm here as long as you need me."

After they had talked to both of the children and called Timothy and Jimmy they made another drink and drank that and then went upstairs. Sarah followed Jack into his bedroom. He opened a dresser drawer and took out a bottle of pills and swallowed one. He held one out to her. "Take it. It's a sleeping pill. It won't hurt you." She took it from him and swallowed it without water.

"How am I supposed to do this, Sarah?" He lay down on the bed and loosened his tie. Sarah went to him and removed his shoes and set them on the floor. Then she lay down beside him. They were not touching, just lying side by side looking up at the ceiling.

"I don't know," she answered. "I don't know how we are supposed to do anything. We are so brave, all us people of the earth, knowing we will die and not thinking of it all day every day. Then one of us does die and there we are, faced with it, loss without end, loss that cannot be reversed. Our own loss coming. I don't know why I can't cry."

He reached beside her and took her hand and pulled it across his body and held it there.

Sarah kicked off her own shoes. It was the last thing she remembered. He had given her ten milligrams of Ambien and she was not used to taking sleeping pills.

Jack had been up for several hours when Sarah woke. He brought her coffee and sat in a chair while she shook herself awake. "I went to the hospital. We'll cremate the body today. As soon as the children get here. Get it over with. Get it done. Ashes to ashes. I don't want anyone getting any ideas about this."

"Did you talk to Hap?"

"Yes. I'm sorry I told you about that. Don't worry about it. Just believe her heart stopped. It did stop." He put his hands on his knees. "Thank you for staying here with me. It helped. I'm glad you're here. I forget about friends. I have to make rounds at ten. The children will be getting here by noon. Johnny's driving. Elise is flying in. Jimmy's going to meet her. He called a while ago but he didn't want me to wake you."

"I'll get dressed. Then maybe I can help."

"Just answer the phone until I get back. My partners will cover for me but there's one woman in the hospital I need to see about."

"What's that music?" It was coming from a stereo downstairs.

"Philip Glass. She loved it."

"I love it too. She liked that album? *Glassworks?*"

"It's the one she played all the time."

"I play it too. It's a fugue, like Bach." She moved near the chair where he was sitting but she did not touch him. She was still wearing the clothes she had put on the day before in New York City. The morning had a surreal quality, timeless, still, out of orbit. It seemed right to be waking in a bed that had not been turned down, wearing clothes she had worn for twenty-four hours. "I need to call my office," she said.

"Use the phone in the upstairs office. We put it there so they wouldn't be in the bedrooms." He stood up, let her pass him on the way out of the room. He went downstairs and Sarah went into the blue and white room and unpacked her wrinkled clothes and then got into the shower and stood a long time in the hot water trying to make sense of the events of the past day. The intense, haunting music of Philip Glass filled the house and she gave up trying to make sense of anything and just listened.

Beat, beat, beat, the sound of a heart, the sound of the sea, the moments of our lives, then silence. All the rest was data, surprise, exchange. Jimmy's coming in a moment, she told herself. If death is true, then there is only DNA or else there is no meaning. If Jack guessed Jimmy is his son he has forgotten or no longer believes it. What does it matter? He's my son. Someday he will love me. I wonder if I care. He's so different from me. So foreign and cold. Perhaps I have never forgiven him for what he did to me, for how he changed my life.

The maid appeared while she was dressing and asked what she would like for breakfast. "Scrambled eggs and toast would be nice. I feel like I haven't eaten in a long while."

"Is there anything else I can do to help you?" The maid was kind, an older, demure white lady named Mrs. Lane.

"I could use an iron if there is one. I never unpacked. Everything I have is wrinkled."

"Let me do it. I'm good at ironing. I did all of Dr. McAllen's things, even her silk blouses."

"Then take this. Thank you. Just get out the bad wrinkles. I hate to look like a refugee." Sarah handed the dark silk dress and jacket to the maid and smiled.

The bathroom was large and well appointed and Sarah took her time fixing her hair and putting on more makeup than she usually bothered to wear. By the time she went back into the bedroom the breakfast was on the desk on a tray and her dress was hanging on the door. She sat down at the desk and ate the food gratefully, grateful for anything on this strange, bad, confusing day.

It had still been raining when she woke but the sun was coming out now. Outside the windows it looked clear and pretty, if still very cold. Sarah put on the long-sleeved navy dress, added a white collar and the sleeveless jacket, and put on her shoes. She went downstairs to wait for her son, Jimmy, and for Jack's daughter, Elise, the god-child she hadn't seen in years. "Dost thou, therefore, in the name of this child, renounce the devil and all his works, the vain pomp and glory of the world, with all covetous desires of the same, and the sinful desires of the flesh, so that thou wilt not follow, or be led by them," the minister had read, as Sarah held the baby, Elise Louise, by the font, and, she, Sarah Louise, had answered. "I renounce them all; and by God's help, will endeavor not to follow, nor be led by them." Our dreams are so far from our deeds, Sarah knew, but at least we used to dream.

Jack returned before the young people arrived. "You look very nice," he said. "Did Mrs. Lane take care of you?"

"Wonderfully. Is it all arranged?"

"As soon as the children see the body we'll cremate her. The sooner the better. We don't want any of that mortuary stuff. Have they called?"

"Not yet." The doorbell was ringing. They hurried to the door. It was Jimmy and Elise. They came into the hall. They all embraced. Jimmy was taller than when Sarah had seen him in the summer. Filled out, matured. He seemed tan and fit and he was being kind. Elise stayed near him. Their hair was the same color, a dark auburn red. They had the same hands, the same half frown. What was attractive on a man, however, was somehow homely on Elise. Eugenie would never love a daughter who wasn't pretty, Sarah knew. Not with her pride. I doubt if she ever thought about this girl. An hour before her death and she didn't mention her children to me. No note, no message. I'm too analytical. She's very pretty really. If she would smile she would be pretty but how can she smile, her mother is dead.

"I love the room you did, where I'm staying," Sarah said to Elise. "Maybe when this is over you will go with me to my farm. No one's renting it this year. It might be the time to fix it up. I want Jimmy to go too. It's his anyway. It's in trust to him."

Jimmy took her arm. "I'd like that, Mother. I haven't been there in years. I can't remember it. It's stone, isn't it? A stone house?"

"Partly stone."

"What did Mother say to you?" Elise asked.

"She said she'd had a good life and that she loved you. She said she was proud of the work you're doing. She seemed happy and at peace. She seemed like herself. I'm glad I was here if it had to happen. I would never have believed she looked that well."

"I saw her last week. I was coming this weekend anyway."

"You gave her everything you could, everything a mother could want." Sarah kept on lying. She held Elise by the hands and told her what she needed to hear.

There had been a night in October, the year they were seventeen. They were on the roof with a new system of extension cords that let them take the good radio onto the roof and not the battery-operated one that always went dead in the middle of their favorite songs.

They were waiting to see if Dick Martin would play "Sabre Dance." They had written him two letters requesting it. The month before he had played "There's a Small Hotel" for them and read out both their names. They thought they were in now. They were sure he would play "Sabre Dance," but it was almost twelve o'clock and he hadn't played it yet. "We have to find a way not to get pregnant or else we can't get married," Eugenie was saying. "After I'm in medical school I won't have to have a baby if I don't want one. There are ways to get rid of them if you're a doctor but ordinary people have to have them no matter what happens. I heard Mother talking about it to her friend Stephanie. There are ways to get abortions if you know where to find the doctors. They call it a D and C. But not in Tyler. You have to go to the cities."

"Then you can't do it with anybody. If you do it, you get pregnant."

"Not me. I'll never have a baby as long as I live."

"Me either, if I can help it. Why should we spend our lives cooking and cleaning up after people? I don't even want to have a house. I want to live in an apartment or a hotel."

"We'll live together in Mexico, or maybe London. I'll be working in a hospital and you'll be writing articles and things. We'll have plenty of boyfriends to take us places but we won't marry them. Swear to it, Sarah. Swear by the stars, our only gods."

"I might want to have one baby someday," Sarah said. "Just to see what it is like. And so I could name him. It would be nice to name someone."

"You can name dogs," Eugenie said, and rolled over on her back and held out her hands to the skies. "Name the stars, for God's sake. Why would anyone want a baby? Why would anyone do that to themselves? It's beyond me. It really, really is."

So here we are, Sarah decided, and returned to the present. And here are the fruits of our labors.

Johnny arrived soon after Jimmy and Elise. He was disheveled and unwashed. He had already started using the funeral as an excuse to get drunk. By dark he would be asleep.

When the family was assembled they went to the funeral home and there was a service and a cremation. Then they went back to the house and there were drinks and food and visitors. Several of Eugenie's friends were presiding over the kitchen. One of them was a girl Sarah had known at Vanderbilt, a fellow Chi Omega who had been in engineering school when Sarah knew her. A tall, bespectacled girl who had seemed above the others. Sarah had always been sorry she had not had time to know her better.

"Lelia," she said now. "It's me. Sarah Conley. Do you remember me?" They were in the kitchen. There were platters of meats and cheeses and bread, homemade casseroles and pies, cheese straws, petits fours, all the foods that make up the tables of funerals and weddings in the South.

"Of course, we all read your books. Eugenie was proud of you, Sarah. So were we all."

"How are you? Are you married? What do you do?"

"I'm an engineer. I built the new student center on the campus. Have you seen it?"

"That's wonderful. I knew you would have an interesting life.

I'm very glad to see you." Sarah stood back from the table where the women were preparing food. She admired them for being able to do that in good clothes as she truly and deeply admired all women who happily did menial work in kitchens and houses. She thought it was a flaw in her character that she didn't like to do such work. Never volunteered to do it. Wasn't good at it when she did. She watched the women now, Lelia, Sally Ames, Betty Hollis, people she knew or slightly knew. She felt very distant and left out.

Jack came in the doorway to save her. "Sarah, could you come here a minute? There's someone who wants to speak to you." She made her escape and he took her into a hall and up the back stairs and lit a cigarette and offered her one. She took it and they stood there smoking. "I know I don't have to say this," he began. "But don't say anything about what I told you. About potassium. Hap's here. He isn't going to say it. So, maybe I was wrong."

"It doesn't matter. Why, do you want to know?"

"Yes. I want to know. She left a mess about the will. It wasn't like her. She should have fixed that."

"What sort of mess?"

"All of it to me. It should have been left to the children."

"Maybe she thought the insurance money would make up for it."

"It will. Half a million dollars. I don't think they'll contest it." He took her hand and held it. "I'm sorry you have to hear this. So glad you're here. I have to talk to someone about it. Timothy's in the living room, by the way."

"Well, then I have to go and see him, don't I? Because this is our culture and we serve its customs. Let's go down."

They put out the cigarettes and went down the front stairs and found Timothy and his wife, Jennifer, who was a nice woman with a pretty smile and an intelligent face. She taught dance to little girls and had kept her figure. Also, she had had face-lifts and they had worked. Sarah had first met Jennifer on the day they had gone together to put Jimmy into his new school, after Sarah had lost the custody battle. Jennifer had been kind then and not gloating, not taking sides, only doing what Timothy made her do. Sarah had liked her for that and liked her still.

"Hello, Sarah," Timothy said. "You remember Jennifer, don't you?"

"Of course. We talk on the phone about Jimmy. Thank you for all your kindness to him, Jennifer. I appreciate that more than you will ever know. He's so fond of you."

"I'm fond of him. Is he still here?"

"In the other room with Elise. How did you get him back in law school?"

"He went back on his own. We didn't do anything."

"He's doing fine," Timothy put in. "He's on law review now. That's the main thing. He'll make it now. He's over the hump."

"Good. Well, you did it and I thank you for it more than you know." She was quiet then, searching for something to say, looking at Jennifer, not Timothy.

"Are you staying here, with Jack?" Jennifer asked. "Because you could stay at our house if you wanted to. We have a guest house. I mean, if you're not comfortable staying here."

"Elise asked me to stay with her. I promised Eugenie I'd do what I could for her." Sarah sighed, she had forgotten how to do this, to fend off and parry and thrust and be in society and have small talk at funerals. "I might take Elise tomorrow to see about an old house I own here in Tennessee." Sarah raised her voice, took over the group, put the conversation where she could control it. "An old farm that belonged to my grandparents. It's Jimmy's actually. I only have the usufruct. I'm going to take her if it will help her to go. I'm thinking of redoing the house."

"Oh, you might be moving back here then?" Jennifer moved closer to her husband, took his arm. Jack rescued Sarah.

"The bishop wants to meet you, Sarah. He and his wife are fans of yours. Excuse me, Tim." He pulled Sarah with him into the dining room and introduced her to a tall, handsome man and a woman in a white dress and the conversation drifted into better waters. Talking to them about her work, Sarah felt herself draw a deep breath for the first time in hours. Why must I stay here another moment? her best judgment told her. Flee, Sarah, while there is time.

*   *   *

They will all talk about my staying here with Jack, Sarah knew. Because of the book. I know Nashville. They will speculate, although nothing about it is in the book. That was the problem with the goddamn book. I was mean enough to write it and then I left out the most important part. That's the problem with using real people in fiction. You have to leave out the most important parts. All the things that make a human being into the player he becomes, the things that truly explain what happens next. I wrote the book and made everybody mad and the book wasn't good because it wasn't true. The next one will be true, if I ever write another, and it will be pure fiction. I won't have to leave out why Eugenie became a doctor to fulfill her father's unfinished business. I won't have to leave out Jack and how much he is like her father was, and mine. How I am always doomed to lose the men I love because I lost the one who counted most.

I thought I had forgotten about that book. Now here I am in Nashville thinking I wrote it yesterday. Karma is karma, but I have suffered enough about that goddamned book. To hell with it. I need to go home and get some air.

The bishop drank too much sherry. On his third glass he found Sarah and engaged her in an argument he was having with a lawyer. "I say our status is determined by our machines," the bishop argued, "just as once it was determined by our servants. What sort of machines we own, how expensive and state of the art they are, who services them, how often we replace them for newer models. There is no difference in that and slavery because men and women have to slave to make the machines and service them. Their manufacture pollutes the atmosphere, the power to run them causes war."

"I say it ends war," the lawyer answered. "We don't blow up the Mideast because of oil. We kowtow to the Arabs in every way and pretend to like them, we send people to live in those godforsaken countries and the only wars we will fight are to protect our oil interests around the globe."

"It should be nuclear power," Sarah said, laughing. "Read Freeman Dyson. If we'd done it right to begin with, built lots of small plants of different designs and not been greedy, we would have dependable nuclear power now."

"But there's the nuclear waste," the bishop put in. "What are you going to do with that?"

"Store it in tanks. At least it isn't spewed out into the air and water every minute of every day like the residue of fossil fuels." Sarah was engaged. This was one of her favorite subjects.

"Eugenie would have agreed with you," the bishop said, and put a hand on her shoulder. "She was a friend to St. Andrew's even if she never attended. She never turned down our requests when we needed help."

"She was my childhood friend." Sarah covered his hand with her own. The bishop was the only person in the room she wanted to talk with about Eugenie. "We were together every day from the summer we were fourteen until we were married."

"She spoke of you with kindness," the bishop said, and Sarah knew it was true. Later, when she thought of the cremation and the funeral service and the aftermath at the house she always remembered standing with the bishop by the blue velvet sofa and holding hands. I stayed by him, Sarah knew, the way criminals hid in churches in the Middle Ages. To protect me from the village and the law.

CHAPTER 8

Jack left the house before seven the next morning. Johnny was gone by eight. Sarah and Elise woke later, had breakfast together in the kitchen, then left in Eugenie's car to go to Harkin, Tennessee, to see the farm. It had rained in the night. The fields outside the city were glistening and wet, sunlit and cold and still. Even in winter some of the trees stayed green, a dark rich life against the lifeless winter fields. The farther they drove from Nashville, the more familiar the landscape became to Sarah, comforting and real. This was farmland and there were barns, gravel roads, schools, old mailboxes, drooping telephone and electric lines.

"I've been too long in the city," Sarah said. "I've forgotten the real United States."

"I learned to drive out in this country. Dad would take me out here on Sunday afternoons and let me practice. Well, he took me twice. I didn't see much of him when I was growing up, Sarah. I think about it now. How little he was at home."

"When we had the custody suit, Jimmy told the judge that he wanted to stay in Nashville and learn to drive. I almost came to peace with the decision when I'd think of that. The selfishness of children. They know what they need. He wanted his father because he was turning into a man. Perhaps that's true."

"Jimmy's fine, Aunt Sarah. He's very important to me, you know. We spend a lot of time together."

"You always did like each other, even when you were small."

"It's more than liking. He's part of my life. I love him."

"Good. I'm glad. That makes me happy." Sarah kept on driving, looking straight ahead. Whatever Elise would tell her about her son she wanted to hear but she didn't want to seem to pump her for information. They were both quiet for a moment. "The gardener finally taught me how to drive," Elise said at last. She turned away from Sarah, looking out the window. "He taught me to parallel park between two sawhorses. Then he took me to get my license. Neither one of them was ever home in the daytime but Mother was there at night. She was usually there when we went to bed."

"She loved you, Elise. She had a career. I thought young women understood all that now. I'm sure she thought she was taking the best care of you in the world." Sarah kept on looking straight ahead, glad to have the excuse of driving. If Elise was going to turn this into a desecration of the dead, she would not be a part of the conversation.

"I'm not complaining. It's just an observation. I just meant, I doubt if Jimmy got many driving lessons. He might have had more of them with you in Atlanta."

"Your mother loved you very much, Elise. You mustn't ever doubt that."

"I loved her and I will grieve for her but I know the bad parts about her too. She wasn't a saint, Sarah, although a lot of people think she was. She didn't want us. She was never interested in us when we were young. That's a fact. I don't mind it. I understand it. I agree with it. I'm going to have a tubal ligation, maybe soon. I don't want children and I don't even like them very much. I'm serious. I don't want to take a chance on getting pregnant by accident and being stuck with it. I want my career. More than you can imagine. Everyone I know who has a baby ends up losing their edge. They become obsessed with finding sitters and day care or they just quit work. You can't do both things. Besides, there are enough children in the world. If I ever start wanting one I'll adopt a child in need."

"I won't argue with you about any of that. But I think a tubal ligation may be going a bit too far. There are reliable methods of birth control, aren't there?"

"I always admired you for letting Jimmy live with Uncle Timothy. I thought you did it voluntarily. There was a custody battle?"

"Of course there was. Didn't Jimmy tell you that? Timothy and I fought over him for three years. Finally, a judge in Nashville gave him custody. Jimmy testified that he wanted to stay here."

"I'm sorry. I got it wrong, I guess. Jimmy always says he was better off being here but he doesn't say he testified."

"The darkest day of my life. He told the judge I left him with the au pair and that Jennifer was home. I didn't leave him *ever* unless I had to. When I went to work to make our living. Anyway, that's all over. The past, where we wander at our peril. Does he say I *let* his father have him?"

"No. He's proud of you, Aunt Sarah. I think he'd like to be a writer too, but he doesn't dare. You cast too long a shadow."

"Not a very big one. I don't take up much space. The job I'm doing at *Time* is a dead end if there ever was one. But a well-paying one."

"Why do you do it then?"

"For the money. I live from hand to mouth about money, Elise. There's a job in Paris I'm thinking of doing, writing a script for a film. The problem with that is, I'd be writing the script but in the end they'd only use scenes from it. I know those bastards. Still, I think I might do it. It would pay to restore the farm. Then I'd have a retreat if I ever need it. It's a wonderful old house. You'll see. I think you'll want to work on it."

"That sounds exciting to me. Going to Paris to write a film. What could be better?"

"Writing a book. The real thing. The thing that hurts and scares you and makes you laugh and makes you learn and be challenged. All of that. I haven't done it in five years."

"Because mother got mad at you?"

"No, that was long ago. Because of the thought of anyone reading it, anyone at all, commenting on it, bruising it with reviews, misunderstanding. Writers act so tough. All the writers I know act tough but actually they are the most sensitive people I know. More sensitive than painters or musicians."

They came around a curve into a long narrow stretch of highway. Sarah speeded up. In a few miles they turned onto a two-lane blacktop road, then onto gravel, then they were at the house.

It sat in a grove of trees, at the end of an oak-lined drive. It was square and forthright in design, with a long porch across the front and a chimney on each side. There was a slate roof. Four long windows sat on each side of a thick double door. There was an overhang that extended beyond the porch and cast shadows in the early morning sun.

Elise and Sarah parked in the driveway and started up the steps. "Heartwood," Elise said. "God, the materials they used back then. Nothing will be made like that again."

"These doors were made on the place. Granddaddy always bragged about being a child when they were made. My great-grandfather was something of a dandy, a farmer, and a scholar. He wore a black suit and tie and had the first automobile around these parts. He had gone to college in North Carolina and come here and married my great-grandmother. The land was hers but he built the house."

"Why have you never come here?"

"My father died here, in the fields, hunting in November. It spooked me. And yet, what a death, suddenly, without warning, alone in the fields with a horse and guns and dogs, the things he loved. We should all dream of such a death, without lingering or fear."

"How old were you?"

"Thirteen. I met your mother six months later and her father became my father. I grieved over his death as much as I did my own father's. I'm glad they weren't here to see your mother ill. I thought that yesterday. I'm sorry."

"It's all right, Sarah. I want to talk about her. Anything you say. Did Dad tell you about the will?"

"Yes."

"He's going to give us the money as soon as he gets it straightened out. It's funny. She was so careful about things. It's unlike her to have left a mess like that. I guess she thought she had time to fix it." They walked up the steps, sharing their sadness and their separate lies. If it were Eugenie we would know this is also funny, Sarah thought. We would laugh to save ourselves, but this big, sad girl is not given to laughter. Whose genes created her? She doesn't resemble either of them. Goddammit, Sarah, don't be cruel, even in your mind.

"I loved your mother, Elise. And now that love is yours if you would like it." They stood on the threshold of the door and were quiet. Sarah took out the key and opened the lock and they walked into the wide, oak-floored hall. "Part of my childhood," Sarah said. "What do you think?"

"It's marvelous. I could make a showplace out of it if you would let me."

Sarah smiled and shook her head.

"Well, at least a comfortable home."

They explored the house for a while, then boiled water on the stove and made tea and sat on an old sofa in the front parlor and talked about the house.

"First of all I love it and can't wait to work on it. Give me a budget."

"No. Tell me first what you would like to do."

"Add a modern bath to the master bedroom and a walk-in closet. Tear off the back porch and rebuild it. That would all be one job. Redo the kitchen. Aside from that, just paint and varnish and some work on the chimneys. I'll need an engineer to look at the foundation and the roof. But they seem firm."

"The roof is only ten years old. I'd had a run of luck the year it needed doing. It's the best roof you can buy. The fireplaces were worked on at the same time."

"I'd like to keep the well and the barn and maybe the stables. They add to the grounds. Would you ever want to keep a horse?"

"No. But someone might someday. Jimmy might."

"I wish he had come with us. I have a hard time getting him to do anything since he got on law review. He's always busy."

"Well, you can bring him later perhaps. It thrills me to think he's taking school seriously."

"Well, he still needs to find time for me." Elise sprawled on the old sofa. It was some sort of challenge but Sarah wasn't in the mood for games so she decided to write it off as funeral nerves and change the subject. She walked to the front windows and opened one and stepped over it onto the porch. It was past noon now. Shadows were beginning to fall across the front lawn from the tall old oak trees. "Come look how the shadows move toward the house," she said to Elise. "I tried to describe them to a painter once. These were the shadows that I feared after my father's death and why I never wanted to come back here. I thought those shadows had taken him. Nature and the wilderness had taken him back from us, wild grasses and squirrels and snakes and bugs and rabbits and foxes and coons and turtles and even birds, especially mourning doves. I believed the mourning doves had taken my father and put him in a grave and left my mother weak." She put her hands into her pockets. "So I had to be strong and make up for all of that, make perfect grades, write for the paper, make money and go to a city where excitement was always going on and there was no nature to contend with. It didn't exactly make me into a hypochondriac but it made me cautious. I used to get annual physical checkups in my thirties. Then it's Eugenie who dies. No one knows what will happen next, Elise. It's all random, chaotic, inexplicable."

"I don't believe that," Elise said. "I believe we have free will, that we can order nature, protect ourselves. Mother died as her parents died, from cancer in her fifties. So I think that will happen to me too, but it probably won't. I don't even look like her. I look like Daddy. Tell me how much you can spend and I'll make you some plans for this place."

"Would eighty thousand do it?"

"God, yes. I surely think so."

"Then plan on that. With twenty more if you need it. It's going to be my first real home that isn't a condominium or an apartment. It's a good investment, whether I live here or rent it or just go on and give it to Jimmy."

"It's so exciting." Elise got up and began to walk around the room. She walked out into the wide central hall and into the facing living room. "We can make it into a showplace for that kind of money. I have to return to Atlanta tonight, then I'll be back for several weeks to finish a job here. When do you leave?"

"Tomorrow morning. It will be Eugenie's memorial. A beautiful home. We will make a piece of the world more beautiful in honor of her beauty and her taste."

The two women stood in the hall and joined hands. It seemed possible, a future that was better than the past. It was possible for Sarah.

By the time Elise had been on the plane to Atlanta for thirty minutes she would be getting drunk. In Sarah's presence, with Sarah's strength to lean on, she could plan and dream and think. As soon as Sarah disappeared she went back to her reactions.

"Would you like a drink?" the stewardess asked.

"A Scotch and water," Elise said. "I've just been to a funeral. My mother died."

Jimmy McAllen was sitting in the kitchen of his favorite law professor getting over a lingering hangover and trying to recover from seeing both his parents in one house. "They have always thought I was a fuck-up," he was saying. "Even when I start accomplishing something they both act like they think it's going to end at any moment."

"So why did you get drunk then? I thought you quit drinking. I haven't seen you drink in months."

"I don't know. Just to keep them away from me. Besides, I was with my cousin. She's fallen in love with me. On top of which I owe her eight hundred dollars. I fucked her a couple of times, to tell the truth. She's crazy. She'll do anything. So we just got drunk. She keeps coming here on the weekends. She just shows up."

"Why do you let her?"

"Hell, I don't know. She's fun to party with but not much fun if she's sober. Her mother died. It was her mother's funeral. Now I've got to get rid of her."

"Then go on and do it."

"I'm afraid she'll tell our folks we fucked each other. My uncle Jack might kill me."

"Jimmy."

"Yes."

"I don't know much about human behavior but I can recognize passive-aggressive females when I see them, having married two or three and had one for a mother."

"So, go on."

"You sound guilty as hell. If you sound guilty and you feel guilty, someone's trying to make you feel guilty. You didn't make her fuck you, did you?"

"Hell, no. She thought it up. She showed up one weekend with some hash and we did it and then we got in bed. Tell me more about passive-aggressive. That's starting to sound right."

"If someone makes you feel guilty then they want you to feel guilty. It's their trip. You can get off the boat any time you want. They'll find another rider."

"What if she tells our folks?"

"Say it's a lie, or say she thought it up. You're almost out of school, Jimmy. You'll have your own life soon. Don't care what your folks think. If it was me and she told them I'd say it was a lie. And eat those eggs before they get cold. And go to a meeting tonight. I'm not going to have you start backsliding on me."

"I think it was the last time I'll get drunk. I didn't even like it. It was like some old shirt that didn't fit."

"Go to a meeting anyway."

"Okay. I will. I'll go to the one at the Unitarian Church at seven."

After Elise had left for the airport, Sarah took a long bath and dressed in a skirt and sweater and loafers and went downstairs to read. At six-thirty Jack returned and joined her.

"Thank you for staying another night," he said. "I don't want to be alone here yet." He got up and went to the bar and began getting out things for drinks. "Do you want a martini?"

"No, I don't drink much anymore. Too hard to handle now. Go ahead." He poured himself a Scotch and came to the sofa and sat by her.

"We'll go out later and get a steak. There's a place near."

"There's plenty of food here. We could eat here."

"Are you sure?"

"I'm sure." She waited. There was nothing to say, nothing to do, it was too complicated, too exciting, and too sad.

"She was throwing us together."

"Do you think she ever knew?"

"She might have guessed. From my part, not from yours. She never knew about the afternoon on the river."

"Jimmy could be yours."

"I know that. I've always known it."

"Is he in love with Elise?"

"I have no idea."

"Because I think she's in love with him. I spent the day with her, Jack. She's going to redo the house. She talks about him. I don't know. It's difficult to explain. She's going to have a tubal ligation. Did she tell you that?"

"She talked of it. I let it go. I thought Eugenie could deal with it."

"What if they guess?"

"They think it's dangerous enough to be cousins. Perhaps it is. Maybe we're making too much of a friendship."

"Someone could have said that of us."

"Yes, they could, couldn't they?" He turned to her and took her hands. His were almost trembling. "This isn't the time or the place, Sarah. I wouldn't despoil you or Eugenie by speaking of it here, in her house, in what I suppose is her wake. Who else in the world is there to really mourn her, but you and I?"

"Let's go out," Sarah said. "I've changed my mind. Maybe we should get out of here." She took back her hands and stood up. Jack drank the rest of his drink. "Come on. Let's go somewhere downtown and eat dinner and come home and go to sleep."

The phone was ringing. Jack answered it and handed it to her. It was her agent in New York wanting to talk about the Paris deal. "I don't know," she told him. "I'm at a funeral. I'm coming home in the morning. Tell them I think so. I don't know but I might. It depends on the deal you can get for me."

She listened, shaking her head. "All right," she answered. "Yes.

That's good. I have a use for the money. Of course. I'll talk to you tomorrow then. Thanks, Freddy. It's all right. I'll tell you later."

Jack was standing by the sofa waiting for her. Thinking how far apart were the worlds in which they lived. "I'll go wash up," he said. "Then we'll leave."

Later, when they returned to the house she asked him for another sleeping pill and he gave it to her and she kissed him on the cheek and went upstairs and got into bed and went to sleep. Not in this house, she vowed. Not because you thought it up, Eugenie. Not in your way, in your scenario. Not with your ghost on the pillow.

In the morning Jack insisted on driving her to the airport. He carried her bag to the car. He drove her across town. He carried her bag into the terminal. He was so close to her it was as though they had always been together. It was embarrassing and painful and confused. They kept going through the scenes. At last they were standing by the gate where she was to board the plane and at last she went into his arms and let him be close to her. "Come to New York and see my world," she said. "Whenever you can come. On the spur of the moment. If you get lonely."

"I will," he said. "As soon as I can." Then she boarded the plane and left him there and found her seat and sat looking out the window for two hours, thinking of the past and the present and the house Elise was redoing for her and the long drive up through the oak trees and Jack's body against her own and their strange, confused children and how odd and mean life had become. Why did I leave him? she wondered. What sort of insanity is this thing I call a life in New York City?

CHAPTER 9

Robert was full of questions when Sarah got home. He took her bag and carried it into their bedroom and began to undress her. He talked while he took off her jacket and her blouse and her skirt. He pulled off her pantyhose and kissed her knees and her belly. Then he began to kiss her breasts and neck and face. She let herself go into it. She tried as hard as she could to love him.

Afterward, he lay beside her and she patted him as she would a child.

"You're unhappy," he said at last. "It's the Paris deal, isn't it? I think you should go on and take it. You aren't going to stay at *Time*. Go on and get it over with. Go to Paris. It's good money. I'll go with you if you want me to."

"No. It isn't that. Why? Did Freddy call here? Did you talk to him?"

"Twice. He said you had to let them know."

"Then I might. I need the money. I want to redo my grandfather's farmhouse. I went up there and looked at it with an architect. It would be a good investment. It would always pay me rent even if I didn't want to live there."

"You're thinking about living there?" He got up and lit a cigarette and came back and sat on the edge of the bed. He looked very beautiful and young, vulnerable, smart. Sarah sighed, trying to know what to say that he would not find threatening.

"Only when I want to go away and write. I might want to write a book when I come back from Paris. Who knows? Anyway, I can always rent it after it's restored. The world comes to Nashville now. I could name my price to music publishing people. It has a creek and a waterfall. It's really lovely property. Of course, it belongs to my son. I couldn't sell it." She sat up on her elbows and tried to keep on loving him. Tried to love him as a man but all she was feeling was maternal. He seemed so terribly, endlessly vulnerable. The young. My God. How to love them, how to help them. Not in this stupid, May-December romance, she decided. I'm too good for this. Slave labor.

"If you wrote them a script and it was successful, you'd be fixed for life. You could get work from them whenever you wanted it."

"But I like what I'm doing. I've been a journalist all my life. I like being at the place where the news comes in. I used to watch the Reuters tape like brokers watch the market. Now it's on a screen but we're still the first to know."

"Keep a lot of balls in the air. You can leave for a few months. I'll come with you. I told you that I would."

"We could rent the apartment while we're gone. I'd hate to have two households and a building project."

"Don't worry so much about money, baby. There's plenty of money. I'll be making more soon. As soon as the season begins I'm going to do some soap opera rewrite work. Freddy said he could get me something. I just hate to start hacking until I get a better start on this book."

He pulled her over into his arms and caressed her. He was lying as usual, but she listened to it. He didn't think it was lying. It was how out-of-work writers talk. She relaxed into his arms, thinking about the bottle of sleeping pills Jack had given her. She didn't want Robert to know about them or he would want part of them. I'll get up later and take one if I don't go to sleep, she decided, and cuddled down into his arms.

This is over, she decided, as she was falling asleep. It's over. I knew it months ago. Goddammit, I hate to break up with him in the winter. I'll have to give him money for an apartment. There won't be anyone to light the fires. No one to buy groceries. No one to make me come.

CHAPTER 10

In the morning there was a snowstorm and moving around New York was impossible. Sarah's agent called twice to talk to her about the Paris offer. "They hold out carrots that usually turn out to be turnips," he said, meaning movie people in general. He was seventy years old and he had been writing contracts between writers and movie people for forty years. He was as cynical and cautious about that relationship as it was possible to be, and Sarah depended on that caution. "On the other hand, this particular backer often holds out money that turns out to be money and he's behind these producers."

"Why do they want me?" she asked. "I haven't written a book in five years or a script in seven."

"Because they like that script you wrote for Tri-Star that we sold several times. They're fans of yours."

"I might do it. I could ask *Time* for a leave of absence."

"Do you want me to call them?"

"No, I'll do it myself. I'm still mad about the Pakistan piece. I spent two months researching it and then *Life* scooped us. That's how it is now. James doesn't have the power to help me anymore. I don't know who has the power. So, who are the producers of the movie? Tell me again? . . . Okay, that's good. . . . She's done good work. I could work with her. Well, I'll think about it. But don't let me start believing in fairies, Freddy. Watch out for me."

"You'll believe in two hundred and fifty thousand dollars if I can get it, won't you?"

"I already do. I have my part spent."

"A new car? A new apartment?"

"No. I'm going to rebuild my grandfather's farmhouse in Tennessee. I may live in it and write a book when it's finished."

"That's good news. When did you think of that?"

"While I was at the funeral. My father died on that farm. In the fields, hunting quail with his dogs. I was thirteen."

"You've never written about that."

"I know. I might now."

"Dangerous waters. See your analyst before you wade out into that."

"Well, I won't do it soon. When would the movie people need me to leave?"

"In the next few months. They want something by September."

"I'd drop everything and write it by September. Then I'd wait around while they formed a committee and flew people in from around the globe and maybe hired Dick Morris to take a few polls and licked their fingers and put them up in the air to see which way every wind was blowing and then they'd have someone read the script and tell them what it said and then they'd say they were going to give me the millions of dollars as soon as I wrote it over again from scratch. Isn't that how they work, Freddy?"

"We'll get a hundred grand up front if you want to do it. As soon as you begin writing. That's not peanuts. I'm not advising you to do this, Sarah. It's up to you."

"I'll read the book again. If I can bear to read it. And I'll talk to James and see what he says. My finger in the air. See, Freddy, the minute you start entertaining the idea of messing with these people, you begin thinking like them. It's catching."

"Greed is always with us. Why do you think the old Jewish priests were always warning against it in the Bible?"

"Why do they want to change the title? What do they want to call it now?"

"*Souls in Paris.* They read somewhere that movies with Soul or

Paris in the title have the best sales over time during the last twenty years. So they decided to have it both ways."

"The producer told you that?"

"Over lunch at Ici. I know, I know." He began laughing like a child.

"And this is the producer you think can be trusted?"

"To pay. He can be trusted to pay."

"I'll talk to James. I'll let you know something next week."

Robert was standing by the door when she got off the phone. "You told him yes? You're going to do it?"

"I may." She got up off the sofa and went over to the window and looked out into the still-falling snow. A few taxis were moving, but very slowly. There were a few hardy souls on the street, bundled up, wearing boots. "It's the classic conflict. Journalism versus striking out on your own. I've always liked to be adrift without an oar, but I also like to be where the news is coming in. It's seductive, getting to be the one to tell the news. The other truth, 'the gigantic idiosyncrasies of the human heart,' is what the fiction or script writer tells. You never know if you get that right, all you can do is tell the truth about everything you've known. If you tell it well enough, you can make someone believe you. All you have to do to report an earthquake or tornado is write clear sentences. The material is provided."

"Which would you rather do?" Robert moved near to her.

"I want both. I want to put on my good shoes and go down to *Time* and be an important editor and I also want to be in Paris and take a chance on making a good film. It's an embarrassment of possibilities. Hell, I don't know what I want to do."

"Go over there. You'll make a success of anything you try. You're lucky, Sarah. If I wasn't in love with you I'd be jealous of your luck. Well, you're lucky because you're good." He was sitting with his elbows on his knees looking like a cross between an angel and a Marlboro ad. Sarah smiled at his beauty and the generosity of the moment, then turned back to looking out the window at the snow.

There was three feet of snow on every car, every lamppost, trash can, newspaper vending machine, tree. It was beautiful and holy.

"I want to go out," Robert said. "You want to try to make it to Stacio's for breakfast? Or one of the hotels?"

"No. I like it here. I might try to work in a while. Read the book they want turned into a script. I ought to read the book if I'm thinking of doing this, don't you think so?"

"I thought you read it."

"I'm going to read it again. Go on. Have fun. I'll see you later." She kept on watching out the window. She heard him in the hall putting on his boots and coat. She watched him leave the building and start down 62nd Street with his green hat pulled down over his ears and she loved him again and knew why she had stayed with him. He swept the snow from the top of a mailbox and fashioned it into a small fat figure and stuck it on top of a garbage can. Then he went sliding on down the street, her young and hopeful and outrageous lover.

I can't stay here and read a book for the movies, Sarah decided. I'm going to the office. I can't quit *Time* magazine to write a movie. If they'll give me a leave of absence, I'll go. If not, I won't. We're doing that cover story on the Bosnian refugees. I want to see if that's set. I'll get to the office. I'll even take the goddamn subway. I'm not a quitter. I don't quit.

The summer Sarah was eleven her parents had driven her to the farm so that she could go to a wilderness camp put on by her grandparents' Presbyterian Church. It was held every summer near a waterfall on a branch of the Tennessee River. There were permanent cabins and a lodge and hiking trails that wound through miles of virgin woods.

They drove to the farm on Saturday afternoon. The camp was supposed to begin on Sunday. Sarah was in the backseat of the old Packard eating a bread and butter sandwich and worrying about going to the camp.

"You're going to love the lake up there," her father was saying, "and they'll take you to see some caves." He was driving the car with one hand and turning around every now and then to look at her. He was very handsome, with his hair cut short and his freckles standing up on his face. Her mother was beside him wearing a dotted Swiss dress she had made the week before. Sarah moved to the side of the backseat so her father couldn't look her in the eye. There were no seat belts back then. People slid around on the car seats and took their chances.

"I used to swim three miles in that lake every afternoon when I went to that camp," he continued. "I met a girl I liked there. She had a bathing suit as thick as a blanket. I thought she must be the strongest girl in the world to swim in that suit. I liked her for being strong."

"I don't know if I want to go or not."

"Of course you want to go. After you get there you're going to like it. You can't just stay home forever and let your mother spoil you to death, Sarah. You've got to get out and see the world."

"Leave her alone, Claiborne," her mother had said. "You don't have to stay at the camp if you don't like it, Sarah. There's a phone there. If you don't like it, I'll come get you."

"You're spoiling her to death," her father said. "Don't be a quitter, Sarah. For God's sake, whatever you do, don't quit."

Sarah went into her bedroom to dress. She was going to the office and she might have to stay all night to get caught up but that was work and that was what it meant to work for a living.

While she was dressing Jack called from Nashville. "I wanted to make sure you got safely home," he said. "I saw the snowstorm on television."

"I'm trying to figure out a way to get to the office. I guess I'll call for a dog team." She laughed gaily, a silly, young girl's laugh. The sound of his voice was so comforting. It changed her chemistry to hear him speak. "I'm sorry for the reason I was there but it meant a great deal to me to see you. Don't think I don't feel that too, because I do."

"Then when will you come back here?"

"When I can. It may takes weeks to clean up the messes I left last week. Also, it looks like I'm going to agree to go to Paris. Take some time and go with me."

"Oh, I couldn't do that anytime soon. I have to arrange for Eugenie's patients to be taken care of. Most of her practice was gone anyway, but there were a few she still counseled with, mostly older people, the parents of friends. They depended on her. She saw them as recently as a month ago."

"But she was a pediatrician."

"These were special cases, favors to friends. Anyway, there's a lot to do."

"Could you come to New York for a weekend?"

"Not right away. I was hoping you'd come back here. I thought you and Elise had to do things about the house."

"As soon as she gets plans drawn. Then I'll come there."

"Come back anyway. Come for me." His voice dropped a level and Sarah felt the stirrings of desire, real desire, terrible, old, threatening, life-changing desire.

"I will," she said. "That's certain."

They talked about trivial things. Then she hung up the phone and threw on some warm clothes and boots and a fur-lined parka and went out into the snow-covered city. She walked down Madison Avenue in the thick deep snow. The day was filled with magic because Jack had called her on the phone. I am fifty-two years old, she told herself. I should be able to analyze this. She would say that to herself and then she would laugh out loud and think about the way he had looked when he left her at the airport. I have to stop doing this. I can't do this. I can't go to Nashville, Tennessee, and be a doctor's wife. If I did it would start a scandal. Maybe he'll come to Paris. No, that's not what he wants. He wants a replacement for Eugenie. What am I thinking? What am I doing? I'd better get over to Fifth Avenue and find a taxi. If I can't find a taxi there I'll get the subway at 59th Street.

CHAPTER 11

The snowplows had cleared Fifth Avenue and she was able to get a taxi downtown. She stopped at the cafeteria and bought a sweet roll and carried it up to her office and began to read the mail and faxes and sort through the messages. She wasn't as far behind as she had thought she would be. Most of the messages were irrelevant. She ate the sweet roll. She tried to decide where to start to answer the mail.

The fax machine turned on. She walked over to it and read the message it was printing.

> Dearest Sarah, have plans drawn. Am so excited. Where are you? I'll Fed Ex them this afternoon if you tell me where. I can do it for seventy thousand dollars. Maybe less. I want a new gravel driveway between the oaks. Three flower beds. I made the bedroom and bath as large as possible without ruining the shape of the existing house. Call when you get this. I'm excited. Elise.

"So am I," Sarah said out loud. "Real world, real boards, real house, bedroom, sleeping under the sheltering oaks. I wonder what the weather is like there now." She walked to the window and looked down upon the snow-covered city and loved it as never before, loved it as she loved Robert, as one loves the thing one is about to leave.

She imagined the farmhouse in the winter, with fires in both the fireplaces and a long white sofa in the living room. And Jack.

She went back to the desk and filed letters and left notes for her secretary and edited a story and called the author and then began to walk all around the office, straightening things, putting things away, making mental lists. I could be gone by June, she decided. I could finish every single thing I've started. I'm not a quitter. Being a quitter was when I took this job instead of taking a chance on my own talent. I have always trusted my talent to make a living for me. She was standing by a wall of bookcases and filing cabinets when her boss came in and started laughing at her. "What are you doing here in a snowstorm? I thought you took a week off."

"I'm going to quit." She turned around and faced him. "In June. I'm going to Paris to write a movie. I mean it, James. I was going to tell you Monday. Stop laughing. It isn't funny."

"It's classic, that's all. Every time I go to a funeral I know I'm wasting my life. We are wasting it, but that's what it's for. Don't quit, Sarah. I need you here. And for God's sake, don't write a movie. They won't use a thing you write. It's fodder. At least we inform the public around the old *Time* magazine."

"About what, James? Junk science, movie stars, the Princess of Wales. We did a special on tornados the week Warner Brothers put out their tornado movie. That was not a coincidence, James. Who did they think they were fooling? Who made that decision? Did they think no one would notice or are we so far gone at every level that it doesn't even warrant notice anymore? In the same issue there was a long article about corruption in the Congress. It's *Saturday Night Live* every day now at the old *Time* magazine, isn't it. Maybe that's it, maybe it's a subtle form of social satire and I just haven't been paying enough attention."

"Did you fall in love at the funeral? See your ex-husband and decide you'd made a mistake? I've been there. It's heady."

She picked up a statue of Amenhotep and pretended to be getting ready to throw it. "You cynical bastard," she said and started laughing. "That's why I'm quitting. Because I'm tired of all this goddamn journalistic cynicism. I bet you would miss me. After the way I covered your ass in that Bosnia piece."

"My mum was sick. What can I say? Put down that Egyptian god and let's go get some French food. Come on, I want to talk to you about next week's cover story. Wait till you hear the new idea."

"Which is what?" She put down the god and walked over to him and hugged him. He was tall and lanky and fabulously Jewish. He was the reason she had come to *Time* to begin with. She took his hand.

"I'll tell you when I have a drink. Come on."

She turned off some machines at her desk and grabbed her parka and followed him out of the room. They went down an aisle past rows of desks where public opinion was being manipulated and formed, day after day, week after week, month after month, year after year.

"You can't leave now," James was saying. "It's an election year. Where will you watch the results? In some bistro in Paris or did you see yourself in a little house with your beloved?"

"Okay," she said. "That's it. You do that one more time and I'm telling your wife about your blood pressure." He held the door open for her and they went down in the elevator and through the lobby of the vast building that news had built and out onto the snow-covered streets. It had stopped falling now and the massive operations of New York street maintenance were in full swing clearing streets. There were clear lanes all up and down the Avenue of the Americas and a bus was running.

"Le Périgord is open," James said. "Want to have an adventure and try to make it across town?"

"Sure." She giggled and took his arm. He was wearing a thick gray cashmere sweater and a greatcoat that matched it perfectly. He was married to a wealthy girl named Betty. It was clear Betty had been dressing him for the winter. "James, where did Betty get that sweater and coat? It's not good for magazine editors to dress like dandies. It gives the field a bad name."

"There's a taxi," he answered. "Run. Come on." They hurried across a bank of snow and got into the taxi, which was being driven by a Russian émigré, and talked to him all the way to the restaurant about the upcoming Russian elections and if he thought the Communists could stage a comeback.

"President Clinton is advising Yeltsin," the driver said. "He is sending his people there to win the election. They are telling him how to get on television and putting the makeup on him. He will win."

"Are you sorry you aren't there?" Sarah asked. "Do you want to go back?"

"I'm happy here," the man said. "I'm buying this cab. When I get it paid for I'll buy another one. Is this it? Is this the place? Are you sure it's open?" He had come to a stop on 52nd Street, across from a plain white door that looked as though it led nowhere. It led, of course, to the best French restaurant in Manhattan. The maître d' opened the door for them and led them into the beautiful small foyer and took their coats and then took them to a table by a window and brought them water and menus. There were only three other customers in the restaurant but there was a full staff.

They ordered coffee and the waiter brought the beautiful home-made bread for which the restaurant was famous, and they ate it and drank the coffee and talked of their work.

"But I am leaving for three months in June," Sarah kept saying. "Don't forget I told you that. If Freddy gets me enough money and a war doesn't start, I'm going to do it. I have to do it, James. I'm not making enough money at *Time*."

"Do you want more money? Is that what this is about?"

"No. I want to write without interference or having meetings."

"Jesus, Sarah. What do you think the movie people will do to you? They're carnivores. They eat writers alive. They have writers for appetizers before they start on actors. It's the carnival. It's not writing. *All* it's about is having meetings."

"You think their meetings are longer than our meetings? How about that two-day cover meeting? I'll hold that meeting up to any Hollywood meeting and besides, their meetings pay more. I'll make three years' salary in three months and if they make the movie, I'll have a percentage."

"Percentage of the proceeds, not the gross. Added, subtracted, multiplied, and I might add *divided* by their accountants."

Sarah giggled and fell into his spell. "Imaginative, daring, bold, innovative, Hollywood accountants. Numbers are so reassuring in an otherwise corrupt world. Let me see the books, one might say. We'd rather not, they answer. They're confidential, but here's a check. We're sure it's right. We've checked it twice. Santa Claus is a good metaphor for Hollywood. Keeping the account books, slipping down the chimney, drinking the cocoa, leaving the presents. I want enough money to take a year off and write a book, James. I deserve that. Every writer gets to take a chance on writing their book. What the hell, it's the big reward. So let me go."

"I'll let you do anything I can, Sarah. I'm on your side, remember that. I don't belong to Time Warner, Turner, Ford, Carnegie, Merrill Lynch, MGM, Mitsubishi. I'm for Robert Frost and Mark Twain and Ernest Hemingway. I'm an old man from the old school."

"Will you marry me?"

"No. I'm already married."

The food arrived. They had sole meunière and pommes frites and drank half a bottle of white wine and then went back to the office and worked until dark. Two other editors came in. They talked to people in offices around the world. They watched the world and reported on it. They passed judgment. They planned its future according to their needs and what they called ideals.

All over the world, as they did what they called work, men and women slept and woke and made love and dug in the earth and looked up into the skies and fished in rivers and in oceans and built houses and fought and bought and sold weapons and gave birth and touched and loved and enslaved one another and gave each other happiness and disease and filled their automobiles with gasoline in the countries that had such things and were kind in places and in others performed acts of such cruelty the editors of *Time* magazine would not have been able to print the details in their pages.

The world in which we live, Sarah thought, as she made her way out of the building into the dark snow-covered city. Now I'll go home and see what my baby lover has found to complain about today.

And so, almost without noticing it, Sarah was pulled back into her complicated and enviable existence. With or without love I am happy here, she told herself. With or without a "real man." I'm a real man, who am I fooling? How did I think I got to where I am now? It was certainly not by being nice or looking pretty. Still, who knows, maybe it was partly because I was nice and pretty. Then she would laugh and shrug it off. It was irrelevant data and she was too busy to care one way or the other.

CHAPTER 12

Five weeks went by before Jack found the excuse he needed and called to say he was coming to New York and wanted to see her. He gave her a date.

"I have to attend meetings all day on Wednesday, but I should be finished by five. I was wondering if you would have dinner with me afterward."

"Of course. Where are you staying?"

"At the Hilton. Is that all right?"

"It's not a bad hotel. I have tickets to a concert that night. You might want to go. You used to love music. It's John O'Conor playing Mozart."

"I haven't heard any good music in a while. Our symphony's not what it used to be."

"Maybe it's our ears, ruined by compact discs." She put down the papers she was holding and removed her glasses. She got up from the desk and walked to a comfortable chair and sat down in it and removed her shoes.

"I have been missing you," he said.

"Why didn't you call?"

"I thought I had to let some time pass. It seemed . . . precipitous."

"Come up here then. How long can you stay?" She was feeling it again, the rush of desire. The thing she never felt anymore. It was one thing to have Robert whine and tease and admire and hate her. This was something else. This was immediate, complete, unquestioning. "I want to make love to you," she added. "Does that make me precipitous?"

"It makes you even with me. I'll be there Wednesday, then. That's ten days."

"I'll be here waiting. Did Elise tell you about the plans she made for me? They're brilliant, Jack. Her sense of space is amazing. I suppose the same sense could make a surgeon. Anyway, I'm thrilled with them and the work is already begun. I'll be able to move in by summer. Will you go there and see it with me when I come to Nashville?"

"Of course. She hasn't told me about it. We've had other things to talk about, when we talk. Eugenie left her estate in a mess. We kept our money separate. The deeper I go into it, the worse it gets. She had a woman broker she found in some fly-by-night firm and they were gambling in commodities. There may be nothing left by the time we clean up the messes. Well, I shouldn't bother you with that. It's just an insult to the children, to have left it to me. I'm trying to keep them from knowing the worst of it."

"Maybe she was angry, because of the disease."

"Perhaps."

"What do the children think?"

"They think it was just another way she found to reject them. She never wanted them, Sarah. She would have had abortions if I had let her."

"That's not the vision I had of your life."

"I don't want to talk about it anymore. I wish I hadn't brought it up. And I'd love to go to the concert with you if you want to take me."

After she hung up the phone Sarah sat staring out her wall of windows into the skyline of a gray wet day. Behind every window of every building are other lives, she was thinking. Other people facing problems, lives they are continually creating and altering and questioning. Driven, living creatures. We know not where we go or when. We know not when we go or why. I have never let my life be part of all their deeper messes, have never agreed to stay around for the bad parts. Always watching, never wanting to be with them in their deeper needs and strivings.

So now I am being sucked down into Jack's life. All our conversations end in darkness. Maybe I just want to get rid of Robert. Is that what this is about? No, it's more than that. When I hear his voice or see him it is real desire as it has always been. And that's in short supply at any age. I couldn't stop this if I wanted to stop it and I don't want to stop it.

She went to a closet and got out her exercise clothes and put them in a bag and left the office and walked the fourteen blocks to a health club and spent the afternoon working on her body.

Robert had news when she arrived home that night. "A friend of mine at Trinity Pictures asked me to go to California and help him work on a film," he told her as soon as she came in the door. "I have to leave in two days. I'm on spec at first but it's good pay. I'm going, Sarah. I'll be gone a month, maybe longer. You don't mind, do you?" He stood in the living room of the apartment looking so young and vulnerable and hopeful and excited and charged that she could not say a bad word about the plan.

"That's wonderful news. What friend?"

"Cather Morgan. You don't know him. He works in the art department but we'll be doing writing too. He designs sets."

"Get your money up front," she said. "That's my entire store of movie advice. Let Freddy handle the money part for you."

"Not this deal. I know these people. It's for Brad Pitt. They haven't signed him yet but he's reading the material."

"Then go. What can I do to help?"

"Nothing. Help me pack. Then help me celebrate. God, I love L.A."

"I'll help you remember to take summer clothes." She giggled, then went to him and took his arm. "Where will you be? Do you know yet?"

"Outside L.A. Cather has a place in Topanga Canyon. It belongs to this guy who's one of the producers but we have it for three months anyway. I'm really excited about this, Sarah. Don't get that look on your face."

"What look? I couldn't be happier. I'm just thinking about you out there in shorts and short-sleeve shirts. I'm jealous. It's what you've waited for. So give it a try. I just wish you'd run the money part through Freddy, but that's up to you."

"Mother's sending me two thousand. So I'll be all right."

"That's nice." Sarah turned away from him and went into the kitchen and started getting out things for dinner. There was no getting in Robert's way when he got excited about something. And, besides, that's how careers were started, wasn't it? By young people following insane dreams to points west, even L.A. Especially when they could charm their mother into checks for two thousand dollars for running money.

He followed her into the kitchen. "Don't cook for me," he said. "I have to meet these people later. I thought you'd want to go."

"Not tonight." She reached into a pantry and took out a long apron and put it over her suit blouse and skirt. She was going to cook, something Sarah did about once every six months. "I'm famished," she explained. "I've been working out. I'm going to make pasta and eat it and go to bed." She turned to him. "Not because I'm not glad for you. I'm thrilled at your news. But because I'm tired. I'm fifty-two years old and occasionally I just get tired. We should have ended this years ago, Robert. I'm too old for you. I told you this should end when I was fifty. I meant for it to."

"Because you're tired of me."

"I'm not tired of you. I'm tired. Period."

"Take off that apron, Sarah. That wouldn't fool a ten-year-old child." He was laughing and took the apron from her shoulders and picked her up and carried her into the bedroom and began to make love to her. It didn't work very well. Nothing was working between them anymore.

"It's me," she kept saying. "This is my fault. I'm no good at this anymore. You have to realize that."

"Because you don't want to. It was good last week. The best ever.

You make up your mind to something, then you make it happen. You're the one who taught me that."

"Hormones aren't an idea." She sat up. "The aging body is a bio-chemical system and some of my supplies are drying up. My pussy's drying up, to tell the truth. I'd think it was funny if it didn't hurt."

"Are you taking the estrogen?"

"When I remember it. I ran out a few weeks ago and I haven't had time to have it refilled."

"What's going on, Sarah?" He got out of bed and walked over to a table and stood watching her. He was very, very smart, never more so than when he was frustrated or distraught.

"Get back in bed," she said, loving him for the intelligence and the spoiled-rotten reactions and the thought of him doing this same number on his mother to get whatever he had wanted when he was small and beautiful and learning to manipulate his world. Now he was big and beautiful and sometimes she let him manipulate her because she thought it was funny.

He got back into the bed and they tried making love for another half an hour, then he got up and dressed and left the apartment. He did not return for two days. Then he packed and left for good. His mother had given him ten thousand dollars instead of two, in a fit of thinking the stock market was making her rich, and Robert was taking it to California to pan for movie gold.

They parted friends. She agreed to keep his things in the apartment until he was settled somewhere and he kissed her and held her hands and got maudlin. "These were the best five years of my life," he said several times. "I won't ever forget you, Sarah. Hell, I proba-bly won't ever stop loving you."

"Take good care of yourself," she answered. "Call and tell me where you are."

"I'll do better than that. I'll write you letters."

"I'll believe it when I see it. Real letters, with stamps?"

"I know. You don't need any E-mail."

"I don't. Well, take care of yourself."

"I'll probably be back in a week begging you to take me in." He threw back his head, looked marvelous, looked strong and excited and happy. He threw his bag over his shoulder and walked off down the hall.

Send the boy off to school, Sarah thought. I should have packed him a lunch or given him some rubbers or an inspirational talk. This above all: to thine own self be true. Not that he could wrap his mind around that concept this late in the game. My God, I'm glad he's gone. She went back into the apartment and took a deep breath. The future seemed to spread out before her, full of possibilities. Anything could happen now. In one of the possibilities was a river that ran to Tennessee.

I don't want to control these forces, Sarah decided. I want to let things happen for a while. I want to stop directing traffic.

Sarah had not worried about her body in years. Now, in the days before Jack came, she worked on it like a teenager. Every afternoon she spent an hour at the health club exercising and another in the sauna and whirlpool. It was the same body she had had all her life, not much fatter, not much looser, a charming, big-breasted, wide-shouldered body with pretty legs and a round stomach. She left the stomach alone. Even at this pitch of interest she was not going to do stomach exercises. This is your body which is given to you, she chanted to herself as she exercised. Its purpose is not ornamental.

He was arriving late at night and would be in meetings all day the next day. All day that day she thought about him being in the same town with her, at a meeting he was attending only as an excuse to see her. But he was going to the meetings. That was inexcusable.

By four that afternoon she was angry with him and angry with herself for wanting to see him. At four-fifteen she was packing a briefcase to leave the office when the phone rang. It was Elise.

"Sarah, I'm in town. I thought maybe we could have dinner and I'll show you the blueprints. They've framed in the additions and begun the porch and the drive."

"How did you happen to come to New York?"

"My partner was supposed to be here and couldn't come, so I

filled in for her at the last minute. Mostly as an excuse to see you. I bet you're busy. I should have called sooner but I didn't know until this morning."

"I'm delighted. Your father's here in New York at a meeting. Did you know that?"

"I can't believe it. He never goes anywhere."

"Well, he's here. At the Hilton. I was meeting him later. Come and join us."

"Fine. Where will you be?"

"Come to my apartment."

After she hung up Sarah was sorry she hadn't lied. What am I trying to do? she asked herself. Protect myself with his child? To prove I'm not trying to marry him? And what in the hell will we do about the concert? We'll never get another ticket this late. This is unbusinesslike. I haven't done any work in days. This is why they don't want women in business. This is crazy. I've been neglecting my job to spend the afternoons at a health club. Then, when he finally shows up, I invite his daughter to join us. Jesus, I need to see a psychiatrist. I've lost my grip on things. Not to mention that gown I bought at Lord & Taylor's yesterday. Not to even mention that goddamn red nightgown. I can't believe I bought that nightgown. I am fifty-two years old. It is not a joke that I went down to Lord & Taylor's and paid two hundred dollars for that gown.

CHAPTER 13

He arrived at the apartment half an hour early. She opened the door on the first ring of the bell and reached out and took his hand and pulled him into the foyer. "I'm early," he said. "The meeting was over sooner than I thought." He was looking at her with the old curiosity and she did not let go of his hand. Again, it was as if no time had passed. There is a tenderness between people who have been lovers that dissolves time and judgment and age. What passes between lovers is always timeless.

"Elise is coming here at seven," she said. "She called and I told her you were in town."

"I'm sorry." He grinned and came into the room and began to remove his coat. "I wanted to be alone with you, Sarah. But, of course, you did what you had to do."

"Or what she wanted me to do. She's so excited about the house. I think she's giving me ten times the hours she's billing me for. She's only going to be in town tonight."

"Then we have Elise, don't we?" He handed her the coat and she put it on a chair and led the way into the living room. You have Elise, she was thinking. Who is not as smart or pretty as her mother was and not as smart as you are either. Why? What trick of the DNA sends us children who cannot match our achievements or make us love them. Us mean ones. Us alpha alphas with our remorseless wills and egos. Don't think about Elise. Think about Jack. You wanted him here and he is here.

She sat down upon a long gold sofa and he sat beside her. His hands were folded in his lap, his fine legs in beautiful tailored pants lay beneath his folded hands. She made an effort not to look at his body and was quiet and waited.

"I don't know what to say to you, Sarah," he began. "I keep wanting to ask you to live with me and be my love. Then I think you'll believe and rightly that I'm asking you to fill a void in my life, but it isn't that. It's you and me. It isn't just wanting a woman or a wife. I could have that anywhere. Perhaps I shouldn't even explain this. I keep wanting to say, Now it is our turn. Don't turn it down. I feel there isn't time to wait to say this. I came up here to say this and I think you will turn me down. I keep knowing you will turn me down, but I want all these cards on the table." He looked at her then, straight on, not vulnerable, not scared no matter how much he claimed to be, the same old Jack she had always known, knowing what he wanted and asking for it. "I feel like this is my only chance for real happiness," he continued. "You, of course, may have many. But I don't love easily." He took her hands and waited. She pursed her lips, turned her eyes away from his, then back again. She could not forget Elise and the brooding thought of Johnny with his dark face, a doped-up Hamlet coming to ruin the feast.

"You could come to Paris with me this summer," she said. "It would be a good time to think of all of this, to figure it out. I know it's difficult to leave your practice, but you must take some vacations. I've about agreed to go. It will pay for the house we're doing and if the film is made it could set me up for life. I feel like I have to take this chance, one last big chance. I haven't taken one in a while. And we could be together and see what happens between us. Could you go? For part of June?"

"How long will you be there?"

"Six weeks or more. You could go with me and stay as long as you can, or come after me. We'd be on neutral ground, find out how we are together. If you hated it, you could leave." Now she giggled and grinned. Now it was Sarah who felt unsure. Had he done that to her? It had been a long time since a man had made her giggle or be unsure.

"I'll try to come. I can't promise, but I'll try my best to go with you or to meet you later. If that's what you want. I will do whatever you want that I can. I know you don't, can't, come to Nashville, Tennessee, and be a wife and live in Eugenie's house. That isn't what I'm proposing. I want to know if you can love me, Sarah. Because I have never stopped loving and desiring you and I don't think I will stop."

He stood up and pulled her up into his arms and they held each other for a long time, each thinking their separate, huge, new thoughts. Someone has died, Sarah knew, and our lives spread out from that catastrophe, our mutual fate and loss and terror. Out of our terror we should rush to life and we are trying to, but fear cripples us. Fear makes us hesitant and will make us mean.

She will leave me, Jack was thinking. This is too far away from my world. It could never last.

"We don't need to deserve happiness to have it," Sarah said. "But we do deserve it. We didn't act when we might have acted and I don't regret that. Perhaps Timothy and Eugenie would have been better off if we had. But the fact is, you and I are alive and free to act now. I wish Elise wasn't coming, because I want to make love to you, but she is coming. Maybe we don't need to make love. Maybe I just need to stay in your arms and smell your lovely smell." She had her head buried in his coat so it was easy to make this confession, this vast statement.

"Oh, Sarah," he answered. "Oh, my darling girl."

The doorbell was ringing. They went to the door together and it was Elise, looking very New Yorkish in a dark gray suit and low-heeled walking shoes. She came into the foyer and embraced Sarah and handed her the long blueprints she was carrying. "I didn't mean to horn in on your dinner," she said to her father. "I didn't know you would be here."

"I'm glad to get to see you," he answered. "Let's see what you girls have been doing to that farm. I went there once, did Sarah tell you that? Timothy and I went hunting with Sarah's grandfather."

"Well, come and look. See if you approve." Elise led the way into the dining room and spread the blueprints out on the dining room table and explained what was being done. Then she pulled a fat package of photographs from her purse and spread them out beside the plans. They were color photographs of wainscoting, quarter round, porch railings, trim, the details and craft of carpentry.

The new porch was almost completed, going around three sides of the house. There were wide brick steps. The driveway was lined and filled. Beds for flowers were edged with native stone.

"I can't believe so much has been done," Sarah said. "You must be driving them like a slave driver."

"We've had good weather."

"What I like about this undertaking is that it's in three dimensions," Sarah said. "Unlike the work I do. This is a real house, with real beds, boards, stones, bricks, gravel. I've never had a real home. I've been living in apartments for twenty years."

"Wait until you see the hot tub," Elise said. "I went all out on this bathroom. I made a long window so you can get in the tub and watch it snow in the winter. I spent your money on this tub, Aunt Sarah, but you'll be glad I did."

"We have a reservation at Le Cirque," Sarah said at last. "We can cancel it if we don't want to leave. There are plenty of restaurants nearer to here."

"Oh, no, let's go there." Elise was beginning to roll up the blueprints. "We can look at these when we get back."

"Fine," Jack said. "Whatever you two want to do."

They found their coats and went out into the hall and into the small elevator and stood very close, and then out onto the sidewalk and found a taxi and were driven through the dark streets.

The evening was doomed to begin with, Sarah decided later. Not all the civilization in the world could have saved that night from disaster. She called and ruined our party and no matter how hard we tried to be nice she was bound to pay us back for not wanting her there.

They found the beautiful restaurant and were served a wonderful meal in grand style. Jack praised his daughter's work and was more than kind to her. Sarah and Jack were both turned to her in every way. There was no hint of intimacy or conspiracy between them and still, Elise got drunk. She drank two martinis before dinner and she drank wine and more wine until finally they had to help her from the restaurant and take her to Sarah's apartment and put her into bed.

"She shouldn't drink at all," Jack apologized. "She's been mildly hypoglycemic all her life. Not a real problem, just a low tolerance for sugar. I've told her not to drink."

They were in the living room of Sarah's apartment. Elise was passed out in Sarah's bed. They were on the sofa again, only this time they were not touching.

"She senses something. She's an intelligent girl. She knows there's something going on. Maybe she got drunk to keep from knowing it. Maybe she just got drunk and there's no deeper meaning."

"We've had trouble with her before," Jack said. "With both of them. I keep thinking it's over, that they're grown and over the hump, but sometimes I'm not sure that happens in the modern world. They live in chaos. We had hoped this new job, new responsibilities, would give her the impetus to finish growing up. She had barely begun the job when Eugenie became ill. I'm sorry you had to see this."

"She's my goddaughter. I love her. She's yours. She's Eugenie's. I don't care if she gets drunk one night."

"It's not one night, Sarah. It's a continuing problem. You should know that, especially if she's doing work for you."

"Especially if I'm in love with you." She sat back, waited. He moved to her and pulled her back into his arms. But it was late now and Elise was in the next room. In the end he left, having extracted a promise from her to meet him the next day before he left.

Sarah walked him to the door and watched until he had boarded the small elevator and the elevator doors had closed. Then she went back into her apartment and spread out the blueprints and the photographs and looked at them for a long time. Then she made up the bed in the guest room and climbed into it and went to sleep.

She dreamed terrible dreams. She was in a wide field before a storm. Eugenie came walking toward her and said, "Well, you fell for it,

Sarah. I was sure you would. You always were a fool. Now I will show you what it was like to be me and have children that I hated. She'll get drunk every night and you can bring her home. See if you can make love to my husband after that. And wait until Johnny comes over. He'll be wearing earrings in his nipples and he will move in and redecorate your life."

"I didn't do this, Eugenie," Sarah kept trying to tell her. "You did it. I thought it was what you wanted."

Finally Sarah gave up talking to her and walked away across the field in the direction of the storm. It was a line of tornadoes but Sarah didn't care. Let them blow, she decided. Let them blow it all away.

Sarah woke at six. Elise was already up and dressed and sitting at the kitchen table writing her a note. "My God," she said, when she saw Sarah. "I'm so sorry. I should never drink. I know better. I always pass out, especially if I mix gin and wine. Will you ever forgive me? What did I do? Did I say something stupid?"

"No, but we were worried about you. I want to talk to you about your father and me, Elise. We have been friends since we were in college, you know."

"I know all that. It was just sort of a shock, finding him in New York. He never leaves Nashville unless he has to." Elise looked down at the note she had been writing. "So what is going on between you?"

"Your mother asked us to be friends. She asked me to stay in touch with him." Now I'm lying, Sarah decided. Every time I get around these people I start to lie. Even with Robert I didn't have to lie. Well, lies of omission maybe. "Please let me make you some breakfast," she continued. "You haven't had anything to eat. You didn't eat a bite of food last night."

"I'm okay. I'll get something later. I'm really sorry I got drunk. I guess I felt like I was horning in or something and so I got drunk because of that. I shouldn't have come over here but I was so excited about the photographs and I wanted you to see them. I have another set, by the way. I brought those for you. You can keep them if you want."

"Of course I want them. I'm excited about the farmhouse, Elise. I feel it's a gift you're giving me. Please eat something. Let's have some toast and eggs." Sarah moved toward the table, held out her hand to the girl.

"No, I have to go. I have to be somewhere. I'm really sorry about last night. I really am."

"It's over. Gone and forgotten." Sarah moved to Elise and tried to embrace her. She could smell the sour smell of old wine. Elise was nervous and she was shaky but she tried to let Sarah hug her. Then she was gone.

She left the note on the table.

When she was gone, Sarah lay down on the sofa and read the half-written note.

Dear Aunt Sarah, I shouldn't have come over here last night. I didn't realize you and Dad had a date. I was embarrassed to be horning in and that's why I got drunk. No one in our family can drink, as you may have noticed. Mother had to stop, but I guess you know all about that. Well, I hope someday you will forgive me. It means so much to me to get to work on your house. It's the most exciting project I've had. Well, I don't know what else to say except to ask you to forgive me . . . Please don't feel guilty about this. It isn't your fault. It's just another part of this messed up year. You didn't do . . . anything.

Sarah got up from the sofa and dressed and made coffee and went downtown to work. The walk to the subway, the hurrying people, the traffic, the subway ride, the newspapers, the wide walkways into the Time-Life building seemed like a wonderful, clean, new world, so impersonal and busy, so cheerful and useful and easy to understand, so far away from the events of the last twenty hours.

She worked hard until noon, returning phone calls, answering letters, agreeing to meetings. Her hair had fallen down out of its chignon and her brain was running at full speed by the time Jack called to ask if she would meet him for lunch at one.

"Come up here," she said. "Do you know where this building is? The Time-Life complex?"

"Yes, it's right down the avenue. What floor are you on?"

"Go to the security desk and they'll call me. We can go to Osteria del Circo. It's in the neighborhood."

"How was Elise?"

"Alive. She left at dawn, hungover and remorseful, so, if you can, call her in Atlanta later and cheer her up. I guess she thinks she let us down."

"I will. All right then, I'll be there at one. Is that too late?"

"That's fine. See you then." She put down the phone and got up from the desk and went into the ladies room and combed her hair and applied lipstick and put on a pair of earrings that were in her purse. She stared at her reflection a long time. Then she went out to the receptionist and asked to see the book. The afternoon was full. There was nothing that could be canceled.

"Is James in his office?" she asked the secretary.

"I think I saw him a moment ago."

"I'm going to talk to him. Hold my calls." She walked across the corridor and spoke to his secretary, then went into his office and sat down in front of his desk. "I really need a leave of absence to write this script," she said. "I'll work twenty hours a day until I leave to get you ahead. You know you can count on me for that. Also, I want to take this afternoon off to see an old lover. There's nothing wrong here, James. I love this job. I want it waiting for me when I get back. But this isn't just another movie scam. They have the money and the producers are people with honest work behind them. I want to take this man with me to Paris. Can you deal with this, James? Talk to me about it."

"Are you all right?"

"Yes. I just have had things offered to me that I can't bring myself to refuse. I'm a writer, James. If I turn down life, I'm dead. You know that. I shouldn't go off this afternoon. We're supposed to talk to Jerry. Can you do that without me?"

"I'll change it to another day. Think how relieved he may be to cancel it. Don't you know he gets tired of playing Solomon?"

"I'll come back in at five and work until ten. I'll make it up."

"Go on. And don't quit this job, Sarah. This job isn't going to show up every day."

"How could I quit as long as I have you for a boss? But I need time to write this film. Think it over for a few days and let me know. I'd need two months. At least two months."

"We'll talk about it tomorrow. I came and found you, Sarah. I wouldn't have you here if I could replace you." He stood up. She went around the desk and kissed him on the cheek and stood beside him holding the sleeve of his blue oxford cloth shirt.

"Who's the guy?" he asked. "Anyone I know?"

"Someone from the distant past. A physician." She smiled back.

"Oh, playing doctor. Well, it works for me, always did."

He began to laugh his wonderful, cynical journalist's laugh.

"I'm just trying to see if I want one last boyfriend." She pulled her already short skirt up a few inches and held out her leg. "See the high heels. You're the one who told me if I didn't stop wearing snow boots I was never going to get another lover."

"You have great legs and a great ass. I always tell people that. They say Sarah Conley's a great writer. She can really do it and I say, She has great legs and a great ass, which will get you further in the end."

"Shut up." She sat down in the chair before his desk and crossed her legs. "So are you going to let me leave?"

"You know I probably am."

"Then I'm going back to work." She left the room and went back to her office and worked hard for another hour. Then she combed her hair again. The phone rang and Jack came up on the elevator and she met him there and they went down twenty floors together holding hands.

"Are you hungry?" he asked, when they were out on the street.

"No. Are you still in the hotel?"

"Yes."

"Let's go there."

They walked down the Avenue of the Americas holding hands. They were both so unused to real happiness they were embarrassed by it. They walked to the hotel and went into the massive lobby and found an elevator and went up six floors and into his room and took off their clothes and got into the bed.

For a long time they lay in each other's arms without speaking. His body was as she remembered it. She remembered his body as she remembered his face, indelible impressions, the skin, the heat, the texture, as if she had been his lover forever and not once, years before, on a wild afternoon.

Her breasts and the softness of her skin were what his hands remembered. He felt her soften beneath his touch and he began to make love to her, tenderly, expertly, and she gave herself to him without sadness and afterward they slept in each other's arms and when they woke they went downstairs and sat in the hotel coffee shop eating sandwiches. "My plane leaves at seven," he said. "I don't want to leave you. I have surgery in the morning or I would stay. Will you come home with me? Will you come next week? When can I see you?"

"I told my boss today that I needed a leave of absence to go to Paris," she said, and laughed. "Putting in jeopardy the job anyone would kill to have. My boss is James Redfield, the man who wrote *Fields of Fire*. He's an angel, an old friend. He may give me the leave of absence but he can't guarantee the job will be there when I get back. We both know that. Anyway, I did it."

"Then you'll have time to come to Nashville?"

"Not right away. I wouldn't leave until June and I'd have to go straight to Paris." She pursed her lips, looked down.

"Oh, no, I remember that look."

"I'm thinking. It's my thinking look."

He reached across the table and held her hand. "It's all right. Anything you do. If you will love me. I don't ask for anything but that, Sarah. For now, just love me."

"I will, I do, I have. I just don't know what we should do next."

"When you finish that sandwich, you can come upstairs and help me pack."

"I don't want any more to eat. I'd forgotten how happiness takes your appetite away. I've forgotten so much, Jack, and here it is and now you're leaving." He kept hold of her hand and pulled her up beside him and they went back to his room and she watched while he folded his clothes and put them in the suitcase and closed and locked it. Then he sat beside her on the bed and they held hands and talked of trivial matters until it was time for him to leave.

After his taxi had pulled away she walked back to the Time-Life building and went up on an elevator and went into her office and worked until two in the morning.

At two-thirty she was home in bed. At three Robert called from California. "Where have you been?" he asked drunkenly. "I've been calling all night. Don't you pick up your messages?"

"It's the middle of the night. Are you drunk?"

"A little drunk, not too drunk. What the hell. It's going to happen, baby. We have a meeting with Brad tomorrow. I think he's going to sign on. Do you know what this will mean?"

"Can I talk to you tomorrow, Robert? I've been working all night. We had to change the cover story at the last minute and I was the only editor there. We changed it between seven at night and two. Cover and all. It's probably a world's record."

"I don't give a damn about *Time* magazine, Sarah. I'm calling about you and me. I've been calling you all day. I left you six messages. Brad's going to sign on. Did you hear what I said?"

"Robert, I'm hanging up."

"Don't hang up on me. This is Robert Hayden, baby. The man you've been living with for five years. Remember me? We have a good thing going. I'm not going to let you break this up, throw this away. People don't find people to live with and love every day. This isn't some used tampon or old milk carton."

"Oh, Robert." She had rolled her legs out of bed and was searching for her glasses. She found them, turned on the lamp and shook herself awake. "Wait a minute. Let me get a drink of water." She walked across the room and found a bottle of water and brought it back to the bed and drank it as she listened.

"You're fucking someone, aren't you?"

"No, I'm not."

"Then come out here."

"I can't. I'm too busy. I have to get ahead so I can go to Paris."

"Am I coming too?"

"To Paris?"

"Yes."

"I don't know."

"I am coming there."

"All right. If you are, you are."

"Come out here next weekend."

"I can't. Robert, I'll call you in the morning. I have to go to sleep. Where will you be at ten?"

"Writing the letter I'm writing you. A short story, an epistle. You better not read it if I mail it. If I send it to you, be careful when you read it."

"Is that some sort of threat?"

"It's a wake-up call."

"Oh, please, save the dialogue. I am hanging up. I am going to sleep." She hung up the phone, then took it off the hook and let it buzz. She snuggled down into the pillows.

Jesus Christ, she was thinking as she lost consciousness. I can't believe I lived with that rotten spoiled child for five years. Who am I anyway? What have I been doing? Where on earth have I been?

Whiskey, whiskey, whiskey, wine, and beer. Why does it always end up with alcohol and someone's drunken phone calls?

Of course it's how they get attention. It's how they get the courage to confront someone like me. Whiskey, wine, and beer. I came from sober, happy people even if my dad did die. What am I doing listening to drunks and placating hungover remorse? Well, I won't do it. I will not be a part of that.

CHAPTER 14

There had been whiskey at the farm the weekend that Sarah and Timothy and Jack and Eugenie had gone up there so the men could go fishing with her grandfather. Mr. C, the farmhands called him. He was a tall, rangy man with sandy-colored hair and wide, strong hands. He was six feet four inches tall and as lithe as when he was a young man. Seventy-five years of riding horseback and farm work had kept him young and seventy-five years of living on the land he owned had given him a courtesy and power that is hard to find in the modern world. He lived for work and duty and expected nothing less from anyone around him.

The whiskey was served in small glasses before dinner. One or two shots, then the bottle was put away. They all drank it except Sarah's grandmother, who had promised a Presbyterian missionary when she was young that she would never touch a drop. She was small and pretty and kind. She giggled like a girl when she told the story of the missionary. She had been fourteen and the missionary had come to collect money for missions in China. He had told them stories of foot binding and slavery and prostitution and in her horror she had promised never to touch a drop of liquor.

"What did the Chinese missions have to do with whiskey?" Eugenie had asked.

"I've forgotten. Somehow I thought the two things were connected."

It was ten days before Eugenie and Jack's wedding. A week after all their final exams at Vanderbilt. It was June in eastern Tennessee and the fields were green and luxuriant and the trees were full of squirrels and the rivers full of fish. "Bring the young man up here for us to meet," her grandfather had said, and Sarah had asked Eugenie and Jack to go along.

They had arrived in the afternoon and walked the property with her grandfather, then sat on the screened porch, sipping the small glasses of whiskey and talking about politics and land and the future. Jack had sat very close to Sarah's grandfather, facing her, and she had been quiet, already feeling queasy from the pregnancy and so confused she didn't understand her own actions. She had given up. She was married to Timothy and that was that. Eugenie was going to marry Jack and that was that.

"Those sapsuckers in Nashville and Washington, D.C., are going to run every farmer in the country out of business," Mr. Conley was saying. "You wait until you start paying taxes, you'll sing another song. They rob you blind, year after year, but they don't help you out when the crops are bad or the market falls for cattle. Sooner or later the Jews will own the world. Well, let them own it, is what I say. If white people won't stand up for themselves, let them work for the Jews."

"Granddaddy, please don't say that. Jews weren't allowed to own land for hundreds of years in Europe. That's why they became bankers. They have wives and children like other men. The best teacher I had at Vanderbilt was a Jewish man from New York City. He taught me more than ten other teachers."

"They're smart people. I'm not mad at them. I'm just telling you who runs the world, Sister. You can believe it or not. It's fine with me."

"I'm not sure anyone runs the world, no matter how many people think they do. Things happen, Granddaddy, and the world changes because of them. Machines are invented or drugs that save lives and the human race follows those events like the waves in the sea. The moon rules the sea. We don't know what rules human affairs. It's complicated. It isn't just some race or idea or group."

"Is that some of the stuff the Jew was teaching you?"

"Yes, as a matter of fact it is." Sarah faced him. As queasy as she felt she was still up to arguing with him. "It's all that right-wing literature you get that warps your mind. Is he still taking all those papers, Grandmother? That *Lighthouse* paper?"

"I sent you some things out of it last month," he said. "But you didn't read it, did you?"

"I don't read propaganda . . . ," she began, but her grandfather shook his head and turned away from her and directed his conversation to Jack, who was smiling and laughing and not arguing with him.

Sarah and Eugenie and Timothy and her grandmother talked of other things.

Before they went to bed they walked out across the front lawn to look at the stars. There were no streetlights for miles around and the stars were as bright as they are in the desert. There will be no more stars like that, Sarah always thought, when she thought of the farm. Those stars are gone forever from the modern world and with them all the mystery they engendered.

As they were leaving the porch Jack took her arm and walked with her. "I like your grandfather," he said. "He's a strong man."

"He likes you too," she answered. "He's picked you out. He's pretending not to be able to remember Timothy's name."

Sarah's grandmother was up at dawn the next morning cooking breakfast, biscuits and eggs and bacon and grits and thick black coffee. The men ate with her, then struck off across the pasture carrying fishing poles.

Sarah rose sleepily from her bed and watched them from the bedroom window. She watched them until they were out of sight beyond the barn. Then she ate some soda crackers for her morning sickness, then fell back into a deep hard sleep.

*　　　*　　　*

The men walked back across the pasture and along a path until they came to a place where the creek wound down through the woods past a grove of elm and oak trees. They set up camp and fished until noon. At noon Sarah and Eugenie joined them, bringing a basket with sandwiches and a jug of cold milk. The hired man had milked the cow at ten, the milk had been cooled and now it was being tasted. "I had forgotten there was anything in the world this good," Jack said. "This is nectar for the gods. Tell me about this cow."

"A Guernsey I bought upcountry four years ago," Mr. C said. "She's a sweetheart. We have to give the milk away. I drive ten miles a week giving away her butter and milk. There aren't enough people here. I may have to go into town and ask someone to give me some children."

"That would be a great idea, Granddaddy," Sarah said. "Call Kathleen Madison. She's in charge of foster homes in Harris County. She came to see me in Nashville last year right after she started the job. You ought to call her up. I bet they'd love to have children stay here with you and Grandmother."

"I might have to do that," Mr. C said, and Sarah went to him and stood in the shadow of his tall body. She put her arm around his waist and remembered for a minute what it was like to be completely safe in the shadow of a man. Her own father had been that way. And Eugenie's father, and Jack. Timothy gave off no shelter. In his arms she felt like a shackle, a mistake, no more important or permanent than his belt.

Why was that? She was standing out on the Avenue of the Americas smoking her one afternoon cigarette and sipping coffee from a cardboard cup. Why did I never feel safe with him? Why did I marry him? Well, they didn't have abortions and I was scared to death and maybe I was mad. I have to quit feeling guilty about Timothy and Jimmy. I love Jimmy and I always will. He was better off with his father and his stepmother. Anyone would be better off than being dependent on me because I don't want any dependents. I want peer relationships. It's all I've ever been good at having.

That's me. That's who I am. I have to quit thinking I should be somebody else.

A cold wind was blowing around the corner of the building. She put out the cigarette and threw away the carton of coffee and went back inside the building and up to her office and cleared off her desk and went to work. There was pride and happiness in work and she was good at what she did. There was nothing to compare with it. Making something out of nothing. A book out of ideas in her head, a magazine out of the ideas and acts and opinions of many men. In a finite world of mostly selfishness and fear, it was high on the scale of things a man or woman could be proud of doing.

A screenplay is all right too, she decided later, when she was sitting at her desk finishing her musings on whether or not her life had meaning and whether she had to feel guilty for going off to Paris, France, to turn a so-so book into a movie. A screenplay might make someone happy when they have the flu. It might cheer people up or teach them something. Maybe I'll make the hero into a college professor. A geology professor, then I can teach a little geology. The geologic time scale is made possible because of the fossil record. That's a bit I've always wanted to find a way to teach.

CHAPTER 15

Sarah and Timothy stayed at her mother's house for Jack and Eugenie's wedding. The wedding was at ten. At eight o'clock Eugenie's father came and picked up Sarah. He put the box holding her dress into the backseat. He took her arm and put her into the car and drove six blocks out of his way going back to his house. "I am so glad to get to talk to you alone, my precious girl," he said. "I don't think she should be marrying him, Sarah. He's too cold, too hard to reach. I know you like him and you're married to his brother and I've about forgiven that one for knocking you up, but not quite. You are my little girls. This is hard on me. This is too soon to give you all away. I wanted to take you to New York and Philadelphia. I wanted to take you to Europe. I wasn't planning on this happening so soon."

"You took us to Chicago and Yellowstone Park. We've been plenty of places together. Besides, she's marrying him, today. I guess that's it."

"You don't sound too happy about it."

"I don't feel very well. I wouldn't want anyone else to feel this bad. If she gets pregnant, how's she going to finish medical school? I wouldn't say that if you hadn't talked about it first."

"She doesn't have to marry him. Ask her if she wants to. If she has the slightest doubt we can call this off."

"I can't ask her. You ask her."

"She'd marry him to spite me if she thought I wanted her not to do it."

"Oh, Douglas." Sarah reached over and touched his arm and left her hand there. "You're my father too, you know. You have me now."

"I do, don't I? And that means more to me than you know, Sarah. I'm so proud of both of you. Timothy's a nice young man. I didn't mean to say anything bad about him."

"I know you didn't. See that vacant lot over there. My dad used to teach me baseball and football there. It was our special athletic field. Every time we pass it I think about him getting his things out of the truck to play with me. He was so serious about it. We took athletics very seriously but I wasn't good at team sports. I wasn't interested in them. Just swimming. The only success he had with me was swimming."

"I'm sorry, Sarah. Sorry you lost him. And the rest of it. What did you tell the people at the *Atlanta Constitution?*" They had pulled into the Moores' driveway. Mrs. Moore was on the porch with two maids. They were standing there looking either busy or lost. It was two hours until the wedding and Mrs. Moore was sure she had forgotten to do something but she couldn't decide what she'd forgotten to do.

"I told them I was pregnant and married and had to stay in Nashville. They said they were sorry. So, that is that. All the money you spent on me and Momma spent on me and I'm pregnant."

"You'll have another chance. There are newspapers in Nashville. You can work and help Tim with medical school. It will be all right, Sarah. I'm sure it will." He turned to her and looked at her with deep, kind eyes and she believed he loved her and was on her side. She didn't completely believe it would be all right, but at least she believed Doug Moore was still her ally.

"Let's go help them," she said and got out of the car and asked Mrs. Moore what she could do to be useful.

"Go upstairs and help her dress. You look lovely, Sarah. How are you feeling? Are you feeling all right?"

"Yes. I'm fine." Sarah took her dress box and went into the house and up the stairs to Eugenie's room and stood in the doorway watching Eugenie arrange her hair. "You sure you want to do this?" she said. "We could climb out on the roof and run away."

"Except we can't." Eugenie got up and came to her and took her by the hands. "We've done it. You're married and I'm going to be. It's over. We found these men and now we've married them and a different time is going to happen in our lives."

"It's a different time in mine. I don't mind it all that much, Eugenie. I'm getting used to the idea."

"You do mind it. It's rotten luck. It's bad timing. It's the worst thing that could happen to you. You're the one with the possible great future, Sarah. You're the one who could have gone somewhere. Well, you still will. What time is it?"

"You've got an hour and fifteen minutes until you're walking down the aisle. Come on, get the hair fixed. Start acting like a bride."

"Put on your dress. Start acting like a bridesmaid." Sarah took off the sundress she was wearing and stood in the sunlight from a window. She was wearing a pale pink half slip and a beautiful pink brassiere. She was twenty-two years old, a dream of health and beauty and perfection. She reached down into the dress box and took out the blue silk bridesmaid's dress and dropped it over her head. As it slithered down over her body she was completely happy for a moment, as if the insanity of the moment and the year had reached a peak that resembled happiness.

I wish I could write that and understand it, she thought many times later. How we were happy getting ready for the wedding. Until we went down the stairs and got into the car to go to the church. We were even happy then. Douglas and Janet in the front seat and Eugenie and me in the back with our dresses taking up all the room. As long as it was pageantry and dressing up we were having fun. Then she had to go off on her honeymoon and I had to dance with Jack at the reception and be unhappy. Everyone was unhappy. It was a stupid, unhappy day. Except for getting dressed. Except for the blue silk dress falling down upon my body.

CHAPTER 16

The following Monday James called Sarah into his office and told her Time Inc. had agreed to a leave of two months. "Without pay, of course," he added. "It was easy. They're sending me someone's nephew. Don't feel threatened by that."

"I do feel threatened. He'll use my office?"

"Maybe not. He's been at *Newsweek*. They just want him in the company, so the timing's good."

"If we died how long would it take them to replace us?"

"Probably until morning. They'd wait until the next day."

"All right. I'll leave in June. The first week in June. Can you protect me? Are you telling me everything you know?"

"As long as I'm in this office, your job is safe. I can tell you that." He looked tired. He played with his pencils. Then he looked up again and smiled at her. "I might come over and see you. I want to go down to Santander and see my ex-wife and my little boy. He's ten. He barely speaks English. Did you know about her, Sarah? My French wife, the bitch."

"I'd forgotten about her."

"I met her in Vietnam. She was with the embassy. She won't let him come to the United States. She thinks I'll keep him."

"So, if he doesn't speak English you can't kidnap him?"

"Something like that."

"Come on over." She stood up. "Well, then, it's done. I'm leaving for June and July and someone's nephew's moving in to do my job?"

"Go on. I wish I was going somewhere. At least you don't have three ex-wives."

"I don't, do I? I'll keep that in mind if I get worried. And James . . ." She went around the desk and kissed him on the cheek. "Thanks for this. When I'm rich and famous in a mansion in Beverly Hills I'll have you out to interview me." She walked around the office pretending to have a face stretched thin by face-lifts. She clowned by the filing cabinets. "Okay, thanks a lot. Onward and upward, et cetera." She left his office and walked into her own and sat at her desk wondering if she had just made the biggest mistake of her life. Probably, she decided. The odds on this one are not good, but, after all, I'm fifty-two. The air is getting thin. That's no reason not to keep on climbing.

CHAPTER 17

The Paris story was made for Sarah. Turning the book into a screenplay would be child's play if she were left alone to do it. It had everything a screenplay needed, a beginning, a middle and an end, in that order, an unhappy ending, bright characters. It lacked danger in the sense that American audiences had come to expect it but the producers assured her that what they wanted was an old-fashioned love story. "Setting, setting, setting, that's all I can say," the older producer, a man named Stefan, kept repeating. "Use the city. I'm not sending a film crew to Paris to film background. I want the city to be a character in the film. I want the city to influence the behavior of the characters, change them. Not jarring, juxtaposed images like most Hollywood films but long, thoughtful pans and quiet images."

"That's in the book," Sarah said. "That's easy. Just use what's there."

"But expand it," Stefan said. "We have two hours to fill, maybe more. I'm thinking this could run two and a half. Summer audiences will go for it."

"It's set in the early fall."

"Don't worry about that," the second producer said. She was an older woman who had come out of retirement to make this film. She was beginning to be sorry she had done it until they brought Sarah on board. Sarah had written two small novels when she was young that had had a certain success among New York intellectuals. One of her greatest admirers was the woman producer, whose name was Dean. She smiled at Sarah and decided not to talk too much until the contracts were signed and a draft was in. Save it for later when it's needed was her credo when working with writers, and she had worked with some of the best of them.

"Why haven't you made a movie in so long?" Sarah asked, turning to her. "Your work was the best being done. The reason I signed on was you."

"I stopped to be a grandmother, but it became boring. I couldn't control their lives. They went right on being themselves so I decided to go back to fantasy."

"This book isn't fantasy." Sarah laughed and shook her head. "It's too close to home. Successful older woman with young lover thinks all will go well if they go live on the Left Bank. Who hasn't dreamed that?"

"It's a comedy," Dean said. "Essentially, it's a comedy."

"With an unhappy ending?"

"A true ending. Where would they go? It has to end like that. She has to send him off to find his way."

"We could have her jump in the Seine," Stefan suggested.

"Don't be ridiculous." Dean gave him a stern look.

"He's kidding." Sarah stood up. "Well, I'm getting excited. I may start writing before I leave. I got tickets for the third of June. I may be able to get away before then. I'll keep you informed."

"We're thrilled you're writing it." Dean stood up beside her. "You can do it, Sarah. You can do it and then we'll all go collect our Oscars together and then go off and live in the Gritti Hotel for a month to celebrate."

"I'm restoring an old house in Tennessee." Sarah looked into her eyes and smiled, waited. "I'll probably go there to celebrate."

"In Tennessee?" Dean looked bewildered. Like all native born New Yorkers it was impossible for her to imagine the middle or southern states without becoming mired in every imaginable filmed and written cliché and fantasy. "Oh, is that near the country music place?"

"It's near Vanderbilt University, where I went to school. It's one of the great universities of the South."

"Well, it must be if it produced you." Dean walked Sarah to the door. Stefan followed her. They had just sent a check for one hundred and fifty thousand dollars to Sarah's agent. They weren't having second thoughts. They were hopeful. It was just hard to let go of Sarah now that they had hired her. Hard not to want to tell her what to do. "Just write it. You know what we need."

"I hope I do," Sarah said, and turned at the door and touched Dean's hand. "We'll see. Call if you get worried."

She left the office building, which was on Lexington Avenue, and walked a few blocks before she caught a taxi to take her downtown to have lunch with her agent.

It's the boldest thing I've done, she thought proudly. It proves something. Who knows, it might win an Academy Award. It might be a beautiful film. If they film what I write. Don't get crazy, Sarah. This is Hollywood. It's the same mire that captured Faulkner and Fitzgerald and every other writer who went on that block and bartered their talent for the chance at big bucks. *It's a business and it's about money.* Say that like a mantra.

Still, if I begin with the city and its charm and powers. If I stay in a small hotel and Jack comes to be with me. Will I work if he is there? I need to be in love in Paris. How can I imagine a love affair in Paris if I've never had one there? Well, I could just remember what it was like when I first met Robert and we transformed Manhattan with our excitement, i.e., lust. I need to read the book again. It's a character named Cary Milligan's love affair in Paris. Not mine. And I can imagine anything. Well, we'll see.

She had lunch with her agent and they talked of the screenplay and how she could arrange it. He had read the book she was working from and was helpful about how to arrange the material. Also, he told her he had received the check. "So quit worrying," he said. "You're set for the next two years. If you don't spend it all in Europe. We can't go over this summer, so you can have our apartment if you like. I asked Camille this morning and she said she'd love for you to stay there."

"You're too generous."

"I have a stake in this too. I think this might really come to something, Sarah. Even if Twin Films doesn't make the film you would have the script."

"But not the rights to the material."

"That's so. What did James say when you talked to him?"

"He said they were all right with it and that someone's nephew was going to be in my office while I was gone. That scares me, of course, but I'm going anyway."

"Do you want me to call and get something in writing?"

"Not yet. Later in the week you can call. He's been good to me, Freddy. He believes in me and he wants me back. He believes in *Time* magazine but I'm angry about what goes on there. That tornado cover was so blatant."

"What was so bad about that? It's public information. It's good to disseminate that sort of information, isn't it?"

"Not the same week they release the Warner movie. It isn't journalism as I was raised to think of it." Sarah looked up and smiled. "God, to think I don't have to go to those goddamn meetings. It will be like leaving prison. I should just quit. Why hang on with it?"

"You were excited about it when you got the job. Don't quit. Take the leave of absence since it's open to you. You can quit later if the movie project takes off or if you don't want to go back."

"I've fallen in love, Freddy. I'm in love with someone I knew many years go. The husband of my friend who died. This is the first time I've told this to anyone. If you think I'm acting strangely, this is the reason."

"Take him to Paris with you." Freddy smiled at her. "I thought something was going on."

"I will if he'll go. How big is the apartment?"

"There're two large bedrooms. It's on the Left Bank, near the Luxembourg Gardens. You could have him there and still work. How much room does he take up?" Freddy was laughing now, pleased at her happiness. "How much space does he need?"

"A lot. He's a powerful man. I don't know if there's enough room anywhere for both of us." She hung her head, looked at her hands. It was the most vulnerable Freddy had ever seen her be.

"Does he love you?" he asked.

"I think so. I have always believed he did."

"Always?"

"We should have married each other years ago when we were young, but it was too late. We were already involved with the others. She was my best friend. Her father paid my tuition to Vanderbilt. I was going with his brother."

"The things we do. The secrets we keep. What fools we mortals be."

"All of us. And now we're here and it's so much later and I sort of halfheartedly think we can fix it up. Oh, that's not true. I think we can fix it up or I wouldn't be telling you about it. Half the time I think the reason I want to go to Paris is to see if Jack will go with me."

"Jack?"

"John McAllen. We'll see. Thanks for being here, Freddy. For listening to all this, for helping me."

"I want to hear it, Sarah. It's exciting. I don't know anyone right now who has this much going on. Most of the people I know are fighting disease or infirmities. This is a story I want to hear."

They ordered coffees and a dessert to share and sat looking out on 61st Street. They were friends, compadres, partners. There was work to do and Sarah would do it and Freddy would sell it and somewhere value would be created in a space that had been empty. Which is what art is, Sarah was thinking.

I hope she will be happy, Freddy thought, and sighed. God knows she deserves it. No one goes after life harder than Sarah Conley.

At nine that night she put a portable computer on the dining room table and began to write the screenplay, blocking out the scenes. She worked until twelve, and then, leaving the notes in disarray on the table, she climbed into bed still half dressed and fell asleep. An hour later Robert called from California. He was angry with her because his dreams weren't coming true.

"I'm writing you a letter," he said. "An epistle. Be careful when you read it. It's dynamite."

"So you said the last time you called. Why haven't you mailed it?"

"Because it isn't finished. I want to get this right, Sarah. It's a position paper. It will require an answer. I don't want us talking off the top of our heads. We have been together too long just to chuck it away. Are you listening? Are you awake?"

"Sort of. Have you been drinking, Robert? Why do you keep calling and waking me up?"

"Because you never answer the phone. I get tired of leaving you messages. What's going on, Sarah? I want some answers."

"I'm writing a screenplay and I'm trying to get James ahead before I leave the magazine. I'm working twenty hours a day and I have to sleep, Robert. I'm hanging up this phone. Don't call and wake me again." She sighed and lay back into the pillows. She was deeply tired and she was getting mad.

"I'll send the letter soon," he answered. "Promise me that you'll read it."

"I'll read it if I can. If it's harmful or insulting I won't read it. Or if it's mean. I'm about to start asking you to think about the money you owe me, Robert. You wake me up one more night and that's going to be what we talk about."

"Your money will be repaid."

"Good. That will be good for both of us, won't it? I'm hanging up."

"Go ahead." He hung up first and she clicked the receiver and left the phone off the hook and curled back over into her pillow listening to the clicks and the operator's voice. *If you want to make a call please try again. If you want to make a call please hang up and try again.*

CHAPTER 18

I am living my life on the telephone, Sarah decided one afternoon. Always at a remove from the real thing. Robert is in California calling me in the middle of the night. Most of my work is done on the phone or fax machine. I communicate with the world through machines. Even Jack, who I am thinking of *marrying*, isn't here. Poor baby, at least he doesn't call me often. He doesn't like to chat. He just wants to know when I'm coming there. The phone doesn't bring good news to physicians. No wonder he hates it. At least, half the time for a normal person, it's someone in a good mood with a good idea or something nice to report. No one calls a physician to tell them how well they feel. So him not calling me doesn't mean a thing. He wants me there. I should be there, but I'm not.

Sarah had left her office early and walked down to Elizabeth Arden to have her hair cut. She had left the number with her secretary and she was in the process of being combed out when a young girl in a black uniform brought her a telephone and told her there was a call. "Where is it from?" Sarah asked, knowing it would irritate Joseph to be interrupted in the middle of a comb-out.

"It's your office," the girl said. "Shall I tell them you'll call them back?"

"In fifteen minutes. I'm so sorry," she said to Joseph. "I have been meditating on the role of telephones in our lives. It's my fault. I shouldn't have left the number."

"You're an important woman." Joseph caressed the curve of her hair with his hand, pulling the sides down half an inch. He stood back to survey his work. "Your friend, Mrs. Bennett, was in the other day. She said you were in love."

"She didn't." Sarah smiled widely, looked at herself in the mirror. "This looks beautiful, Joseph. It's perfect."

"You are a beautiful woman. I want this top to grow out. Don't go cutting it any more when you are in California." He smiled at her and stood back to receive his well-earned praise. He was an artist and his clients adored him.

"That was a mistake made in the heat of battle," Sarah said. "Don't worry. No one will ever cut my hair again but you. I adore it. Thank you."

She got up from the chair and examined her hair in the mirror. The young girl was still holding the phone and Sarah took it from her and phoned her office and half listened while someone gave her a problem to solve.

I am losing interest in this well-paid, useful work, she decided and hung up the phone and then gossiped with Joseph for a while and took her time getting dressed and going back to the building. I am losing interest in it and I know why. I never meant to be an editor. I am only doing it for the money. I will write that script and go back to being free.

Only I'm not free. I'm in love and that's the worst bondage of all, only I'm not able to bear bondage. Can barely stand to keep a job. Much less be a wife to a busy man.

Time for the Zen prayer bench, she decided. Time for a retreat. Time to get the hell out of Dodge and get some writing done.

She walked back down Fifth Avenue to 49th Street and then down to the Avenue of the Americas and back to her enviable, supposedly exciting job.

CHAPTER 19

"I don't love anyone and no one loves me," Elise was telling the psychoanalyst her father had insisted she see after the night she got drunk in New York City. "You shamed me," her father had said. "I thought we had that all behind us, Elise. I thought you had decided to have some pride and make a good name for yourself in the world. We are not a family of drunks and wastrels. My father and grandfather were respected in this town. We have been here since before the Civil War and people here have treated us with respect because we earned that respect. . . ."

"You selfish bastard. You had Sarah staying here in this house at Mother's funeral. Sleeping in my room. I didn't make her move out of my room. No, I went into the small bedroom. Then I go to New York and you're up there dating her. What was I supposed to do? Getting drunk was about all there was to do."

"We are people of breeding and restraint. We do not get drunk at funerals and make fools out of ourselves in restaurants in cities."

"What are you doing with Sarah?"

"I was in New York for a medical meeting and I called her to have dinner because she is an old friend of your mother's and of mine."

"You can't tell me what to do. How dare you even say a word about it? I'm rebuilding her house for her. I'm giving her the best workmen in the state of Tennessee and barely charging for it. What was she doing there anyway, when Mother died?" Elise was screaming into the phone. She would never have dared to say these things to her father in person.

"Your mother called her to her deathbed. She came because your mother asked her to."

"You both hated me. You hated me all my life. Mother could have called me to her deathbed. I'm the one who came down every weekend when she was taking chemotherapy. I'm the one who held her while she was sick from the poison you let them give her. Oh, Daddy, I'm so unhappy. I'm sorry I got drunk, but I couldn't help it. Everything's falling apart."

"You need to get some help, Elise. I know a man there who might talk with you. I'll pay for it if you will go and talk to a psychotherapist. I'll pay as long as you will go."

"That's never worked. The last one told Mother I had a learning disability."

"That was years ago. Just talk to someone once. Promise me you'll go one time and talk to a man I know about. I don't know him personally, so you'd be safe about that."

"Okay," Elise had said. She had made the appointment, and she had kept it. But she had approached it with the feeling she was agreeing to go into the enemy camp. She had not believed for a moment that every word she said wouldn't be reported to her father.

"It's true," she repeated now, sitting in the office of the psychotherapist her father had found for her. "Neither of them loved me and no one else does either. I don't have any friends. The only person I really trust is my cousin, Jimmy, and I can't marry him because he's my cousin."

"Where is he?"

"In Lexington, in law school. It's his last year. I go down there and see him. It's the only thing I like to do."

"Why do you like him? Because he's your cousin?"

"I don't know. He looks like my dad. He has reddish hair. He looks like me. I don't know. I just always liked him, that's all. He used to party with me but now he's quit drinking and he won't come see me because I still like to party. He blames everything we ever did on me."

"Maybe you should quit drinking too, help him with it. Be the one who helps him quit."

"I lent him a thousand dollars. He paid me back part of it. His parents are rich. His father's a surgeon. His stepmother has an antiques business. Why should he borrow money from me?"

"I don't know."

"Because I offered to lend it to him. I always do that. Give everybody money. Why are you looking at me like that?" She sighed, leaning back in her chair. The psychotherapist reached for his pad. *Needful*, he wrote on it. *Passive-aggressive. Suicidal?*

"Is it time for me to leave?" she asked, and bit her lip.

"No, not yet. We have plenty of time. Tell me about your mother's death."

"She did it. We all know that. Doctors do anything they want to do. She weighed about ninety pounds. She was a skeleton. She could have called me and said goodbye. She could have left us a note. She didn't give me a thought. I know that. She didn't care if I live or die." She curled a piece of her hair around her finger and pulled it until part of it came out. It was something she hadn't done to her hair in many years.

"That bastard had me pulling out my hair, I mean, literally," she told Jimmy, when she called him that night. "I'm never going back. You should have seen that office. There were fifteen thousand dollars' worth of antiques in the waiting room. I felt like the hour lasted six days."

"I'm sorry it was a waste of time."

"He said I should quit drinking if I want you to like me."

Jimmy didn't answer that.

"Should I?"

"Not for me. Don't do anything on my account."

"So when can you come to Atlanta again? They're building the Olympic Village. You should come and see it."

"I may have a job interview there soon. I'll come and stay with you if I do."

"He was such an asshole," Elise continued. "He kept looking at me like he wanted me to tell him something worth writing down."

"Then don't go back. That's simple."

"When do you think you might come?"

"When they call and set it up. It's Walton, Eyers and Lindley. Have you heard of them?"

"I know a woman over there. She does our title work. You want me to give her a call?"

"Sure. Every little bit helps."

"We'll take her out when you get here. And hurry up. I have something I want to show you." Elise giggled. She wasn't flirting. The sex between them had always been pure rebellion, never passion, except occasionally in Elise's starved, romantic imagination.

"Oh, yeah, like what?"

"Bad girl underpants. No, no kidding, come on up here. Let's have some fun. I won't get drunk. I promise. If you want to quit partying it's all right with me. I can have a good time sober."

"We'll test that theory." Now he was laughing. Jimmy and Elise had secrets going back to when she was ten and he was twelve. They had been bad together since puberty. It was their relationship, only now Jimmy was outgrowing it and Elise was not. She did not believe he was outgrowing it. She thought she could pull him back in anytime she got him to come visit.

"I'm serious," he said. "This is an important interview for me, Elise. Maybe you better not say anything to anyone over there. Just let me do it."

"But you'll stay here, with me?"

"Sure I will. I'll be glad to save paying a hotel."

CHAPTER 20

Elise was calling Sarah at least once a week to keep her updated on the progress of the house. The supports of the roof had proven to be sound and the floors were being refinished. Finally, one morning she called to say, "The floors will be dry by Friday. Come and see the work. I won't be here but Dad will drive with you. I talked to him this morning and he said to tell you if you come he will take you there."

"I'll try. If I can finish this week's stories I'll get on a plane and be there. I wouldn't know when. Leave the key with your father."

"There's a bed in the back bedroom. With sheets and things. I had it moved in last week. It was one I had in storage. Also, a dresser and a chair. We have a storage bin in Nashville for pieces we buy and don't use. So I decided to give you a start in case either of us needs to stay there."

"A bed. What sort of bed?"

"Luxury mattress from Sears. Something I picked up when I was doing a job last year. The sheets are in a bag on the mattress. If I were sure you were coming I'd try to stay over."

"I can't be sure. I'll call later in the week and see how things are coming here. Don't stay. I know what to look at, I think. And, Elise, thanks again for everything. For all of your work, and now, for the bed. Imagine me sleeping in Grandmother's room. I used to sleep there. I used to cuddle up to her back and feel the skin on her arms. It was like velvet. I suppose her ghost will be there now for sure. She liked things to be pretty."

"She would like this. So will you, I think. Did I send you the photographs of the floors?"

"Yes. I want to make an album. Put all the photographs you've taken in a wooden box and sit it on the mantel."

"Not my new mantel. I don't want anything on it."

"Aside from that, how are things going?"

"All right. Jimmy came here last week. We went to watch them building the Olympic fields. It's pretty exciting. I think he's coming here to see the events this summer."

"I'm glad you're friends."

"We're more than friends, Aunt Sarah. I don't think you understand what we mean to each other."

There was a long silence. Sarah walked across the room, carrying the phone. I will not ask, she decided. If Jimmy wants me to know this, he would tell me. If it's true. I don't believe it's true.

"You wouldn't need me to say there might be problems," Sarah said at last.

"We don't want any children. Neither of us does. Everyone doesn't have to have children, Aunt Sarah. It's not the only way to live."

"I agree with that."

"Does it bother you if Jimmy and I see each other?"

"Of course not, Elise. You are grown people. What would I say?"

"It bothers Uncle Timothy. He thinks we're bad influences on each other."

"I'm sorry to hear that. Well, thanks for the update about the house and the furniture. I really might stay there one night when I come. Give it a test run."

"You're going to be surprised."

"I'd better go now. I have to get back to work."

"Don't worry about what I told you about Jimmy, Aunt Sarah. It's nothing new."

"I never worry about him. I'm sure he doesn't want me to."

*   *   *

When she hung up the phone she walked around the room for a minute. Then she called Jack's paging number and then she walked out of the office and went down the elevator and out onto the street. She walked over to a Korean bodega on Seventh Avenue and bought a package of cigarettes and took them back to the Time-Life building and sat on a wall facing the fountain and took out a cigarette and lit it. Well, I've started smoking again, she said to herself. That's what the McAllen family does to me. This whole incestuous mess. Jesus H. Christ, what am I doing in this? This isn't like Jimmy. I don't believe he's involved in this. And I can't ask him about it. What is the date? How many weeks has this madness been in my life?

She went through her old tennis countdown, life lessons, sports metaphors, wisdom. No weird serves, play your own game, don't wonder what the opponent is doing, keep your eye on the ball, be strong, be fast, keep moving, get ahead, stay ahead, play to win.

She sat on the stone wall with her feet hanging down and enjoyed the cigarette and the cold wind coming down the Avenue of the Americas. She had put the mobile phone in her pocket when she left the office. Now it began to ring. Jack was returning her call.

"Jimmy and Elise are screwing each other," she said, when she heard his voice. "That's it. We have to tell them. There have to be tests done. We have to know."

"Could you come here?"

"I'm trying to come this weekend. We'll tell Jimmy first. It's his information. If he wants to tell Elise he can."

"I don't know about this, Sarah."

"She could be his half sister. This is serious. We have to know. It's gone too far. It's gone far enough. I don't want this turning into a Greek tragedy."

"Let me know when you're coming. I'll meet your plane."

"We can tell Jimmy and ask him to stop screwing her. It's that simple."

"Then he'll tell Timothy."

"To hell with Timothy. This is the welfare of our children. They could have a one-armed seal or a blind daughter, God knows what could happen."

"Slow down. Don't get crazy. What are you worried about specifically?"

"God knows. Recessive genes. You're the scientist. Tell me what there is to worry about."

"They had different mothers. They're probably only first cousins, at worst half siblings. We don't have any degenerative diseases."

"There could be recessive genes that won't manifest until there's incest."

"Calling this incest is going a bit too far."

"Then what would you call it? I'll be there Friday night. On that nine o'clock American flight if I can get a seat."

"I'll come get you."

He called a geneticist at Vanderbilt. "What happens if first cousins marry, Larry? Or half siblings?"

"We aren't sure. We know that inbreeding usually produces less viable progeny. Less vigorous. The genetic loads of deleterious, recessive genes. Not a good idea. Half siblings would be worse than first cousins by about a seven point five degree. I've forgotten the exact statistics. I could look it up and let you know. Why, are you planning on breeding with your sister?"

"Don't have one. It's not entirely academic, Larry. Elise is in love with her cousin, Tim's son. Don't spread this around. They're talking sterilization. Would that be necessary?"

"If I married my cousin I wouldn't breed with her. Do you know of any degenerative disease in your background?"

"No. Just anxiety and obsessive tennis." Jack laughed. Larry was an old friend from college and had attended medical school with him for a year before he quit to become a geneticist. Larry could be trusted.

"Of course, it's also how you breed for genius. Look at the Jews. You get bad eyesight after a hundred years of a small gene pool. We see that in lots of groups. Then, sometimes, you get an amazingly vital immunity to certain environments. Take the individuals out of that environment and you get autoimmune reactions. I used to be interested in this. I could do some research for you."

"No. We'll wait and see."

"What's this about half siblings?"

"I knew a case. I was wondering. So Timothy will vary from me by seven point five. That's all?"

"It's a lot to the DNA."

"Thanks, Larry."

"Nothing to it. Call back if you get worried. It worked for the Franklin Roosevelts."

"Thanks again, Larry."

"Take good care of yourself, Jack. I was sorry to hear about Eugenie. This could be a backwash from that."

"I know. Well, thanks again. Goodbye." Jack hung up the phone. He went to the hospital and made his rounds. Disease and sickness, diagnosis and the long attempt to cure and heal. All around him people making themselves sick, making stupid decisions day after day, taking chances, riding motorcycles, drinking, smoking, overeating, fighting, causing pain. Elise and Jimmy off somewhere hating things together. Getting ready to cut through Elise's fallopian tubes to punish her mother, who is already dead and wouldn't care if she were alive. Maybe Sarah cares. Or maybe none of us does. Just do your work, Jack. Just get your work done. Sarah will be here Friday. We'll see what happens then.

Sarah's plane was delayed because of weather. At ten-fifteen on Friday night it finally landed and Jack came walking down the ramp to find her and took her home and they went into the house and made love to each other. Sarah was distracted from worrying about the children and Jack was worried about not pleasing her but they were able to give each other the thing they both needed. To mend the past, the loss, the tear in the fabric, the rent in time. To be together made them whole. Even for an hour it seemed to be worth any cost.

Afterward, they returned to the world where there were problems to be solved. "Elise says she doesn't want children anyway," Sarah was saying. "But I think she's using this thing with Jimmy to punish all of us for not loving her enough. I care about her, Jack, because she's yours and because she was Eugenie's. But we can't let them marry each other without telling them there's a chance they could be half siblings. I'm determined about this."

"Slow down. It doesn't really matter if they are half siblings or first cousins. I talked to this guy at Vanderbilt who's slated for a Nobel in genetics. He said to hell with it. It's not as if they were carrying Tay-Sachs. Homozygosis of genes is six point two five for first cousins. It doesn't go much higher, maybe two points, for half siblings. They could have an extremely bright child. There can be a late-term amnio. This isn't as dangerous as you think it is, Sarah."

"Inbreeding? You just don't want to tell them. I want to tell them. Is there anything we can learn from blood tests?"

"Jack and I are both O positive."

"So am I."

They lay back against the pillows and were quiet for a while. "There *are* problems that *can't* be solved, Sarah," he began at last. "I don't believe Jimmy and Elise are planning on getting married. If they screwed each other a few times, so what? I'm her father. I'm the one who should be upset about this. I'll talk to her. I'll tell her if she gets pregnant to let me know and I'll get her an abortion. Do you want me to do that?"

"No. I want to tell them the truth and let them make decisions based on full information. That's how I treat my friends. That's how I wish to treat the world. Why would I cheat my own son of information I would give to any friend, if I had it?"

"Just wait awhile. That's all I'm asking. Just don't tell them yet."

"If we aren't going to Lexington to tell Jimmy, why am I here?"

"To be with me." He got up and went to sit in a chair by the edge of the bed. He was wearing a striped cotton robe of some very soft thin material. His strong shoulders and the curly, still reddish hair on his chest and his elegant legs and his black eyes and all the power and energy and maleness of him was very beautiful to Sarah.

"I'm in love with you," she said, and got up and went to him and knelt beside him and lay her hands upon his knees. "I suppose I always have been. I don't think I have stopped thinking about you for a minute since I was here. Please come to Paris with me this summer. Let us have that much out of all the time of our lives. I want that with you. So very much."

"I'll take you to your farmhouse tomorrow." He covered her hands with his. "If you won't make me tell Jimmy I might be his father. I don't have much in the world, Sarah. My brother, Timothy, isn't that close to me. We don't play tennis together much anymore or call each other a lot, but he's my only close living relative. I don't want to do this unless we have to. If Jimmy and Elise marry and she gets pregnant, we'll insist on an amnio or an abortion. That's as far as I can go."

"Then I'll start hoping she goes through with this ligation. I think she's going to, Jack. She seems adamant about it. It's as though she intuits something."

"I don't know what they want with each other, to tell the truth," Jack said. "Neither of them ever seems happy to me. Every time I see either of them they're complaining about something."

"Elise likes the work she's doing for me. She's happy about that. Let's get up early in the morning and go and look at it."

"I have to make rounds. I can leave by ten, I suppose. Ten-thirty at the latest."

CHAPTER 21

The day dawned bright and clear. "The warmest day so far this year," Jack said, as they were leaving the house. It was ten-fifteen. They were dressed in slacks and boots and wearing sweaters. The sun was drenching the earth in light and kindness.

"Do you remember going there to fish with Granddaddy?" Sarah asked him. "I mean, do you really remember it? Tell me what you remember."

"I remember walking about ten miles to the river and he was ahead of us all the way. Tim said, 'I'll be damned if that old man will outwalk me,' and I said, 'I don't care if he outwalks me, tell him to slow down.' "

"You caught fish. I remember because we cleaned and cooked them."

"They caught them. I sat on the bank and watched. I never have liked to hunt or fish. Too bloody. I'm a city boy."

"I know you are." She turned on the seat and watched him drive. It seemed suddenly too good for her, this life, this town, his profession, his power. It seemed too high for her, something she could never have. One night with him, in his house, in his bed, and she had turned over her own power to him, disposed of it like some sort of biomedical waste. Here, this life I've led, my accomplishments, are fluff, window dressing. A magazine that has lost its usefulness, outlived its time, is nothing but a haze of cardboard advertisements Henry Luce would be enraged to see, a job cutting and pasting and talking on the phone for a gossip rag. Nothing is secured by what I do, nothing of value created, no need is filled. This is not what I meant to have happen. I meant to be somebody. Jack is somebody. We are back where we were when I came to Vanderbilt, a girl who had to be given tuition, whose mother had to scrimp and save to buy me party dresses, who didn't have an automobile or any hope of having one.

"We'll be out of this mess in a minute," Jack said. "God, I hate the traffic now. It's Saturday, for God's sake. Where are all these people going?"

"Out to the country to see the grass and trees." Sarah laughed and came out of her musings. "The same place we're going."

She sat back. Jack found an exit from the main highway and went down a ramp and onto a less crowded road where he could drive faster. The closer they came to the outskirts of town, the faster he drove. Finally they left the highway altogether and were on an asphalt road she remembered from when she went to the farm with Elise.

The fields were green now, planted in corn and alfalfa and soybeans. The trees were beginning to have small reddish-colored growth where there would be leaves. There were fields that had been turned and plowed. Here and there was a farmhouse, set back from the road, with barns and butane gas tanks and tractors and fences. There were horses grazing behind fences, a feeling of the earth waking up for spring.

"We are both going to keep on being nervous about changing our lives," Sarah said. "I don't think there is any way we can deny that. Whatever it is I have, it's all I have, it's what I have."

"You're not giving us much credit. We're stronger than that, Sarah. If we want this, we'll take it. How long do you think this Paris thing is going to take?"

"It's a chance to make a lot of money for a small amount of time. Also, it has a chance of being a real film, something I could be proud of. The producers are good people, they've done great work. Especially Dean Tinnin. She's the woman who created *Playhouse Ninety*. The first serious drama on television. There hasn't been anything better since. I don't know how long it will take. Not more than a year. Six months to write it. Then revisions and so forth if they start filming. I only have to be in Paris and at their beck and call for two months. Maybe not that long. I should have it all behind me by fall."

"Would you come and live here?"

"I don't know. Part of the time I could. Not all the time. And the farm will be here. If I start a novel I have a feeling that would be the place to write it. I'm funny about where I can write. It has to feel right to me. I can write anywhere. I just can't feel inspired and without that there's nothing. I know it sounds silly." And suddenly, because she had said it to him, it did seem silly. This profession, avocation, that had been the earth and sky to her since she was thirteen years old, which had always seemed the highest thing a person could aspire to do, seemed like some second-rate job.

"It's not silly. I can understand that. Actually, it makes sense in a psychological manner. One has to be very comfortable to create, I'm sure."

"Thanks." She laughed and became girlish. Except he can't understand because no one can understand unless they do it, unless they are driven and talented enough to do it, blessed. It is only words to Jack. Only an idea. It is not an idea when it happens to you. It is possession, magic, excitement, hope, fear. It is not something I should ever talk about and I am talking about it to him because if he doesn't understand this, there is no hope for anything permanent between us.

Then I won't let him talk of it because I can't let this go. I want this excitement now. I want to belong to this exceptional man.

"Don't talk about what I do," she added. "It makes me nervous to talk about it."

"I just want to know when I can expect to see you every day." He reached out and took her hand. "You don't know what this means to me, Sarah. What hopes I have around it."

"Yes, I do," she said. "I have them too."

*　　　*　　　*

They turned from the asphalt road and onto a secondary road and went up through trees for a mile and they were there. The new gravel road to the house was almost finished. It was built with red crushed stone and was much grander than Sarah had imagined it would be. She began to laugh out loud. "Granddaddy would have a fit," she said. "He would think that was the most wasteful thing he'd ever seen in his life. Oh, I love this, Jack. It's transformed. I never paid much attention to Grandmother. She was in his shadow to such an extent, but this is her revenge. She would have loved to make this place look like this. Her mother was from Virginia and she had ideas of grandeur that were never realized. Well, Elise is doing it for her. Look at the porch, the brick stairs. I don't know how she did it for so little money."

"She's been down here working on it every week. She likes you, Sarah." He was beaming. It pleased him to think one of his children had accomplished something. There had not been many accomplishments. There had not been much chance for parental pride.

They parked the car and got out and went inside. The doors were unlocked. Men were still working inside and had left their tools behind on Friday. The front rooms were painted off-white and the hall was a deeper ivory. The kitchen and breakfast room were a pale grayish blue and farther back the master bedroom and bath were the same blue. "If I had known a decorator could do things like this I would have used one years ago," Sarah was saying. "Oh, Jack, this bathroom is for an Egyptian princess. I wish Grandmother was here. I think I'll find a photograph of her and have it enlarged and hang it here so she can look at this bathtub for eternity."

Jack's pager was going off. "Excuse me, Sarah. I'll just return this call." He went over to the bed and sat down and made the call. Sarah came and sat down beside him. When he had finished talking they lay down upon the bed, using the plastic bag of bedclothes for a pillow, and giggled and were silly and happy.

"I'll call Elise," Sarah said. "Give me that high-tech phone. I bet you have it programmed for her number."

"I don't think so," he said. "I don't call people unless I have to."

*   *   *

Elise answered the phone on the first ring. A television was on in the background. "We are in the house and I adore it," Sarah began. "I don't know how to thank you for this, Elise. It's more than I imagined it could be. The driveway, the flower beds, the wainscoting in the bathroom, the little marble sills in the windows. I feel like a sculptor made this bathroom."

"I'm glad you like it. Wait a minute. Let me turn down this television. I'm watching the news. We're having storms and Jimmy is flying in at seven."

"Give him my love. How's he doing?"

"He's going to a second interview for a job here for next year. So he'll be nervous about that but I'm holding his hand."

"I'm glad you have each other to hold on to."

"How's Dad?"

"I'll let you talk to him. He's right here. He's so proud of this house, of the work you've done. I guess he never saw a before and after of your work, has he?"

"He's never seen anything I've done."

"Here he is." Sarah handed Jack the phone and listened as he had a conversation. Then he handed the phone back to her.

"I'll call you next week from New York," Sarah said. "Is there anything special you want looked at? Other than being amazed in general?"

"I don't think so. See if there's anything you want done to the small barn we decided to keep. I think it can just be propped up and painted. It's sound enough as it is."

"I'll get my script written and paid for. Then we'll see about the rest."

"Let's go for a walk in the fields," Sarah said, when they had finished talking to Elise. "I need air and movement. I brought some insect spray. If we spray our boots and socks maybe we won't get chiggers. I hate chiggers. The worst thing about the country is chiggers."

"It's too early for chiggers," Jack said. "Chiggers come in June."

"That's right. This is the time of year to swim in ponds."

"Buy a houseboat. Fall in love." He came to her and took her in his arms and kissed her long and slowly and held her against his body. But when she moved to take off her clothes he stopped her. "Not yet. I want to desire you for a while."

"Is that so?" She laughed and put her hand on him. "Could you imagine how sexy a pair of khaki pants is to a woman who likes to fuck? Your M.D. has left gaps in that kind of knowledge. We can wait to make love if you really want to. Or we could do it now and do it later. Who have you been screwing, by the way, who thinks it's a good idea to put it off to make it better?"

Then he took her to the bed and laid her down upon it and made love to her like a young man would. The red hair on his body was as exciting to her as the memory of the afternoon when he had been her first lover.

"Couldn't we have this?" he kept asking. "Can't we have this, Sarah? Would you throw this away? Would you let this end?"

"Marriage won't be like this," she said at last.

"It could be, if we wanted it enough."

Later, they went for a long walk. They went out the back door and down across the property to a low fence and climbed it and struck out for the pastures and the woods.

"There were always three or four riding horses," she said. "Granddaddy had field trials here in November. Once I came and rode with them. We were gone all day and Grandmother put cookies in my pocket. It's hard to know how to feel about one's childhood."

"How do you feel?" They were walking beside a small creek, skirting the edges, heading toward a stand of oak and maple trees beside a pond.

"I keep remembering a boy who lived near here who used to come and ride with me. He was a silent boy. With crooked teeth. He helped Granddaddy out sometimes and he would come over without warning, just show up, and we'd go off and he'd show me things. Snake skins, a cow's skull, things he thought were interesting. I never knew what to say to him. He was so foreign to me and yet I was always glad when he showed up. Glad to go off with him and see his treasures. I wonder where he is. If he still lives around here. They lived on the next farm."

"It would be easy to find out. We'll ride around in the car in the morning and see if his house is still there."

"It was his parents' house. Yes, we might do that. If I'm going to live here I should know who the neighbors are."

They skirted the pond and went on to the edge of the woods and walked along the edge looking for a path. The overgrowth was dense and full of briars. No one had cut a path into the woods for many years. "Who was renting it?" Jack asked.

"I don't really know," she answered. "I got a check every month, but it came from the lawyers. I didn't even see the check. My CPA collected it and put it in the bank. Somewhere in there is the place where my father died. There's a cross there. I'm glad we can't get in. It does no good to make outward signs of mourning. The dead are gone. Let them sleep with the Egyptians. Nothing matters but the present and the memories we keep in our hearts. All the rest is no longer true. We should go to the Swiss Alps if you come to France. We could climb and drink chocolate in thin china cups. I need to go there while I'm in Europe. I could plan it for when you're there. We could ride the train to Grenoble. Have you ever been?"

"I've hardly been anywhere unless there was a medical meeting. I'm a provincial, Sarah. You know that."

"Say you'll come to France with me."

"If it's that important to you, I will try to come. I don't know how long I could stay, two weeks, maybe a month. You want to leave in June?"

"I want you to fly over with me. I know that's silly and romantic of me. We have my agent's apartment. He has fabulous taste. I promise you it will be nice."

"Then I'll try to go. Now let's go back to the house and eat some of those groceries we put in the car."

They walked back to the house and unpacked the car. They turned on the new stove and boiled water and made tea and ate the sandwiches and cake they had brought from Jack's house. After dinner they sat on the porch steps and watched the sun go down. Then they went inside and got into bed and slept until the sun rose again. "If I slept like that every night it would change my personality," Jack said. "Let's move in, Sarah. Why would anybody ever want to leave this place?"

"The Orientals believe houses have spirits, powers left there by their makers and their owners. A good life was lived here, Jack. My grandmother was a funny, happy woman and she adored my grandfather. My daddy rode a quarter horse to school. He got up every morning and saddled it in that barn. All that is here. All that goodness remains for me. And now, the goodness Elise is adding will be here too."

"If she stops drinking."

"She drinks because she wasn't wanted and wasn't loved. That isn't something Eugenie did. Eugenie took care of her. She couldn't help it if she didn't love her. That's nature's cruelty, Jack. Nature does what she goddamn well wants to do and we can just pick up the pieces."

But I can't pick them up, Sarah decided. I love this man but I will not take on the whole family. It would do no good. Nothing I could do would be enough. I would end up being a dumping ground and I won't be in nature's plan. I'm in my own plan. Goddammit, I will do what I can but I'm too smart to think it could never be enough.

"That's the fate of the strong," a psychoanalyst had told her once. "To be the prey of the weak or unhealthy. Of course they gravitate to you and want to latch on to you. Positive and negative charges. Can't you see that?"

"How do I protect myself?" she answered. "One can't just leave the world and not love people."

"You keep the proper distance," he had told her. "That is more difficult than it seems because they are always thinking about you. Devising ways to move into your sphere, to get closer, to make you guilty."

"I attract passive-aggressive personalities," she had giggled. "Beware the weak. Is that the credo?"

"Yes. It doesn't help them to weaken you."

"And then the whole tribe is weak and gets taken over. It's easy to say all this, Jerry, but when they need you, you don't think about these things. They are so . . ."

"Seductive is the word, Sarah."

"God, that's cold."

"This is a gift I'm offering you. Remember it."

"I wonder if I will. I hope I will."

"But two strong people could love each other and make a bond, couldn't they?" she asked him later. "A friendship or a love affair? Two equal forces who would be in synch, not opposition?"

"Well, that's the ideal," he answered. "That's what we are always striving for. But early on the strong get in the habit of having the weak for satellites, so it's hard to break those habits, hard to learn to share power with an equal."

" 'Sabre Dance,' " she said.

"What's that?"

"Oh, nothing. Just a piece of music I used to love to listen to. A real relationship would be like that. Two equal people who can dance among the swords and not get cut."

"Why should there be swords?" he asked.

"Because that's how it is. There are always edges because everything is made of crystals."

CHAPTER 22

In a house in Topanga Canyon, in a downpour of rain, Robert was working on his letter. He was on page five and he was starting to warm up.

Dear Sarah,

You used me and then you threw me away. You gave your son away to his father and now you're giving me away. So much for anyone wanting you for a mother figure.

I thought you were the one who believed in karma. Well, it's bad karma to use people, then throw them away. I know what you're doing. Bill Knight was out here and filled me in. You're going to quit your job and marry some doctor in Nashville for his money. Money? Status? Respectability? What? what? what? I can't decide. It won't be as simple as it seems, baby. You'll be bored to death in a month. You'll gain twenty pounds. I kept you young, sweetie. I kept the juices flowing. Maybe you want to get old. Go on. The only reason I care is that I love you and you're breaking my heart.

Dear Sarah,

I am starting over on a more rational tack. This will be in fragments, perhaps even scenes. Begin at the beginning. Isn't that what you're always telling me? But where is the beginning? That's where we differ in our understanding of what happened.

You think I want you for a mother. No matter what happens you can't let go of that idea. You don't listen to me, or else, you don't believe what you hear. Here is the beginning, from my point of view. I'm not retyping this. Pardon the typos and the margins.

A long, long time ago. It's a nice fall day in New York City and an actor friend of mine calls up and asks me if I want to go to lunch and maybe meet the editor of *Granta*, who is in town from London and could be of use to me. Remember, I don't have a publisher and an agent and a name. I'm just trying to write books and make a living as a writer. I'm not able to just blow everybody off when I'm bored with them. I have to pay my dues, do some sucking up. I see nothing wrong with this. I think, this is how the world works. Do you know how difficult it is for anyone to live up to your standards? Do you know how unrealistic they are? No, you do not. You have been lucky and you don't know what the rest of us are going through.

So we go down to the Polo Lounge because Raiford, that's the editor, is staying in the neighborhood and doesn't want to spend his time in cabs, only at the last minute he doesn't show up because his traveling companion has caught the airplane flu and he thinks he's coming down with it and doesn't want to give it to us. I appreciate that and settle down to enjoy a nice lunch and talk with Anthony Arnolfini, who is one of the sweetest men in television and has a son who is a child star. He's got problems with his ex-wife pushing the kid and he's in need of chat. We're happy. I'm having lunch with someone who's in my corner (we went to college together in Texas, in the darker ages) and who has made it. I want to make it, Sarah. You don't seem to care if I am desperate for my own moxie. I never have been able to understand that about you. You are the most ambitious bitch I've ever met in my life. And yet, you act like there should be limits to how far I'll go to get ahead.

Anthony orders a drink and I order a Perrier because I'm not drinking and then you walk in the goddamn restaurant and I fall in love. That's it. The minute I saw you it was like the light coming on in a dark room. You had a squashed velvet hat and some kind of velvet blouse underneath a cotton suit. I don't know what you had on. It was dark red or blue or green. I didn't say, Anthony, how old is she? I didn't say, Do you think it will matter if she is twenty years older than I am? I said, Do you know that woman? and he said yes, and I said, Introduce me, I'm in love.

You were alone and in a hurry but we sat at your table for a few minutes and then I went out and bought both your novels and read them and spent the afternoon tracking down every article you'd ever published and then I wrote to you and asked you to have dinner with me and a month later you called and said you would. Since that time I have not desired another woman.

Morning, Wednesday. You asked me to move into your apartment. I didn't ask you if I could. I didn't want to do it. The only reason I did it was because I wanted to see you every night and morning. I didn't do it for a place to live, although that was nice. If I could afford it I would buy you a *building* on Park Avenue and live on one floor and let you live on the next. Fuck you, Sarah. I am really pissed off about you going off with that guy. I know who is with you. I have had six or seven reports. You owed me more than this. You should have told me.

Afternoon, Friday. I went to a party in Topanga Canyon last night and did drugs with starlets. It was classic. They all have sad stories. They will mostly come to bad ends. They are hungry. They lost interest when they found out I was broke but not before they all asked me to sleep with them. I might sleep with one of them later today. I wish I could describe this girl for you. It might force you to believe that I was (am) in love with you.

Her name is Janko Morales. She is five feet seven inches tall and has blond hair and green eyes and soft skin. She works out five hours a day and hangs out the other hours, except when she is sleeping on Ambien or Xanax or worse. She is just about bright enough to sell clothes in a nice ladies clothing shop in Saint Louis, Missouri, or maybe even Chicago. Instead, she wants to be an actress and have her name up in lights. I think she really just likes to work out. She gets up, puts on her little tights and sports bra and Nike shoes, and heads on out to test herself against the machines at Le Exercise Hotel.

At noon she drinks a sports drink and a vitamin shake and maybe gets a massage if she's in the chips and then she calls around to see who there is to fuck or talk to. It could be me, she wants me to understand. Even if I am broke but not permanently. Just until she gets a part in a movie. She has had several very small parts. She's not proud. She'll work as an extra. Even get a real job when it's required. She would like to have a child someday. Maybe two. But not now. Janko, I say, why me?

Because you're here, she answers. I like that attitude. I will probably spend the night over there and learn some more of this fascinating saga.

Friday night. Before I leave, one more note. You can stop this before it goes any further. You can call me up (917-443-5733), and say, Robert, we belong together. We're right together. I'm going to start thinking of you as a human being with feelings and not some mistake I made who might be useful if I get horny. Hard? Well, yes, but that's how I feel, Sarah. Used.

Because I love you I have studied you. I know you better than anyone you ever knew. I know how you operate, how you change. You change like a genie when you get scared. Who did you ever love who left you unless it was your father and I think we have all about used up that Freudian bullshit. Let's get on with the life that's here, Sarah. I want to come to Paris with you. I want you to go over there and write a script that will knock them dead and then we'll celebrate. CELEBRATE. Remember that word, along with gratefulness and charity and karma. This is bad karma to do this to me.

Robert sat back and thought over what he had written. He was definitely going to mail it to her. And soon. For now, he was invited to a party and he was going to go to it. He had decided not to go because it was raining but now that he had written to Sarah and gotten so much weight off his chest he didn't care if it rained or not. He imagined his letter being published someday, in her memoirs or his. Companion article in the *New Yorker*. Everything happens, as they say in Los Angeles County.

He put on a clean white shirt and his Teva sandals and went out to the garage and got into the car and opened the garage door with the genie and drove off down the hill in the rain. Get high, get laid, spend some time. What the hell? He wasn't old. He was a good-looking young man in a seller's market. Let Sarah stew in the situation she had made. She'd be sorry. She'd be begging him to come to Paris before the year was over. He knew her. She hated to be alone, especially in a foreign country, and she sure wasn't going to be taking some doctor there.

Robert turned on the radio. He put on his seat belt. He was going to where it was happening.

CHAPTER 23

Sarah and Jack decided to walk the mile to the neighboring farm to see if the boy with crooked teeth still lived there. "His name was Sam Martin," Sarah said. "And he was the bravest boy I ever knew. One day he picked up a snake from the grass and beat it to death against a tree. We were walking and he just bent over and picked it up and killed it almost as if he didn't have to think about it. I was terrified of snakes. After that I would follow him anywhere he wanted to go."

"He was how much older?"

"A year or two but it seemed more than that because this was his home and I only visited here. My grandmother could get me to do anything by promising to call and ask his mother to let him come and play. I don't think he really came over to play with me as much as for Grandmother's cakes and cookies. He ate a lot of them when he was here."

"What else did you do?" They left the house as they were talking. Sarah had gone back inside and put on lipstick and added a scarf to her blouse when they had thought up the expedition, an act that was not lost on Jack.

"We used to play being scientists," Sarah answered. "It was my game, my idea. We would pin bugs on cardboard and write their names below them. We got the names out of Grandmother's encyclopedia or just called them anything we wanted to. I don't think Sam really liked to do it very much, but he would help me catch the dangerous ones like wasps and spiders. We tried to kill them with alcohol since we didn't have any formaldehyde but sometimes we'd have to squash them too." She started laughing and took Jack's arm. "It was right over there, by the old side stairs. That's where we put the laboratory. So we could go inside and get cake in between our slaughters."

"I think he came for you *and* the cakes," Jack said, trying not to let the jealousy he was feeling show. Damn her, he was thinking. How dare she make me feel this way.

Yes, it was for me too. Sarah slipped her hand up and down the inside of Jack's arm, feeling as sexy and crazy as a sixteen-year-old girl. She was remembering an afternoon when Sam Martin had lifted her onto a horse and stood beside it with his hand on her skinny leg. She had been wearing worn riding pants and the imprint of his hand on her leg was like an X ray. I must have been eleven, Sarah thought. Before Daddy died. Or maybe it was afterward. I can't remember. He put his hands on my waist and turned me around and lifted me to the saddle. Then he stood with his hand on my leg telling me where we were going. I was on Muldoon. She was as still as a statue while he had the bridle. Then he took his hand away and we rode back to the grove and sat underneath a tree and ate a lunch Grandmother had packed and he lay down beside me on the grass and I think he put his hand on my breasts. They weren't even breasts yet. They were nipples sticking up from my skin but I was proud of them and thought they were better than nothing. Later, he had his hand on my stomach and we weren't talking about a thing. It was before Daddy died.

They walked along the new crushed stone drive to the mailbox and turned onto the asphalt road and walked along in the quiet sweet smells of a spring Sunday morning. Not a car came down the road during the time it took to walk the mile. The mailbox was where it had been forty years before. Martin, it said. The post was new and the mailbox painted a pretty blue. There was a small sticker of a redbird way down on the side, the way a child puts stickers on things they can barely reach.

"He's here," Sarah said. "I don't think he had a brother. Do you think we should go on? Should I tell him who I am?"

"They're your neighbors. They might be wondering what is going on."

"Let's walk down the driveway. If they have bad dogs, can you protect me?"

"No. But we'll chance it. This doesn't look like a place with bad dogs. There're children's bikes underneath that tree. See, and there's a swing."

He was right. There was a swing underneath an ancient oak tree and, as they drew nearer, they could see a tree house cantilevered out over a huge old branch. They walked down the worn drive. As they drew near, a tall man came walking out to meet them. He had a crooked smile and missing teeth and he was wearing jeans and boots and a blue shirt tucked into his pants. Beside him were two small girls, perhaps six and seven, dressed as he was and holding his hands.

"Sam," Sarah called out. "Is that you? It's me, Sarah Conley, from the place next door. Claiborne Conley's granddaughter, do you remember me?"

"I thought you'd be showing up," he said. "My son-in-law's working on your place. They told us you'd be staying there."

"This is Jack," Sarah said. "Jack, this is my childhood friend, Sam Martin." They all smiled shyly and shook hands.

"These are my granddaughters," Sam said. "Jody and Celli. They spend the weekends with us. There're boys too but they're older. Come here, Jody. Shake hands with Ms. Conley. She's going to live in the house your daddy's putting the woodwork into over there."

The little girls came forward and shook hands. They smiled beautiful blue-eyed smiles at Sarah. "They're learning to ride bikes," Sam said. "I got the big one riding a two-wheeler now. But we've still got training wheels on the little one's bike. So why didn't you pave the road to the house?"

"I thought the gravel would look pretty with flowering bushes in the woods beside it. I didn't think about people coming over on bikes. Maybe we ought to make a bike path beside it."

"I'll come cut you one one day," Sam said. "It'll pack down in this red clay. Someone's going to have to cut the weeds along there anyway. That'll grow up like a forest. Come sit down, Sarah. Tell me what your life's been like." They followed him to a set of wooden chairs underneath the tree house and Sam took out his handkerchief and dusted one for Sarah.

"I have a son," Sarah began, "who's in law school in Lexington, Kentucky, at the university. He's almost finished. But no grandchildren, much less pretty girls." The little girls were sitting beside their grandfather on a wooden settee, one on each side. Their hands fell across his long knees. They leaned into his side. His back was straight and his shoulders were wide and his hips were as lean as a man in a cigarette advertisement. Alpha males, Sarah decided. I can pick them. I can find them anywhere. Positive charges. Only Sam has done what a man should do, he has provided vehicles for his DNA.

"How many boys are there? Grandsons?" she asked.

"Four. There's one more baby on the way. Due in three months. We're hoping it's another girl. They're going to take care of me when I'm old, aren't you, sweeties?"

"We're going to roll him around in his wheelchair and take him into town to the movies," the small one said. "We're going to come out here and live."

"My wife's going to want to meet you," Sam added. "She's a big reader. She goes to a book club every Monday night. I bet they've read your books."

"Is she here now?"

"No, she's gone into town for groceries. She won't be back until noon."

"I'll meet her when I get back. It will probably be several months. Maybe late fall. I have to finish some work I'm doing first."

"Late fall's a bad time to move to eastern Tennessee. Just in the worst weather. Well, if that's what you have to do."

"I might need to hire someone to watch the place when it's finished. Maybe you could help me find someone."

"You wouldn't have to pay for that. We'll do it for you. We'll be proud to do it. My name's in the telephone book. Just let us know."

"I'll call you." Sarah stood up and went to him and took his hands.

"It means so much to see you, Sam. To know you are still here, in this house. That this place is still here. And nothing ruined."

"I never did want to go away." He looked at her out of clear, blue eyes that did not wear glasses. "I always found plenty to do right here."

Sam walked them to the mailbox and stood watching as they went down the half mile to the beginning of Sarah's red gravel road. "He's a good-looking man," Jack said. "Even with those missing teeth. I guess something can be said for the simple life."

"But we aren't simple so we could never have led one. It's moot for us. We have to live in all this chaos. It's our fate and nature. At least that's how I explain my inability to imagine giving you up."

"Don't give me up." He stopped and pulled her to him. "I got jealous of that man, Sarah. I couldn't believe it. It was so surprising. I don't even want him cutting the weeds along your road."

"Once I let him put his hands on my eleven-year-old breasts." She held out her hands and laughed a wonderful eleven-year-old laugh in memory of it. "You were right to be jealous. I'm not sure, but I think I let him put his hand on my stomach." She broke from him and began to run toward the house, looking back over her shoulder and laughing as though she had just remembered the funniest joke in the world.

They left the farm at noon. Sarah slept all the way to Nashville. She was sleeping so soundly Jack shook her once to make sure she was all right. She won't stay with me, he decided. I could never trust her not to leave. So, I'll go to Paris with her, but I have to be careful not to love her too much. This is dynamite, this is danger. I have too much to do to stop and get my heart broken at my age.

They spent the afternoon in a sort of limbo. Sarah's plane left at eight, and, although Jimmy had said he was driving up to see her, at the last minute he canceled and didn't come. So there was the afternoon to be lived through. Jack went to the hospital for two hours. When he returned they went for a walk around the neighborhood. There were solid, expensive, respectable houses, on large, well-taken-care-of lots. There were wide driveways and inventive doorways but the place was as quiet as a tomb. There were no children playing outside and no animals. The only people they saw for three blocks were a middle-aged couple who smiled and nodded and spoke to Jack.

"When does this Paris adventure begin?" he asked.

"I should leave the first week in June. Could you go then?"

"If nothing unexpected happens."

"Then I'll go home and work without stopping until then. We'll be happy there, Jack. I've never felt anything so strongly in my life. It's what we should do. We can't arrange a life by tacking it on to either of our present ones. We need to be somewhere new to both of us."

"Then we'll go. I can remember how to be free, Sarah. Don't think I'm completely hopeless."

"Hopeless? How did hopeless get into this? I love you, I want you to go with me to the most beautiful city in the world. I want us to have this time, to have every chance. Not to settle for anything but what we want."

"I just think you are very intent on this. It's not our only chance. I think it doesn't matter where we are. But I'll go. I'll look forward to it." They stopped before a large brick mansion on a high lot. Two black Cadillacs were in the driveway. An American flag flew from a flagpole on the garage. The flower beds were stuffed with blooming flowers. I could use that as a set in a parody, Sarah thought. I would film it just like this and the viewer would know everything that could be known about the owner.

"Daniel Carter lives there," Jack said. "Do you remember him? He was a class ahead of me."

"I think I do. Come on, start walking. Let's go up that hill." She struck off, walking fast, not wanting him to see her face, knowing that in a moment she was going to laugh and keep on laughing and maybe even run up the hill of the brick house and start rolling in the grass.

At seven he drove her to the airport and waited until the plane left and then he went back to his house and they were both free to doubt the wisdom of what they were doing. Sarah's letdown took the form of an essay on contemporary life. All watched over by machines of loving care, a poet had written in the sixties. It's true, she decided. We get out of cars and into airplanes. We go in taxis to buildings with elevators and go up the elevators and into our air-conditioned boxes and turn on the stoves and television sets. I walk in my office and turn on machines. Water is delivered by pumps and pipes. We never question this. Even at the farm, the main thing Elise is interested in is a bathtub with water jets. It is all right to live like this, I suppose, but not to question it would be madness. Not to challenge it, to ever stop being surrounded by machines. It will be better in Paris. Paris is an older, simpler world. Bread is still made by bakers. Food is prepared by hand. I will have a dressmaker make me a dress and I will go and have fittings. I will try while we're there to live more simply and closer to the bone. And I will love him if I can. I do love him. More than he knows. More than he believes.

Sarah was falling asleep. She put the computer away and pulled out the airplane phone and called Jack's house. His answering machine answered the phone. "I'm calling from the plane. I'm falling asleep. I love you. It will be fine. Love is its own protection. I believe that. Please believe it too. I'll call again when I get home." Believe it, because someone has to believe it and I'm trying to. As if belief has anything to do with reason. As if hope and love have more cachet than work and tree and fuck. So young and so cynical, old girl? So old and far from dharma. I have to believe in something, don't I? What did Bill Gates say? I have no evidence for that. Is that all it's going to end up being? Every goddamn thing I try to do under that relentless microscope. Who raised me? Who taught me all this unease?

Then she fell asleep. Thirty-five thousand feet above the ground, in the darkened cabin of an American Airlines 747, lulled by the sound of the motors burning hundreds of gallons of gasoline that had come to the United States on tankers from the worlds where they still veiled and maimed their female children. I'll write an essay on that, she decided. Nothing is ever lost on a writer. She fell asleep thinking of the great presses turning out the essay pages of *Time* magazine for the coming week.

CHAPTER 24

It was eleven in the morning. There were twenty people in the waiting room of Jack McAllen's part of the Sports Medicine Clinic. Twelve of them were patients, in varying degrees of pain and fear. The rest were relatives or friends who had brought the patients there. There were three children playing by the water fountain. There were framed photographs of tennis players, ballet dancers, baseball pitchers, and football teams. Jack was the team doctor for a junior high school and high school football team.

The patients had all been waiting a long time. The clinic was behind because the high school had started spring football practice and there were a lot of injuries. In the surgery were three young men stretched out on tables. It was Wednesday, the day Jack looked at stitches and casts he had put on the week before. The young men were all healing well. They didn't complain. They thought Jack was a god because he had been a quarterback in high school and had broken his arm and had to miss a year of college while it healed. They knew he understood there were things a man did and a man took the consequences.

In the two front examining rooms were an old lady with an arthritic knee, accompanied by her irritated daughter, and an even older man in a wheelchair who was recovering from a hip replacement no one but Jack had thought worth doing. It had probably been a bad idea but the old man had wanted it and he was the father of one of Jack's childhood friends. The old man was not healing. Jack was in the hallway debating injecting cortisone into the old lady's kneecap and trying to decide how much more pain medication he could give the old man without turning him into an addict, when one of the high school football players moaned.

"I bribed my grandson not to play football," the irritated woman told her mother in a voice raised loud enough for everyone in the area to hear. "I don't want him torn up for life to give some middle-aged men a vicarious thrill on Friday night. It's a brutal, stupid sport. It should be outlawed in high schools."

Jack turned from the desk, where he was standing near a nurse, and looked in the direction of the woman. She was standing in the door of the examining room reading her mother's chart. She was the sort of patient every physician dreads, smart enough to know there are no answers and who questions the ones he gives. He sighed, looked at the adoring young nurse who was seated at the desk, and said in a soft voice, "I may be going to Paris for a few months soon." The young nurse giggled. "I mean it. I'm going to start looking for an intern to come in and help out while I'm gone."

"You should do that," the nurse said. "You work too hard. It doesn't help anyone when you never get any rest."

"Okay, let's get through." He turned and walked into the room with the elderly woman and looked at the X rays and showed them to the irritated daughter, then put the woman on the table and injected five milliliters of Depomedral into the joint space of the kneecap, then patted the woman's arm until she began to breathe normally.

"Thank you, Doctor McAllen," the woman said. "I've been in so much pain. I wondered if you would tell the insurance company to get me a nurse for a week so I can stay in bed."

"I don't want you in bed." He looked at the daughter. "I want you on your feet and out in this beautiful weather."

The older woman sat up and smiled widely. "All right," she said, and seemed to lose ten years at the thought. The daughter smiled too. The feeling in the room relaxed.

"I'm sorry I said that about football," the daughter began. "I didn't mean . . ."

"You're right," he answered. "I'm glad to be reminded of it."

Living vicariously. The phrase haunted him all day. Now he was sure he was going to Paris.

CHAPTER 25

Sarah worked unceasingly for five weeks. She finished every project on her desk. She dreamed up and painted a cover for the Fourth of July issue, to be used unless a natural disaster, act of terrorism, or pressing political issue stole the spotlight from the nation's birthday. She managed to include, in legible print, the first three paragraphs of the Declaration of Independence. "People should read this," she said, when she handed it to James. "I hate those copies of the original document. No one can read them. I'm a fool to leave you, James. Now that it's set in motion I have to do it, but I think I'm the biggest fool who ever lived to leave you, even for the summer."

"Go get rich. We'll be here when you get back."

"I love you. You've been good to me." She embraced him. It was her last day in the office. "I am drowning in second thoughts," she added. "But I think these movie people are different than most of them. I think they're really serious about making a good movie."

"One can hope." He raised his eyebrows and Sarah started laughing with him.

"I keep running into that word lately," she said. "Hope and believe. One should worry when one has to look up believe in the dictionary, wouldn't one say?"

"Cut down on the estrogen," he suggested. "Especially around the movie people. Especially if you start believing they are different."

"Want to know what the dictionary says?"

"Why not?"

"Believe. From the base, *leubh,* to like or desire, from *lief* as in love, from the Latin, *libido.* One, to take as true, real, et cetera. Two, to have confidence in a statement or promise of another person. Three, to suppose. Should I go on?"

"God, no. I want to think you're safe, Sarah. I don't want to think I'm throwing you to the wolverines." He kept on hugging her. He meant it. He loved her. He wanted the best for her. He was one hundred percent on her side.

They finished the details of the Fourth of July issue. Then Sarah gathered up her things and left the huge, tall building. She did not look back. I would turn into a pillar of salt, she decided. They would have to put me in the fountain, where I would melt. She walked down the Avenue of the Americas, found a taxi and was driven home.

That was Wednesday, the fifth of June. On the sixth of June Jack flew into Kennedy International Airport at four in the afternoon. Sarah was waiting for him at the gate, wearing a pale blue silk dress and low-heeled sandals. She had a small carry-on bag and a jacket with her passport and airline ticket buttoned into the pocket.

Jack was the third passenger off the plane. She watched him for a second before he saw her. A handsome, red-haired man who looked exactly like who he was, a harried physician hurrying off on a vacation. He was carrying nothing, not even a magazine or briefcase or book. When he saw her he waved and came straight over and took her arm and kissed her on the cheek. "Here I am," he said. "At your service, madam. Not much sleep last night but I made it. What times does this flight leave for France?" He pulled his ticket and passport out of his pocket and handed the passport to her. "At the last minute I had to get a new one. Mine was expired. I barely made it. A friend downtown hurried it through or I wouldn't be here. What else have I forgotten?"

"Nothing. We have two and a half hours. The flight leaves at seven. Would you like something to eat?"

"Yes. That's a good idea. I've been eating in the hospital cafeteria since Eugenie died. I've grown to like it, seeing the interns and the families. I've decided I don't care what I eat as long as someone puts it before me."

"We'll test that theory in France." She took his arm. "Where did you get a passport photo? Did you have to go to a mall?"

"I went to Kinko's. A teenage boy took it. He was convinced I would be vain about the way it looked. He took three before he got one he liked. It was the middle of the night when I had it made." He opened the passport and looked at the photograph, obviously pleased with his adventure. He belongs to a priesthood, Sarah was thinking. His entire life is consumed with healing sickness. There is no time for the ordinary things we do, for taking a day off to pack and get ready for a trip. He is a warrior against death, a priest in our most crucial battle. No wonder he has forgotten how to have fun.

She took his arm and it began to happen again. The transference of her power into him. I don't want my power, she decided. I'm sick of it. I want to lean on this man and let him carry me. I want to feel him beside me. Him and no one else. No other man in this world. I have missed this feeling. This feeling is without parallel.

Two and a half hours later they were on a plane bound for France. "The air is so clean in Paris," Sarah was saying. "That's what I think of when I'm going there. How good everything smells. I can't imagine why. There are as many cars as there are here. Well, maybe not as many, but it seems that way. They are such avid drivers."

"The air comes off the Atlantic Ocean. Oxygen from plankton."

"Maybe it's just the food," she added. "Art and food and that divine Gallic haughtiness. It never puts me off. It just makes me haughty."

"You have a good start in that direction."

"We both do. Maybe that's why we like each other." She sank back into the seat beside him. His presence shut out everything else. I am no different than a veiled Arab woman walking behind her man, Sarah thought. It is wonderful to be this way, how comforting.

I could sleep without being on guard. I could just go to sleep on this plane. He reached over and took her hand and held it and she lay her head next to his shoulder and fell asleep.

When she was four years old her father had taken her to a river and taught her how to swim. There was a small mud beach. The house was a cabin on the river. There were wide plank floors and a fireplace and a sleeping porch with six or seven beds. Her mother was pregnant, with a child she would later lose. It was June and her father took her by the hand and they walked to the water and then he lifted her up into his arms and walked out into the water with her. "Hang on around my neck and we will swim," he said. She held on while they swam out into the deepest water and then back. "Would you like to try it?" he asked. All winter he had been practicing with her in the bathtub, teaching her to put her face down in the water and turn it from side to side to breathe. She stood on the muddy bottom and practiced the breathing techniques. She let him carry her out into the deeper water and when he let go she flailed and went under and he caught her and put her on his shoulder and swam with her holding on again.

Every day they swam in the cold, brown water. The taste of it was good to her and there was no sadness in the world, just her father holding her and laughing and catching her when she went down and every day she swam farther and farther until finally one morning she swam from her father's side to the ladder on the pier and held onto its slippery moss-covered rungs and knew that she had won. She was a swimmer. The river was hers.

Sarah woke in the dark cabin of the plane. She touched Jack's arm and lay her head beside his shoulder and wondered at him being there. It was no longer a long-distance affair. No longer phone calls and letters. No longer Jack in his house in Nashville and Sarah in her office or apartment. They were alone together on this huge plane flying over the Atlantic Ocean to a city where neither of them spoke the language. She looked at her watch. They were four hours out. They might be over Greenland.

Sarah had bought four magazines at the airport. They read them and traded them. They played checkers on a magnetic checkerboard. They told each other stories about things that had happened in the years they were apart. "Don't try to leave out Eugenie," she said to him. "You don't have to leave her out of the stories. I have more stories about her than you do."

"It's true. If we try to leave her out, we can't talk. But don't tell me about your lovers, Sarah. I'm not modern enough for that."

"I never had one. Here, take this *Newsweek*. If you find something good, show it to me." She handed him the magazine. The stewardess came by offering drinks. "I think I'll wash up and then go back to sleep," Sarah said. "I like this long strange interlude and you beside me in the middle of the night."

"It might be dawn in Paris," he answered. "I hope I won't disappoint you, Sarah. I haven't been in Paris in twenty years. I have nothing to offer but naïveté."

"Just bring this shoulder," she said. "Freddy has an English-speaking maid who's going to be waiting at the apartment. She'll take care of us both. It's exciting, being here with you." She kissed him on the cheek, then got up and went to the small bathroom and washed her face and brushed her teeth and got ready for pretending to go to bed. Dawn in Paris, France. The pale light beginning to fall on the bakers making the croissants. Rich, thick coffee beginning to be brewed. Fresh white sheets on beds and pillowcases on pillows, shop owners putting paintings and chairs into windows. Street cleaners sweeping the streets, vegetables and fruits coming into town from the country. She went back to the seat and sank down beside him and fell back asleep. He was already asleep, having taken a Halcion. He shouldn't dose himself all the time with pills, Sarah was thinking. And I shouldn't think that or dream of saying it.

They landed at de Gaulle Airport at nine in the morning. They collected their bags, went through customs, then found a taxi and were taken into the heart of the city. The apartment was in the Latin Quarter, in the Fifth Arrondissement, near the Luxembourg Gardens. It was larger and more beautiful than anything Sarah could have imagined. A uniformed maid met them at the door and took their bags into a large bedroom with a canopied bed. She spoke to Sarah for a while, showing her around the four rooms, then took her leave, promising to return in two days.

"I wonder if you know how impossibly lucky we are to have this place," she said to Jack. "It's the loveliest place I've ever stayed. I should have known Freddy and Camille would buy the best."

"Let me make love to you," he said. "That's all I've thought of for hours." Then they took off their wrinkled clothes and turned down the bed, which was covered with a beautiful silk quilt of many colors. Under the quilt were lace-edged sheets and soft down pillows. They lay beside each other barely breathing and were still for a moment. Then they began to make love. This time there was no embarrassment or fear. This time they were sure of themselves and sure of Paris and sure of love. "I waited twenty years for this," Jack said. "Or thirty or however long it's been. And now I'm going to take it day by day and love you, Sarah Conley. That's all I know to do."

They slept until late afternoon, then got up and dressed and walked the streets for an hour or two. They walked to the Sorbonne and found an outdoor restaurant and sat at a table drinking wine and watching the students come and go. "This city is forever new," Sarah said. "No matter how many times I visit here, each time I am in a new awareness. No matter how many times I walk these streets I always feel there is a side street I have missed, or else a small painting of a flower is missing from a shop window and I must regret not buying it all over again."

"A writer said of Venice there is 'a mystery of implosion' about it, 'as if feeling and intellect had been compelled into collision.' I liked that. I've been saving that to tell you." He smiled at her then, having delivered his gift, having reminded them both that he was her equal and could learn anything she knew at any level.

"I wish I'd written that. It isn't true of Paris, however. Paris is a gathering place of stones and wonders. Perhaps a town has to have a river to call artists to its banks. The thing about Paris that seems most new is that the stones never change. Only the small paintings in the windows. Like a black dress to which one adds different scarves and pins, or one day, in rain, or for a death, just the dress with no adornment."

"What do you need to see to write about?"

"This. Anything that happens. Any moment. This one will do."

"Then I would like to find a real restaurant and start eating asparagus. The main thing I remember from the time I was here is the asparagus. I went home and planted some but I must not have done it correctly. It never came up."

"I know where a restaurant used to be. Shall we go and see if it's still there?"

"Yes, of course." They got up and paid the bill and then walked down the rue de Vaugirard until they came to the restaurant she remembered.

They had foie gras and asparagus, which was still in season, and grilled perch and tiny carrots swimming in butter sauce and coffee and chocolate soufflé. It was their first meal together in Paris and it was superb. They walked back to the apartment hand in hand and went to bed and slept away their first real night together.

"The days run away like wild horses over the hills." The days and nights of the next few weeks were that way. Sarah wrote in the mornings while Jack went off for long walks to explore the city. Her work was going well. She mailed ten pages to the producer and was rewarded with a glowing fax and a box of lilies and roses.

Paris, the divine, the indescribable city of light. Its terraces, gardens, fountains, bridges, esplanades, quays, canals. Its trees, shops, buildings, beautiful people. The Visigoth crowns in the Cluny Museum, the skies above the buildings, wine and bread and lovers. There is nothing to say of Paris. Words roll off its skin like rain on the face of a beautiful woman. Work and love and the wonder of each moment. If I could not be happy here, if I do not know I love him, then I am too dumb to live, Sarah told herself, but she was happy, and knew she was.

*　　　*　　　*

They had been in Paris four days when Jack began to speak what was on his mind. They were in a park at the tip of the Île de la Cité, sitting on a bench beneath the ancient trees.

"When we get back to Nashville we'll go out and find a house to live in. I don't care how much you are there. As long as we have a place together. You can buy anything you want. But we need a place to live without ghosts. Not my house and not your farm, no matter how fine it is going to be. With new furniture in it. Everything brand new, things we pick out together. I don't know where you buy those sorts of things but Elise will know."

"Oh, Jack, that's so thoughtful, so tender. I don't know how long I'll be here. I don't know when I can come to Nashville. Not until a draft is written and then I'll have to come right back. You can't stop and start these things."

"It's important though." He pulled her hands closer to his body, looked into her eyes, would not let her go. "I won't lose you now that I've found you. I won't go back to being alone. But I can't abandon my practice. I have patients who depend on me. I don't know if I can live anywhere but Nashville."

"I wish we didn't have to talk about the future." She pulled back from him, away from his hard, driven, beautiful, longed-for face. "We have this time, these weeks. Couldn't we have them first and then worry about the future? We aren't going to lose each other. We have enough money for what we need to do. I could live in Eugenie's house. I liked her. I like her taste."

"It's not permanent enough. I have to be able to plan. I have to know what we are doing. We should get married, Sarah, and soon. There's no reason not to marry each other. We could do it here. We could do it tomorrow."

"Nothing would change because of that."

"It would change for me. I might stop waking up in the middle of the night dreaming I'm pursuing you through endless chambers."

"You don't have to pursue me. I'm right here. And I'm starving in the city with the best food in the world. If you like me so much, buy me some lunch."

"Don't make light of this. I mean it. I want you to marry me."

"I will if you want it. I will do it in a month if you still think you want me to."

"Then we'll go and buy a ring somewhere. There are jewelry shops here, aren't there? After we have lunch we will go and find an engagement ring."

She shook her head and laughed and pulled him up and they walked to the Pont Neuf and joined the flow of walking people. Beside them a man stopped and pulled his girl into his arms and kissed her.

Paris. Flowers everywhere. Perfection. A door painted blue. Music at the Sorbonne. A soprano singing Brahms and Poulenc. A piano. A bare stage. Black velvet draperies. The sets painted by Chagall at the Paris Opera. Sainte-Chapelle. The Roman baths. The Cluny Museum. Dawn coming in the stone windows of their room. Beauty, peace, order, bluepoint oysters, red walls, breakfasts of croissants and coffee and fresh yogurt and berries.

He stayed with her for sixteen days. It was the longest time he had ever left his practice. Every day his partners called and asked questions. Every day he reassured them. Every night Sarah lay in his arms and tried not to think about the future.

"I will not leave you ever," she told him. "But I don't know how we'll manage the immediate future. You have to trust me and give me time. Let me finish this script and get paid for it. Then I can work at the farm."

"I'm going to buy us a house. If you won't come and do it I'll ask Elise to find one. Would you be satisfied with something she picked out?"

"We need to talk to them. I have written Jimmy but he hasn't answered. That doesn't mean anything. He never answers my letters."

"They know we're here."

"Yes, they do, don't they?"

"Let's go to sleep. We don't have to talk to them tonight, thank God." He rolled over on his side and reached for her and she fit her body into his and was still. This is how he must have slept with Eugenie, she knew. It doesn't matter. I loved her too. I slept with her in my arms when she was afraid of the dark. I used to hold her as he is holding me. My oldest tribe. The first one I created for myself. How I have missed them, not only Jack, but them, the thing we were together when we were four.

Three days before Jack was due to leave, Dean Tinnin called Sarah from New York to say that she and Stefan, the other producer, wanted to come to Paris to go location hunting.

"We want you to show us what you imagine," Dean told her. "I want to see what you see, where you imagine scenes taking place. We don't want to interrupt your writing. Just to walk around with you for a few days."

"When are you arriving?"

"On Friday. In five days."

"I'll meet your plane."

"Oh, heavens no. We'll call when we get to the hotel. We're in your neighborhood, a few blocks from Freddy's apartment. Stefan knows a hotel there he's fond of and we thought it might be easier to be near. I hope you don't mind."

"There's a man staying with me. An old friend, a doctor from Nashville."

"Of course. How nice. Well, we'll try not to take up too much of your time. How's the writing coming? Do you mind if I ask?"

"I'm forty pages into it. It feels good, Dean, it feels right. I'm pretty excited about it. I could write a lot faster if I wanted to but I don't want to hurry it."

"We'll see you Friday then. Are you sure you don't mind if we are in the neighborhood?"

"Of course not. Come on. You'll like Jack, if he's still here. He may have to leave before then. And Dean, I'll fax you what I have on, say, Tuesday or Wednesday, so you can read it on the plane. You'll know where to go if you read it. Except for the villa outside of town. I need to go find that. I made it up from one I visited two years ago. A two-story farmhouse to the north of here. I may go this week and look for it again."

"Just keep writing," Dean said. "Keep writing. Keep writing."

*   *   *

At dinner that night Sarah broached a plan to Jack. "I need to drive outside of town and look for a villa I want to use in the screenplay," she said. "Would you like to drive with me? It's fun to drive on French roads. I'll read the map if you'll drive."

"I'd like that. Could we go up to Normandy and spend the night? My father and uncle were in the invasion. I've always wanted to see those beaches."

"Sure. If we leave by noon we'll have plenty of time. The house I remember is to the north so it's the right direction. It should be simple to find. If not, we'll find another. Supposedly the one I visited is deserted now so it would be easy to rent for a location."

"Does the screenwriter do that too? Find the locations?"

"No. I just have a hard time relinquishing power around my work. Which is why it is so exquisite to go off for a while and write a novel. Just me and my characters and no one else to please." She smiled, to take the edge off her professionalism and air of mastery. It was a habit she was forming around him. If he spoke of his work, it was always as if he were speaking of a priestly occupation, or, if he denigrated it at all, it was to speak harshly of someone who worked for money, or wasn't careful or methodical or scientific enough. He never denigrated what he and his partners did. But Sarah could not stop pretending that her work, the high-powered world of publishing and entertainment, was somehow second-rate. Even when she spoke of writing a novel, the hardest and loneliest and most mysterious work she knew, she always smiled and laughed as if attempting to write a novel was too pretentious to be taken seriously.

"Then we will go find your location and my beaches," Jack said. He didn't know how he felt about Sarah's work. Sometimes he agreed with her denigration and sometimes he wondered at her strange flights of genius and imagination, as intense and immediate as they had been all the years he had known her. She was able to go in an instant into an imaginary world and know it entirely.

The next morning Sarah worked until noon while Jack arranged to rent a car. At twelve he brought the car around, a blue Citroën with wide seats and a horn that sounded like a Canada goose.

Sarah had dressed in slacks and a white blouse. She had a pale yellow sweater around her shoulders and her hair was pulled back with a yellow ribbon. Jack got out of the car and came around to the sidewalk where she was standing and handed her a small box wrapped in white paper. "Take this," he said. "I was going to give it to you later but you looked so lovely standing there that I couldn't wait. You will probably dislike it. That's all right."

She opened the box. It was a diamond set in a plain gold setting. It was very old, very beautiful. She put it on her finger and held it out to him. "This is the most beautiful thing I've ever received and the most romantic. How could I dislike it?"

"Let's go then," he said. "I don't know why I did that. I've never had this much time on my hands. While I was out walking yesterday I was looking at the ties in Sulka's."

"And did you buy one?"

"No, I bought this instead. There was a shop in the building that sold them. Well, I'm glad you like it. I wanted you to like it." He held open the car door and she got in. He got into the driver's seat and started the motor. He pulled out into the sparse traffic. "I have to leave by Monday," he added. "On Monday afternoon. I made the reservation."

"I know," she answered. "Do you want me to try to tell you where to go?"

"If you can."

"I think I know but don't get mad if I make a mistake. First we have to get on the *périphérique* and then we have to find the exit. They are barely marked and not numbered but I marked a map so don't talk to me until we're out of town."

She concentrated on the map and he drove and she waited until they found the exit and were safely headed north before she answered the main question he had raised. "You are leaving Monday for sure?"

"I talked to Reilly this morning. They can't make it any longer without me. I have to be in the office Wednesday."

"The producers are coming Friday. I had hoped you could meet them. Well, never mind. It may be best. I can finish the script if you aren't here. It should be done before they come. I know it's better than anything I've ever written. It's just a matter of typing up what I know."

"Have you decided how it will end?"

"They have to give each other up. There's no other way. I know Dean and Stefan though. They'll want to leave a loophole, some hope for the audience, but I'm not giving in on the end. It won't be memorable if they stay together. And it won't seem true."

"Why not?"

"Because their worlds are too far apart."

"Ours are too."

"Not like that. Not a quantum leap."

"Yes, they are, Sarah. I've been more aware of it here than before. I have loved these weeks. But I couldn't live like this."

"You aren't going to have to. All right, just continue on this highway. In about ten miles there should be a crossroad that goes to the villa. I'll try not to get us lost." She leaned back and watched him drive. The countryside was green and beautiful. Fields of vegetables and vineyards and orchards. Everything seemed deserted, they only passed a few cars on the road. It was noon in France and Frenchmen were at lunch.

"This is exactly what I wanted," Sarah said, stretching her hands out in front of her. The ring caught the light and sparkled on her finger.

"I didn't think you'd like it. It's so plain. You don't have to wear it if you don't want to."

"I love the ring. I mean this countryside is exactly what I need for the long shots at the beginning of the Paris scenes. The road should be right up here. It will say Parthenay or maybe D6. If we miss it, we might have to go back. I'll try not to turn this into a driving farce."

"Just tell me where to turn. What do you mean, a farce?"

"I hate it when women can't navigate and men get mad while driving automobiles. My parents used to do that. Then Daddy taught me to read maps and I would navigate. We used to go exploring on Sunday afternoons. All over western Kentucky and Tennessee. You didn't know that about me, did you? That I am a great navigator and can get you anywhere if I have a map."

"Oh, Sarah, there are so many things about you I don't know. I don't think I knew Eugenie. She might have been anybody. We became, partners, you know. We shored each other up. It wasn't like it is with you."

"You still feel guilty about this, don't you. So do I. I suppose we have to talk of her, don't we?"

"No. And if we do you'll forget to watch the road. Is that the sign up there? Parthenay?"

"Oh, God, yes. Turn there if you still can." They took the turn and found the villa a few miles down the road. It was exactly as Sarah remembered it. A two-story farmhouse at the end of a tree-lined driveway. At one time it had been painted pink but the color had faded to a beautiful soft sheen.

Sarah had talked to the previous owner, the friend she had visited there, and he had told her he thought the house was deserted, tied up in some bureaucratic mess about ownership by a foreign minor.

The friend had been right. The house was vacant but the grounds were well cared for and the gardens were blooming. Sarah picked up the camera and loaded it. Jack parked the car by the front steps and they got out and began to walk around the yard.

An old man came out from behind the house and waved his cap at them. Sarah went to him and explained in French that they were only tourists, not from a magazine. She took forty francs out of her purse as she talked and handed them to him. "It's just for tourism," she told him. "To help the French economy."

The old man took the money and nodded his head. Sarah asked if they could go inside and take a photograph of the "interior."

"The furniture is gone," the old man said in French. "All of it has been taken away, the chests, the rugs, the pans, the curtains."

Sarah nodded sadly and said they would be satisfied with photographs of the windows and beautiful doors.

The old man thought that over. Sarah took out twenty more francs and held them. He nodded, took the money, then led the way up the stairs and opened the door with a large key and held it open while they went in.

It was perfect, exactly as she had remembered it. She pulled a notebook out of her bag and began to scribble on it, leaning the notebook against a door frame.

"No, no," the old man said. "Here is a table and a chair." He led the way to a dining room that still contained a massive oak table and three chairs.

Yes, Sarah thought. This is the house. Here they kissed, here they argued, here made up, on this porch they parted. This is where she walked to pick the flowers to put into the vases when she thought he was going to return. Here was the chair, the sofa, the piano, here is where they danced in the darkness the night it rained and the lights went out.

Sarah wrote as fast as she could, wishing she was alone, ashamed to be caught in the act of writing, of being swept up in her imagination. All her life she couldn't bear to be with other people when her imagination began to feed her.

Jack and the old man stood talking in broken French and English. Neither of them understood a word the other said but there was much nodding and pointing and signs of agreement. They seemed to be talking about vegetables or a well.

"Could you take him outside so I can concentrate?" she asked Jack. "If I don't get this down while I have it it will be lost."

"Of course." Jack took the old man by the arm and tried to ask to be taken to see the garden.

Sarah interpreted, then assured the old man she wouldn't touch anything. Then Jack and the man went out through the kitchen.

She sat back down at the table and wrote as fast as she could for several pages but the spell was lost. If I had been alone I would have finished the script in an hour, she knew. Well, that's why I have to live alone. This is only a movie script, what if it had been part of a novel. This is why I can never live with anyone, not even Jack. I know better than to take someone along when I'm working. It never works. It never did. It's a choice and I thought I had made mine.

She wrote as much more as she could remember of the spell the house had cast on her, then she closed the notepad and went to find Jack and the old man.

They were beside a well. The old man was talking very fast in French and pointing and touching pulleys. Sarah stood on the back steps watching them. She felt she had been violated, interrupted, harmed. It was a terrible feeling and she examined it and suffered it at the same time. She took a deep breath, gave herself a Zen lecture, assured herself that anything the mind imagines it never loses, decided that might or might not be true, then called out and walked down the steps to her lover.

"Sorry," she said. "I had to get that down before I lost it. So, have you learned anything about wells?" It was a false note, the first one that had fallen between them in the months since he first called her on the phone. It was the first real lie, the first real irritation. This is how love self-destructs, Sarah knew. The design flaw, when reality clicks in, the thing all the jokes are about.

Jack thanked the old man for the information. He reached in his pocket and brought out more franc notes and the old man pretended not to want to take them. Jack insisted and the old man gave in.

Jack and Sarah walked back to the car, past a hedge of flowering bushes, a garden with roses. When they got to the car Sarah reached in the backseat and got out the wide-angle lens and put it on the camera and walked back down the line of trees and took photographs of the house from that perspective. When she got to the house she turned and took a photograph of Jack, the first she had taken of him in all their weeks together. In case the real thing disappears? she wondered, then walked back to him and they got into the car and drove away. The old man stood on the porch steps waving.

They continued down the two-lane road to the intersection with the highway. As they were slowing down to turn, a speeding car came barreling down the highway on the opposite side. A farm truck pulled out into its path and the two collided. The sedan hit the side of the truck and then screamed into a ditch. Stones and hubcaps were flying down the road in the direction of Sarah and Jack. They ducked but none of the debris hit the Citroën.

"Damn," Jack said. "Well, I have to help." He drove quickly out onto the highway and crossed the grass-covered divider and pulled up behind the truck. The driver was already out and walking toward the car.

The windshield of the sedan was shattered and a girl was collapsed against the steering wheel. The farmer tried to open the driver's side door but it was locked and jammed. Jack took the handle from him and tried it. Sarah ran around the other side and tried the passenger door but that was locked also and the window rolled up.

"Look out," Jack said and pushed her out of the way. He picked up one of the stones that had been dislodged from the berm and smashed in the passenger side window. Then he reached in and opened the door and climbed into the car. "Tell him to go for help," he yelled. "Give him the Citroën if the truck won't run. See if you can find that bag of mine in the backseat. Damn, I don't have anything. She has a head wound. God knows what else." He was working on the girl as he talked. The impact had extended and bent her neck against the lower bar of the steering wheel. Her forehead had broken against the upper crosspiece. Jack checked for the carotid artery. It was palpable but her airway was obstructed by the steering wheel. He opened her eyes to see if the pupils were contracted. Okay, he said to himself. Do what I can.

He pulled the girl's head gently off the steering wheel. She gurgled. "The trachea's crushed," he muttered to Sarah. She was standing beside the open driver's door. Jack had opened it to give himself more room. "I'm going in," he added. He pulled a small Swiss Army knife from his pocket and cut a V into the cricoid cartilage. The girl shuddered and breathed in a huge intake of air. Jack cursed himself for not having a surgical hose to keep the airway open. Then he did what he could. He pulled a Bic pen out of his pocket and removed the ink cartridge. He pushed the tube into the open V. The air began to move in and out of her lungs.

A carload of students from Nancy stopped behind their car and came over to see if they could help. "Send one of them to call an ambulance," Jack said. "Get me an ironed shirt out of my suitcase."

Sarah opened the trunk of the car and found his suitcase and took out a clean shirt, still in the plastic bag from a cleaner in Nashville. She brought it to him and he opened it and tore off the sleeves and began to treat the cuts on the girl's forehead and right arm. "Did they go for the ambulance?" he asked.

"Yes, they said there was a town nearby. They're gone."

"Good." He went back to his work, completely intent on the girl and the makeshift emergency room he had created in the front seat of the small car.

I've never known this man, Sarah thought. I know nothing about him. I mistake his naïveté in a French restaurant for unworldliness and yet, he is the one who can do this. This sureness, this vast store of knowledge, this power. Nothing I have done in my life equals this and nothing will ever equal it. These are rites I cannot enter. Eugenie was his equal. She entered there. She mastered that amazing body of knowledge and could apply it. What am I doing here? What do I think will happen? How did I ever think the two of us could put our lives together? She stood watching him care for the girl, awed, jealous, worried. She pulled the ring on and off her finger, on and off, on and off.

Finally, after what seemed an eternity of time, a terrible limbo, there were sirens in the distance and an ambulance and policemen were there. Jack talked to the ones who spoke English. They gave him a surgical tube and he used it to replace the Bic pen. Then he helped them load the girl onto a stretcher.

They gave the police their names and address in Paris. Also, they gave them the name of the hotel where they hoped to stay in Calais and asked to be called with a report on the patient.

When there was nothing more they could do they got back into the car. Sarah reached for him and took his arm. "I have never seen anything like that," she said. "How fortunate you are, your gifts, your skills. It makes me feel like a barbarian. With my primitive education and my scattered knowledge. There is nothing in the world I can do to equal that."

"It's what I do," he said. "I suppose she will be all right. I did what I could. If they get to an intensive care unit soon enough I suppose she'll make it."

"What do you think she was fleeing?" Sarah asked. "Going that fast, with no seat belt."

"Who knows. Her mother, her lover."

"Let's drive to Calais," Sarah said. "If we drive straight we could be there by dinnertime. If not, there are other places we could stay along the way."

"You hold the map," he said. "Tell me where to go."

CHAPTER 26

They drove though the beautiful countryside to Calais. Between Bapaume and Arras they passed a field where three skydivers were coming down in brightly colored parachutes.

"I can use that," Sarah said. "If we hadn't already been delayed I'd stop and take some photographs."

"We can stop. We don't have to go to Calais or Dunkirk. We can go back to Paris. Are you tired?"

"No, and you want to see Calais and Dunkirk and I do too now that you've thought it up. The hotel will keep our reservation no matter how late it is."

"I need a phone tonight. Do you think they'll have good phones?"

"I'll find you one if they don't. I promise that." She settled back down into the seat, opened her notebook and began to write.

They see the skydivers. He is excited, wants to try it. She is horrified by the risk. They argue about risk-taking. Risk for the sake of excitement or to prove oneself. She thinks action should be for social good. He is young. He believes in action for the sake of anything at all. She gets more and more self-righteous and critical. He complains she is trying to control him, to control everything around her. I'm not your son, he yells. I am not your mother, she yells back. But of course she is.

It began to rain as they neared Calais. You could almost feel the water rising from the Atlantic and coming onto the land. It was more like a prolonged mist than rain. They stopped on the outskirts of town and Sarah asked a clerk in a service station the way to the hotel. She was given a map and a brochure and they drove over a bridge and into the town and down old curving streets to the shore. They found the hotel without trouble and went inside and Jack signed the register and they took their small bags up to the room and washed their faces and hands and walked out on the balcony to watch the misty rain falling on the ocean.

"It won't matter if you leave if we handle it correctly," Sarah said at last. "We won't let separation harm us. Think of the years we never spoke. You wouldn't want me to come and live with you and not have enough money to support myself. It wouldn't work if I had to ask you for things."

"I want to support you. It wouldn't be a burden to me."

"But it would burden me and you would feel it. Let's go walk in this rain," she said. "It's barely falling. We have a change of clothes. Let's leave the hotel and walk out to the water's edge and look across the Atlantic to England. Think how fortunate we are, Jack. How unbelievably lucky to have each other and to be in good health and to be in this glorious country. Think how amazing all that is. Believe in that. It is ungrateful not to be happy with all our blessings."

"That's why I don't want this to end. You will still be here, with your friends coming. I'll be walking into an empty house, nothing to eat, no one to talk to. I've done that for months now. I can't go back and do it again. I need a wife, Sarah. I want it to be you."

"It will be, Jack. In a month's time. I'll finish this, then I'll find a way. I promise that. Please, let's go walk. It smells so good here. Did you notice?"

"Oxygen from plankton," he repeated and seemed to think that was very funny. "I'm better," he said. "I think I've decided to believe whatever you tell me to believe."

They left the room and went down on the elevator and walked along the piers and the edge of the ocean until dark. The rain came and went as they walked and they had given up talking about themselves for now. There was only one conversation Jack wanted to have and they had already had it.

CHAPTER 27

From Sarah's *Travel Guide to France*. "Calais is an island, a seaport on the Strait of Dover. It began life as a fishing village and is bordered by canals and harbor basins. There are lovely sand beaches. It is the nearest point in France to England. From its beaches you can see the chalk cliffs of Dover. During the Second World War the Germans used it as a base to launch rocket bombs against England. It was demolished in the liberation. One thirteenth-century watchtower still stands to remind visitors of the past. A few miles south at Sangatte is the terminal of the Channel tunnel to Dover. This tunnel was completed in 1994 and is cut through white chalk limestone."

When they returned to the hotel, the concièrge was helpful with their plans for dinner. "La Diligence," he insisted. "My cousin is the chef. It has three Michelin stars. *Très magnifique.*"

They changed clothes and drove to the restaurant and were not disappointed. They had snails with mushrooms and a fricassee of sole and crayfish. They drank the house wine. Sarah flashed her ring around in the candlelight and they were serious and gay and in love.

"In the morning we will ride the tunnel train to Dover," Jack insisted. "I would regret it if I didn't try that out."

"I'll take the Hovercraft and meet you there." Sarah laughed. "It's one of the most beautiful boat rides in the world. Why would anyone want to do it underwater?"

"We'll go one way and come back the other."

"In the morning I'll decide," she said. I am getting girlish, she was thinking. I am definitely backsliding and sliding and sliding.

CHAPTER 28

In Atlanta Elise McAllen was lying in bed doped up on Demerol and waiting for the swelling in her stomach to subside. At ten that morning she had gone to a gynecologist's office and had a tubal ligation, effectively ending her chances of ever having a child. She was not having second thoughts but she was lying in bed thinking someone should have told her how much it was going to hurt afterward. Also, she was wishing Jimmy would call. She turned on the light and looked at the clock. It was twelve-thirty. Too late to call him. She got up from the bed and went into the bathroom and examined her tongue. She took the last of four Keflex she was supposed to take for the day. Then she took another Demerol, then she turned off the lights and got back into the bed.

Momma's dead and Daddy's in France with Sarah and no one cares if I live or die. Only Jimmy cares. Maybe he cares. He's been acting so funny lately. He didn't want me to have the ligation. So what does that mean? I don't care if he's in love with me. As long as I can get him to marry me, so I won't be lonely. Sarah hasn't even come to see the house. I work my ass off for her and barely charge her for it and she doesn't even come to look at it. What time is it in Paris? Six in the morning. I can't call Daddy. I swore I wouldn't call him. It's a simple surgical procedure. Nothing's going to happen to me. I'll be all right in the morning.

Just as the Demerol was kicking in she picked up the phone and called her father's paging service and told them to find whatever doctor was on call and have him call her.

By the time one of her father's partners called her back she was going down. The next morning she barely remembered talking to him, but when Jack called his office the next afternoon the partner reported the incident. "I hate to tell you this but your daughter called from Atlanta. She had a tubal ligation. What's that about? Anyway, she was incoherent. Pain medication. I'm sure she's fine but you'd better call and check. And get the hell on home, Jack. I need you badly."

It was nine in the evening in Atlanta when they got Elise on the phone. She had been up and taken a shower and was feeling somewhat better. She was still groggy and still depressed, however, and now she had someone to take it out on.

"How did you find out?" she asked her father.

"Jay told me you called last night. Are you all right?"

"I don't even remember calling him. Why didn't that bastard tell me how much it was going to hurt? I'm going to sue him. I don't think he did it right."

"Do you want me to call him?"

"He probably wouldn't return your calls. I have an appointment with a woman gynecologist tomorrow. I'm not going to him again. He told me it would be nothing. My stomach's still swollen like crazy, Dad. I think it's infected."

"Are you on an antibiotic?"

"Yes. Keflex."

"That should handle it. I'll call you back after you see her tomorrow. I'd like to talk to him, honey. To see what was done."

"I cut the fallopian tubes. The line to the future. I don't want to be in the future of the human race, Dad. Not that I don't like all of us. I just don't want to cause any more suffering. Is Aunt Sarah there?"

"Yes."

"Put her on." Jack held out the phone to her. He shook his head as if to say, Watch out. She pursed her lips, returned his look, then took the phone.

"Elise, my dearest girl. I'm so sorry you are suffering."

"When are you coming to see the house again?"

"The minute I can. As soon as I finish earning the money to pay for it. Do I owe you any more right now? If there is more, let me know because I'm not at home to get mail."

"No. That's all right. We're even. I just want you to see it. There are some more things to finish but we can't do them until you choose the colors."

"I told you you could choose them. I love your taste. I'll love whatever you do. But don't talk about that now. The important thing is your health. Do you think this was badly done?"

"I think so. I was unprepared for what was going to happen. They should have told me how much it was going to hurt."

"Is it better?"

"I suppose so. It doesn't hurt as much but my stomach is still really swollen. I can't wear my clothes."

"I'm sorry."

"So am I. Put Dad back on. What are you guys going to do? Is he coming home?"

"Day after tomorrow. Here, you talk to him."

"I'll be home next week," he said. "If you need me, I'll come through Atlanta and see about you. I don't know about this, Elise. I hope this is reversible. What exactly did they do?"

"They cut it all out. It's not reversible. Every woman doesn't have to be a brood mare in nineteen ninety-six. There are enough starving children in the world. Starving for love, starving for food. I knew you'd start criticizing me. I didn't mean to even tell you."

"I'm sorry you feel that way. I want to help you, Elise. Tell me what I can do." He sat down in a chair, looked at Sarah. His face was as cold and unmoved as stone.

"What are you and Sarah up to?" Elise asked. "What are you planning to do? Is she moving to Nashville? Are you two going to get married? I'm a grown woman, Daddy. I don't feel like being the last to know this week."

"I wanted to talk to you when I get home," he began. "And, yes, we have talked of being married. Not anytime soon. Sarah has commitments here. I didn't want to talk about this yet. If we did decide to marry, how would you feel about it?"

"I don't know how I'd feel. Mother's barely been dead four months. Five months. I don't know what to say. Did you talk to Johnny? Did she tell Jimmy about this?"

"No. We are just talking about it, Elise. Say what you feel. If it bothers you, say so."

"I want to talk to Jimmy about it. I'll call him as soon as we hang up."

"No, don't do that. Don't tell him until his mother tells him. He shouldn't hear this from you."

"Let me talk to Sarah again." Her voice was guarded, dangerous.

Jack considered not passing the phone to Sarah, then decided they had to get this behind them. "There will be some money from your mother's estate," he said to Elise. "I'll call when I get home and let you know how that's coming along. About Sarah and myself, there are no plans made. She has months of work to do here and I have to get home to my practice."

"I want to talk to her, please." Jack turned and held out the phone to Sarah. They exchanged another look.

"Is there anything we can do for you from here?" Sarah began. "If I'd known you were going to do this I could have come there."

"I didn't want anyone around. It was supposed to be a simple procedure. Then I agreed to this balloon bullshit. They forget to tell you they are going to pump you full of gas and you can bloody well figure out a way to get rid of it. I hate doctors. Mother hated being one. She never did like lying to patients and all the bullshit they do. Lies of omission. She had three lawsuits pending when she died. No wonder she got sick. She hated the whole thing. I finally got her to admit that."

"Are you on pain medication now?"

"No. Just Advil. I might take another Demerol tonight. Why, do I sound funny?"

"Just as though you were suffering. I'm sorry your father isn't there, Elise. I feel selfish having him here when you need him."

"He wouldn't be here if he was at home. I don't care if he's over there with you, Sarah. Maybe it will be good for him to get away from the place where Mother died. I think it might be hard on Jimmy if you start talking about getting married. He's going to be upset about it."

"I hope not. And nothing is planned, Elise. We are just comfortable together. We have known each other for so long. It's hard to replace that when you grow older."

I am begging this spoiled child, Sarah decided. I am begging this bad-natured, ugly girl to forgive me for loving her father. She's lying in bed after going out and having a completely unnecessary surgery, probably to get attention, and I'm on a transatlantic call trying to get her to tell me it's all right to live my life. Not to mention she is probably ruining the life of my only child, if he is really crazy enough to be involved with her, which I pray to God isn't true.

"I wish there was something we could do to make you more comfortable," Sarah said.

"I need a video of a live birth, for comparison. That's what one of my friends told me. She said she'd bring one over but she hasn't shown up yet. I've been lying here alone for twenty-four hours. Where are you guys anyway? Are you in Paris?"

"We're in Calais, on the French coast, facing England. It's near Dunkirk. You father wanted to see Dunkirk, then we ran into an automobile accident and he had to help. It's complicated."

"Okay. Well, I need to hang up. I really feel terrible. I wish I knew the rest of the colors to paint your house, Sarah. I can't finish that until you choose the rest of the colors."

"Paint it all white and off white. Make the decisions. I will like whatever you do. I told you that several times. Would you like me to write it to you?"

"No. As soon as I get better I'm going to Nashville anyway. I'll take care of it. You better call Jimmy and Johnny if you are really thinking about getting married. Be careful telling Jimmy. He cares a lot more about you than you think he does, Sarah. Things you do affect him more than you know."

"I'm sure that's good advice. I'll take it."

Elise hung up the phone.

Sarah and Jack spent the rest of the afternoon trying to call Johnny and Jimmy. "Dismal, dismal, dismal," Sarah said several times. "The swamp of family. The quicksand, the miasma." The first time she said it, Jack laughed. The second time he only shook his head. The third time he argued with her.

"But it's all we have."

"No, it really isn't. We believe that because for thousands of years our only safety was the tribe. If Elise wants to lie in bed in Atlanta, Georgia, trying to make you feel guilty because her life isn't perfect, that's her scenario. You and I don't have to let it ruin this day, although, of course, it has ruined it."

"I don't believe you are that cynical, Sarah. You just say those things."

"You're wrong about that. I say them because I believe them. I believe things that are much more cynical than that."

Finally, they left messages, one for Johnny, asking him to call, and one for Jimmy, telling him of their plans. It was late when they finished making calls, too late to go to Dunkirk or to Sangatte to see the tunnel. Much too late to ride across the channel. They took a long afternoon nap instead and then went out and walked along the quay and the piers. "I feel we've been gone for days," Sarah said. "It seems we have left several lives behind. One in Paris and one so far away I can barely remember what we did there." She took his hand and they walked more slowly, their arms and shoulders touching. "Everything seems so strange, Jack. Us being together and the world we inhabit either suspended behind us or pulling us like puppets, I'm not sure which. Habit, that's the thing. Every moment of our lives we are creatures of habit and you and I are trying to create some new habitation."

"We're strong people, Sarah. We aren't children or helpless or that far away from each other."

"Let's go back to La Diligence and eat more snails and sole,"

Sarah said. "Are you hungry? Do you think they will feed us that heavenly food again?"

"Let's go," he agreed. "Come along. Turn around. Let's head in that direction."

La Diligence was near so they walked the four blocks and found it easily. The maître d' was happy to see them back and took them out onto a covered garden and gave them a table by a wall with a flowering vine. Wonderful smells were coming from the kitchen. A waiter appeared and took their orders for drinks. He returned with hot French bread and a bowl of whipped butter. This was followed by a delicious cream soup, then fish and a pâté of rabbit and a plate of cheeses.

They walked back to the hotel in the moonlight. It is done then, Sarah decided. I will be this man's wife and change my life for him and it will not be like these weeks in France. It will be frustrating and I may never work again. So be it.

They got up early the next morning and had breakfast in the downstairs café of the hotel. There was yogurt in stone cups and strawberries and raspberries and croissants fresh from a brick oven that was older than the hotel. There was also brioche and hard rolls and jam and butter and hot thick coffee and cream.

It was nine when they collected their things and said goodbye to the concièrge and told him over and over again that his cousin was the chef "most *magnifique*" in France.

They got into the Citroën and drove up the coast to Dunkirk and walked on the beaches and marveled at the courage and glories of the past. Then they drove back to Paris through the Vallée de la Somme with its battlefields covered with poppies. Sarah began to cry at the sight of the red flowers and Jack was silent and drove very slowly until the flowers were out of sight.

"We have no perspective on the past," he said. "My father and his brother signed up when they were seventeen and eighteen. They walked three miles in the heat of July to get to the registration office. Father had signed Uncle Barrett's release and Uncle Barrett had signed father's. They went off to war because they were hot young men who wanted to see something of the world. Or else because they thought there was a cause worth saving. Or God knows why. I was old before they talked of it to me. Uncle Barrett was under fire for eighty-three days at one point. I never knew what that meant. It must have begun on these beaches."

"And neither of them was harmed?"

"Father brought home a limp. And medals. They had between them a dresser drawer full of medals. Grandmother kept them in a drawer with a star she had kept in the window. Other things were in that room. I wasn't allowed to play with any of it but I would sneak in there and look at it. War. Do you know what it would mean to be a surgeon and watch that happening all around you? I see the results sometimes in my office, old wounds from Korea or Vietnam."

"I'm glad we came," she said and touched his arm. "Now we have something together that neither of us had with anyone else in the world. That may be all there is to love, Jack. Someone to have adventures with, and secrets. All of life is an adventure. I suppose getting old will be too. I suppose degeneration could be interesting if you had someone around who was interested in the details. Mother and Daddy died so young I have never had to witness it."

"Turn on the radio," he said. "Find a station playing music."

Sarah fooled with the dials and found a scratchy station playing Barry Manilow. "My God," she said. "They have been playing Barry Manilow since I first came here twenty-five years ago. The first time I heard Barry Manilow was in a Paris drugstore. I had a yeast infection from the flight over and I was trying to find something for it."

"Who came with you?" he asked.

"No one," she lied. "I was here on business."

Two days later Jack left for Nashville. Sarah stood at the door until the taxi had driven out of sight, then she went back into the apartment and straightened up everything in sight. She bundled up the laundry and threw newspapers and magazines away and made a pot of coffee and then she went into her workroom and took the telephone off the hook and went to work on her script. The visit to the villa had done more good than she imagined. She worked for fifteen hours, completely happy and inspired. The next morning she faxed the draft to Dean and then went back into her workroom and began to edit it.

Jack slept half the way home. As the plane moved over the land mass of northern Canada he woke and went into the rest room and scrubbed his face and hands. He changed his shirt and socks. He went back to his seat and ordered a drink. When it came he used the airplane telephone to call his secretary and his receptionist. He had a life to find and he couldn't wait to get home and find it.

Even when he walked into his empty house it was not as bad as he had imagined it would be. His dog was glad to see him. The maid was there. There was mail and phone calls. He fixed himself a drink at his own bar and took it out into the backyard and sat in a chair and wondered if he really wanted to buy a house and live in a new place with neighbors who had dogs that barked at night or other unexpected hazards. He liked his house. He had struggled to buy it and keep it repaired and it was where he lived.

CHAPTER 29

Dean and Stefan called Sarah at eleven on Friday morning. "Let's meet for lunch," Dean suggested. "We're quite rested. We took melatonin on the plane. It's marvelous. We have lots to tell you. We talked to Laurens Scully and she's thrilled you're doing the screenplay. She has an approval clause but I don't think she'd use it. She needs the money."

"Don't we all."

"But we wouldn't do something we were ashamed of for money, darling Sarah. That's why we wanted you. I adore the draft you sent. It isn't long enough yet but what is there is wonderful."

"Are you sure you feel like lunch?"

"Absolutely. We'll sleep later. Could you come to the Montalembert?"

"Of course."

"At twelve then. Afterward we'll rest."

Sarah turned off her computer and went into the bathroom to do something with her hair. She put on a white silk pantsuit and a pair of sandals and pulled her hair back into a chignon. She applied makeup very carefully and then added a soft blue and peach scarf around her neck. After all, this was Paris and she was going to have lunch with the most cosmopolitan woman she knew. Dean had lived in Europe for many years and been the director of the Spoleto festival. Sarah started out the door, then went back inside and removed the scarf. She nodded at her reflection in the mirror and walked off down the street feeling chic and important and useful, an artist on her way to do what artists do, make something out of nothing.

Although, she decided, in this case, we are trying to make a good film out of a bad novel. Still, I think we are going to. I've never felt this good about a piece of work. Never been this sure, felt such mastery.

She walked down the boulevard St.-Germain and found rue de Montalembert, going past a small shop with a marvelous blue sofa in the window. Everything I need to furnish the farmhouse is in Paris, she decided, and smiled at the thought of trying to duplicate that craftsmanship in Nashville.

She crossed the street and went into the marble lobby of the hotel. Dean and Stefan were at the desk talking to the concièrge. They turned when she came in and embraced her. They looked marvelous, elegantly dressed and completely at home with the language and customs of the elegant hotel, where they had stayed in the 1950s with Buckminster Fuller and his entourage.

They embraced Sarah and moved with her into the restaurant and ordered wine and began to talk about the movie. "It's all excitement," Dean began. "Francie Mankowitz wants to direct it. She's convinced it will be her masterpiece. She read the script you sent me and called the next morning and signed on. You won't believe who she wants for Cary. Cleta Wrightsman. She's reading it now. This is happening, Sarah. And you did it."

"When did all this happen?"

"In the last two days. Francie's agent is writing contracts. We think we can film by September if Cleta comes aboard. She has four months free in the fall and we'll shoot around her schedule. Do you know what that means, Sarah? Fall in Paris. You did it. We have no doubts whose triumph this is."

"So you won't be back at *Time* magazine anytime soon." Stefan laughed. "This is the day we wait for, Sarah. This is the career maker."

"I'm not even finished with it yet." Sarah was laughing, excited. In her mind she saw Jack hurrying through the corridors of the hospital, sitting alone in his house in Nashville, counting on her, waiting for her. Then, in another part of her mind, she saw the script she had been writing brought to life. A great director, a real star, an actress with great charisma and the ability to project and make imagination manifest. Not to mention the money. Lots and lots and lots of money.

"I've never had a lot of money at once," Sarah said. "Funny, all the years I've worked and never really wanted it or needed it but I would like to try it out. Just one time having enough money to stop working if I want to stop. Are you sure of all this, Dean? This isn't just in the air or maybe. Francie Mankowitz is going to direct it?"

"She's on board. She's afraid we'll back out. Her agent called me an hour after I talked to her. He's talking to our lawyer and of course they'll call Friday. But you're already protected in every way."

"Should we order champagne?" Sarah was laughing now, beginning to believe it. She was going to be the screenwriter on a major film directed by the best woman director in the world.

"Half a bottle now, then more for dinner." Stefan was laughing too. There is nothing more humorous in the world than success. He signaled the waiter and champagne was produced and they drank it in the middle of the day and then Dean and Stefan went upstairs to finish unpacking and sleep and Sarah went out onto the streets of Paris to walk and think and celebrate. She went into the shop with the blue sofa and priced it and asked for costs on shipping it to the United States. I may never get back to the United States, she decided. It may be a long time before I get to Nashville.

That afternoon she called Jack to talk to him but got his answering machine so she decided to write him a letter instead. She made a few starts on writing it, then gave up and went back to work on the script.

"I need to go back to the villa and walk around," she told Dean that night, at dinner. "As soon as you are over your jet lag, would you like to go?"

"We're fine," Dean and Stefan both agreed. "Melatonin's marvelous. We started it three days before we came. Would you like to go tomorrow? We'll arrange for a car."

The next afternoon a chauffeur appeared at her door and she got into his car and they went to the hotel and picked up Dean and Stefan and were driven to the country to see the villa. The old man was still there and glad to see Sarah again. They gave him money and Sarah went back inside and once again was filled with ideas. A local habitation and a place, she quoted to herself. Embodied now. Oh, I know exactly how to write the scenes here. If only they use them as I tell them to, but that's the problem with a director. It will be her film now. I'm only a hired gun no matter how much Dean and Stefan try to flatter me. I'm part of a team, something I never was much good at doing.

"It's perfect," Dean said. "We'll have someone start trying to lease it this afternoon. Also, we need to see about an apartment. There's a building on Avenue Gabriel that might be nice. We might be here until after Christmas, you know."

"I don't know if I can stay that long," Sarah began. "I can't just leave everything."

"Of course you can. This will only happen once in a lifetime, Sarah. Your first real film. The first Stefan and I have done in ten years."

"We need to go to Avignon next week," Stefan put in. "I think it might help you flesh that part out if you went with us and stayed a few days."

"I've been there many times."

"Oh, I know but it's always nice to revisit old scenes. We might find something no one's ever used in a film. And we can scout locations there."

"When will you hear about Cleta Wrightsman?"

"I think soon. No one keeps Francie waiting. It will be either yes or no in the next few days. If she says yes, we're in. The studios will fight for this one."

"Look around then. I'm going to walk to the back of the property and see if there's anything else I need."

"Fine. Go on. We brought a picnic. We'll eat on the patio when you come back."

Sarah put on her boots and stuck a notebook and pencil into her pocket and struck out down the dirt road that led from the house to the fields. She went past the courtyard with its massive stone tables and past the abandoned milking barn and down a small road to a vineyard. In the distance was a house with a stone fence. In one field was an abandoned tractor sitting on a broken wheel, listing to one side. The sky was a bright, clear blue. It was so quiet, so untouched. Sarah began to imagine her heroine, alone and walking here after the young man left for good and left her alone to find a life to live.

What am I doing? she was thinking. Letting Dean and Stefan think I'll stay here and be a hired hand to rewrite scenes all fall. I won't do it. They can fax things to me. I never said I would stay for filming. No one does that anymore. But if I don't they'll get another writer and I'll end up sharing a screenwriting credit. Well, who cares? I care, because it could mean a lot of money. I should call Freddy as soon as I get home but it will be the wrong time of day. I need to call him as soon as he's at the office in the morning. I have to know what I'm doing. I told Jack a month. I told him I'd marry him.

She sat down on a large flat rock and took out the notebook and tried to make notes on the landscape but she had no real interest in it. This is not how I work, she knew. Not for money. Not in the presence of other people. Not because some goddamn movie star wants the part. Who am I? Where have I gone? What has happened to me?"

Taking herself very seriously, she wrote on the pad, then drew a tree on top of it. *Since when is there anything wrong with making money?*

By the time Sarah arrived back at the house there was more news. Stefan had called his office from a cellular phone and had the news that a popular actor from the Royal Shakespeare Company had agreed to play the young man. "It's all happening," he told Sarah. "This is how it used to be in the old days. Dominoes. Of course, Francie's strong but mostly it's the script. It's a beautiful piece of writing, Sarah. I told Dean on the plane I thought it was the nicest love story I'd read in years."

"We need to drive to Provence tomorrow," Dean added. "We should keep on before they start coming over and wanting to have meetings. The more we do this week and next week the more the movie will belong to us. If we have concrete scenes, written, and know where they should be filmed, Francie will listen to us. She trusts me. We made *Santander* together, did you know that, Sarah?"

"It's one of my favorite films. I didn't know you had done it."

"I found the book and I produced it. It made Francie. She hasn't forgotten what we can do. So, can you leave writing a few more days, Sarah, and go with us to Provence?"

"If that's what you think we should do. I need a push to write the scenes in Avignon. I've been thinking they might be better at St.-Tropez or Le Lavandou, which is less well known. The cliffs there are so lovely."

"We'll look at several places. This is so exciting, Sarah. The most exciting thing in years."

"Let's go out into the courtyard to have that picnic," Stefan suggested. "I'm famished, ladies. And there's a wine in that basket I'm longing to taste." They went to the courtyard and spread the picnic out upon the table and asked the old man to join them but he refused. They opened the beautiful white wine and ate croutons with rouille and brandade de morue and salade with bread. There were tarts for dessert and when they were finished they packed up and were driven home. Dean and Stefan slept most of the way but Sarah was wide awake, with her mind going a thousand miles an hour. It was here, the big break, the big event, the moment every writer wanted. And she was going to take that ball and run with it and Jack would just have to understand.

The next morning they flew to Aix-en-Provence in a small plane and were met by a car and taken up and down the coast for three days while Sarah took notes and Dean and Stefan argued about sites. They visited the two-thousand-year-old Roman bridge, the Pont du Gard, and agreed to use it for background shots if not for scenes. They went to Monaco and St.-Tropez and down the coast to several small resorts. They went to the Camargue at the mouth of the Rhone delta and looked at the marshlands and white horses.

"It's overkill," Sarah said at the end of the third day. "Let's get back to Paris. I want to write."

"We can get a plane from Cannes," Dean said. "There's a service there." They spent the night in Cannes and flew back to Paris the next day. From St.-Tropez Sarah had sent a fax to Jack telling him what she was doing but when she got back to the apartment there were no calls or messages. She called him at eleven at night Nashville time and he sleepily answered the phone. "Jay Wilson had a stroke two days ago," he told her, speaking of his best friend and partner. Jay was the mainstay of Jack's support system, the one who had covered for him when he was with her in France. "It's been hell around here. I don't know what he's going to be left with. Nothing on the right side. It's as bad as it could be. If it were me I would want to have died."

"I'm so sorry."

"I can't imagine going on without him. I ran things through him. Have since medical school. I wish you could come here. Is there any chance of that?"

"No. It isn't a good time to tell you but there have been some breakthroughs about the film. Francie Mankowitz is going to direct it. They've signed a male and female lead. It looks like it will happen, Jack. I know that's nothing compared to what you've been through."

"Where have you been, Sarah?" There was resignation in his voice, sadness, blame. She felt it like a blow.

"I've been on the Côte d'Azur looking for locations for the film. They may be starting on it in two months. If they can get the cinematographer they want. Are you all right?"

"No, I'm not. Elise is going into a treatment center. She's in bad shape. I haven't had much sleep, Sarah. You caught me at a bad time."

"Did you get my fax?"

"I don't know. I don't think so."

"I better let you go back to sleep. Can I talk to you tomorrow? What time is good?"

"I can't say. I'll call you."

"I won't be here. I have to meet the director. She's flying in tomorrow. I don't know exactly when. Well, we'll find each other."

"I suppose so. I hope we do." He hung up the phone first and then Sarah put down the receiver of her own phone and then she turned around and slipped the diamond ring from her finger and put it in a box in a drawer. It bothered her when she typed. It slid around on her finger and made her transpose letters. I don't want to be wearing an engagement ring when I meet Francie Mankowitz. She'll think it's some sort of joke.

Dear Jack, I can't go through with this. Dear Jack, we have to put this off until after Christmas or next winter. Dear Jack, I'm no good at relationships. I'm no good at living with people. I don't want to live in a house in Nashville, Tennessee. Dear Jack, I'm sorry Elise isn't well. Dear Elise, I hope you're better. To hell with this. To hell with guilt. I'm going to work.

By the time Francie Mankowitz arrived two days later, Sarah had managed to rewrite the draft they were all reading, expanding several scenes and adding three more. The best scene was a picnic in the shadow of the Pont du Gard. Cary and her young lover had gone on a hiking vacation. She was stronger than he was at first and in better shape but as the week wore on she began to have injuries. First her knee and then a toothache. She was a forty-five-year-old woman and things went wrong. He was twenty-six and still a god. To keep him from knowing she was in pain she was taking pills surreptitiously. "I need to talk to Francie," Sarah told Dean and Stefan. "I don't know how these things work on film, how much to show, how much can be done with dialogue. Do I flash back to a doctor's office? How powerful is a closeup of her face when she's in pain?"

"Just keep writing," Dean said. "You're on a roll. Keep writing, keep writing."

*   *   *

Then Francie Mankowitz was there. She moved into an apartment on Avenue Gabriel and they began to have meetings in the beautiful gold and white living room. "It belonged to the Auchinclosses," Dean said. "Whoever bought it lent it to Francie."

The cast and crew were being assembled. Meetings were held every day. In the meantime Sarah kept writing. The second installment of the money was paid to her agent and she called her broker and told him to put the money in treasury bills. She talked to Jack every other day and then every three days. She had not talked to Elise because Jack said the treatment center wanted her incommunicado for a week, nor had she given the farmhouse a thought. If she thought of it at all she consoled herself that it was a good investment even if she never lived there. Elise's firm called and said the work was done. Sarah's accountant sent them a check. She called Sam Martin and asked if he would watch over things. He said he would be happy to take care of the place for her. She had Elise's firm mail him a key. She stayed at her typewriter.

The heroine, Cary Milligan, was alone in Paris now. The young man had left. She walked out along the Seine and ran into old friends and had dinner with them. She went home and fell asleep. The phone was ringing in the other room but she would not answer it. In the United States her young lover gave up letting it ring and went out to a bar and started picking up a date.

In Nashville, Tennessee, Jack finished his rounds and went to a nurse's station to turn in his sheets. A beautiful young girl behind the desk raised a tearstained face to his. "What's wrong," he asked. "Are you all right?"

"My father died this morning," she said. "They just called me. I don't know what to do. No one else is here. The other RN isn't here yet."

Jack picked up the phone on the desk and called the hospital supervisor. Fifteen minutes later he was driving the young girl, whose name was Stacia, to her apartment. He waited while she changed clothes and packed a small bag. Then he drove her to the airport. He helped her buy an airline ticket. He bought her supper while they waited for the plane. She had a beautiful tall body with a graceful neck and elegant long arms. She had a beautiful wide smile, which he only saw once or twice that night. She had the terrible energy and health of a twenty-five-year-old girl. She had a nursing degree from Vanderbilt. The apartment had been tasteful and neat as a pin. She was from Memphis. It took two hours to get her on a flight to Memphis.

When she was finally walking down the ramp to board the plane she turned around and came back to him and kissed him on the cheek. "I won't forget this, Doctor McAllen," she said. "I'll find a way to pay you back when I get home."

CHAPTER 30

Sarah had her first serious discussion with Francie on a Saturday afternoon. They closed the door and the maid brought coffee and they sat at the dining room table and began to go over the script, scene by scene. Francie wanted more changes than Sarah had imagined she would. She wanted to lose some of Sarah's finest lines of dialogue and in their place she wanted bits of action Sarah thought were tacky and degrading. "But they were in the book," Francie said each time.

"Bathroom scenes play to the lowest common denominator," Sarah said. "I can't believe you want a bathroom scene, Francie."

"Do you know how much money this is going to cost? The Japanese are ready to invest fifteen million. That's big money for a film made in France, Sarah. We have to be sure they get it back. I'm not sure the scene will stay in the finished cut but let's film it so they can use it in the trailer."

"I don't believe this. I thought we were trying to make a great movie. I don't care if some pathologically insecure, anal-retentive studio head thinks it's funny for people to be caught with their pants down, he won't do it to my characters. I'm not writing this for the Billy Crystal set." Francie didn't respond so Sarah went on. "I wouldn't have left my job and come here to do this if I had known it was going to be bathroom scenes for the trailer. I won't write it. I'll expand, and if I have to, cut, but I won't write adolescent trash." Sarah got up and began to walk around the room. She had tried to call Jack that morning and hadn't been able to get an answering machine at his house. She had left a message with his service but after two hours he hadn't called her back. "I mean all that," she added.

"We'll have someone else write it then. Jaen Norman is coming over to work on the dialogue. He'll do it if you won't."

"When is he coming? No one told me about that."

"The first of next week. We'll meet with him on Tuesday and Wednesday if that's all right with you."

"I'm not sure I can do that. I have to go back to the States for a few days and take care of things. I had hoped to go Monday."

"Could you go this afternoon and get back by Wednesday?"

"No, that's not good. I have to be there in the middle of the week."

"Stay until Wednesday afternoon. Then take the Concorde. Tell Laymon to get you the tickets. The company will pay for them. We need you back here and in good shape. I'm sorry no one told you about Jaen, Sarah. We thought you'd be thrilled to have him along. He's the best in the business. He worked on *Juniper Tree* last year and *Sunday in the Park*. He's good. He's careful and he won't be harming your work in any way." Francie sat back in her chair, coffee cup in her hand, absolutely in charge and unshakable, and Sarah remembered finally and for all that she was a hired hand in a world run by money.

"Let's work on the sixth scene some more," she said. "I want to try to convince you to leave the dialogue alone." I can play this game, she decided. I am an editor at *Time* magazine. A bunch of trashy, tasteless movie people aren't going to push me around.

The father of the young nurse Jack had aided had been the postmaster in West Memphis, Arkansas, and the town turned out for the funeral. Jack's secretary sent flowers and when Stacia returned on Friday afternoon Jack met her at the airport and took her out to dinner. Then he took her to her apartment and then he spent the night.

The next afternoon he did something he hadn't done in years. He went to talk to a friend who was a psychiatrist. "What am I supposed to do?" he asked him. "I begged Sarah to marry me but I don't even know where she is half the time. I got horny and fucked a young girl and I'm glad I did. I want to fuck her some more. I don't know what I want. Maybe I want them both."

"Of course you do," the friend said. "We all want them all. Tell Sarah about it. See what she chooses, then take what you need. This isn't some gentle, kind species we belong to, Jack. I thought you knew that. Maybe Eugenie's death scared you. Remember who we are, the most bloodthirsty, desirous, adroit, devious, cruel, kind, voracious seekers of sex and safety that have ever walked the face of the earth. How do you think we survived? And don't get that look on your face. That isn't you. Call Sarah. Tell her to give you an answer. If she doesn't want to marry you, forget her. Take that young girl and move her into your house and have some fun. It's all we have, Jack. This is the only run."

It was Sunday when he finally talked to Sarah on the phone. It was seven A.M. in Nashville. It was past noon in Paris.

"How are things in France?" Jack asked.

"Not perfect. The dream director has turned out to be a bitch. I don't know what I thought she would be. I don't know what led me to think I was going to have a different experience with Hollywood than any other writer has ever had. I'm mad at Dean and Stefan too. They want to put a bathroom scene in the beginning of the movie. A birthday party where she locks herself in a bathroom by mistake. Please."

"Sounds nice."

"Do I detect pleasure in your voice?"

"Oh, Sarah, I'm sorry. When are you coming here? I want to talk to you about something."

"How's Elise? Is she all right? I've been meaning to call you about her but I haven't had a minute. I'm fighting for my life here."

"No. It isn't about Elise. Elise is—"

"Wait a minute. Excuse me. I have to answer the other phone."

She pushed the hold button and talked for three or four minutes to Francie's assistant. Jack held the dead phone for a minute. Then he turned off his phone and walked out of his house and went to the hospital to go to work. He was angry as he had not been angry before. Angry with himself and with Sarah and with Eugenie for dying and with his useless bad children and the cold he was catching and the X rays that refused to be crystal balls and tell him the future of the patients he was treating.

There was a message from Sarah on his machine when he got home. "I'm sorry. That was terribly rude. I love you. I'll be in New York on Friday. If you can come and meet me, good. If not, I'll be in Nashville as soon as I can unpack and pack another bag and get a plane. I'll be there Saturday night or Sunday for sure. Tell Elise I'm thinking of her."

CHAPTER 31

Jimmy McAllen had been offered the job he applied for in Atlanta. It was a good firm with an established reputation and they were offering him fifty thousand dollars a year to start. The next afternoon a firm in Lexington that was smaller and did more interesting work called and asked him to come in and talk to them. They were three young men who were bright and full of energy. "We want you because we read the law review piece about the TWA case. We really want you with us, Jimmy. Tell us about your other offers."

"A firm in Atlanta offered me fifty grand with a raise in a year if they like my work."

"What would you be doing?"

"Suing chiropractors and handling corporate accounts." He laughed. He felt wonderful, in the room with the handsome, bright young men. He felt like being charming now. "I'd rather stay in Lexington. Make me an offer."

"Fifty-three," the young man behind the desk said. "And anything else they offered."

That night Jimmy called Elise to tell her what he had decided. "And then you won't come to Atlanta?" she asked.

"I like these men. I want to work with them."

"It's because I came into this clinic, isn't it? It embarrasses you. You're leaving me, aren't you, Jimmy?"

"Goddammit, Elise, you're my first cousin. We have no business getting married. That was always your idea."

"Then why did I get that tubal ligation?"

"Because you wanted to. I told you not to do that. I never wanted you to do that. You did that on your own. Stop blaming people for things, Elise. Calm down. Listen to me."

"Will you come here this weekend?"

"Not this weekend. I have to study."

Two hours later Elise walked out of the treatment center and caught a taxi to a bar and ordered a drink. She had been abandonded so many times in her life she was good at getting mad in a hurry when it happened.

She had a good time in the bar for a while. Then she stopped having a good time and got into another taxi and went to the Four Seasons Hotel in downtown Atlanta and tried drinking in a nicer bar. Then she rented a room in the hotel and went upstairs and drank half a bottle of gin and took three of the Demerol she had been saving in the lining of her purse since the ligation.

She woke up around four in the morning and took the last two Demerol and then she didn't wake up again. She didn't wake up and she didn't dream and she didn't have to think about how mad she was at everyone and how mean they had all been to her.

It was late the next afternoon when the hotel manager found the body. It was seven at night when Jack was notified. He got on a plane and flew to Atlanta, but he did not call Sarah. This will be the end of that, he decided. She's in a world where they only make up death and disease and horror. She has no idea what we suffer because she has always refused to suffer. She's over there with all those fairies and movie people. I can't tell her yet.

So now Elise is gone too who was unhappy every moment of her life. I loved her as much as I could. My daughter is dead. My wife is gone. The woman I think I love is in Paris, France, and doesn't help me in any way. That was never reality. I could never live the life she lives. So I have to go to Atlanta and collect my child's body. My son is useless, doesn't even work. What sort of life am I living? What set me up for this?

Then he was weeping. He was thirty-five thousand feet above the earth and he was weeping.

CHAPTER 32

Jimmy sent the message to Sarah on her fax machine. "Call immediately. Elise is dead. We will be at Uncle Jack's. Funeral Wednesday or Thursday. I'm all right. Love, Jimmy."

"I have to leave," Sarah told Dean. "Explain it to them. I'm leaving on the next plane. This is the man I love, Dean. My godchild. My son. Do what you can. Try to protect my script."

"Of course. What can I do to help? Do you want us to go with you to de Gaulle?"

"No. I can't get out until six this afternoon. The Concorde is full. I'm taking an American flight. It will connect at Kennedy."

"I'll send a car. I'll have them pick you up at three-thirty."

"Thank you. I'll be waiting."

At three-thirty a chauffeur knocked on the door and took Sarah's bag and carried it to the car. Dean was in the car waiting. "I couldn't let you go out there alone. Come, get in. I brought you a little lunch. Something I had the chef at the hotel make for you. So you won't have to depend on airplane food. Now tell me what's going on, if you can speak of it."

"I have to see about my son. That's my main concern, more than Jack, more than anyone. He's all I have in the world, my only kin. I have to let him know I love him."

"He was in love with the girl who died?"

"I don't know what went on between them. She could have been his half sister, Dean. That's the worst thing. They were so alike, both so unhappy. Why are they unhappy? I'm not unhappy, why should my child be? I loved him all I could but he never was comfortable with me. He always liked his father better. So moody, so dark, darkness deep in his heart. I don't know how to save him, Dean. This is the worst day of my life. I can't marry Jack after this. Oh, God, I forgot the ring. What time is it?"

"I don't think you should go back now. Not if the flight's at six. The French are very serious about transatlantic flights."

Sarah rummaged around in her purse for her key. "Will you send it to me by Federal Express? Oh, that won't do. I might be back before it came. I'll make some excuse, say I didn't want to wear it in front of Jimmy."

"Say you were getting it fitted."

"It doesn't matter."

Dean reached out and took Sarah's hand and held it in her own. Sarah was filled with a sense of how stable and intelligent Dean was, how sure of herself, how much a woman at home in the world, sure of what to do, how to conduct herself under any circumstance.

"I can't thank you enough for coming to get me," she said. "This means so much to me."

"We'll take care of the film until you get back. I'm not going to let Francie and Jaen turn this into a farce. I'll fire Francie if she gets crazy. We could get another director. Especially with the cast we've assembled."

"Don't let her put that bathroom scene in the movie. Don't let her film it for the trailer. I want the money as much as you do, Dean, but not enough to film bathroom scenes. It's become the prevailing metaphor in Hollywood movies, the toilet stall. Do you know what that says about the mental state of the studio heads? Terrifying. Healthy people overcome their absorption with bodily functions by the seventh grade. I wish I still had an essay page to fill. I could get an essay out of this. Oh, well. Francie wants to put it in the trailer. The trailer, as if to invite an audience into their own lower mental states. Not childlike. This isn't childlike. It's dark and scary, Dean. This bathroom scene business is really scary."

"There won't be any bathroom scene," Dean said. She squeezed Sarah's hand. "You can rest assured about that."

The driver carried Sarah's bag inside to the American desk, then waited with the car. Dean stayed with Sarah until she went through security. They embraced. "We will be here when you return," she assured her. "We are going to make a wonderful movie, Sarah, if that's any consolation for all this. Bring your son over here. We'll find him a job on the crew. Take him away from the drama."

"I might do that," Sarah answered. "I'll call when I get to Nashville. I'll let you know where I'll be."

The funeral was in the Episcopal cathedral at noon on Thursday. Afterward they went in cars to the cemetery and buried Elise next to her mother. The sun was shining. It was a clear, hot day. Sarah rode in the first limousine with Jack and Jimmy and Johnny. The second car carried Timothy and his wife and a first cousin. Forty people came to the cemetery, mostly older people who belonged to Saint Andrew's.

After the ceremony Sarah and Jack and Jimmy and Johnny stood by the casket as the gravediggers lowered it into the ground and began to pile dirt upon it. Stacia was standing back from them with another nurse. She was wearing a long pale peach dress and a straw hat. She waited behind them until they turned and began to walk back up the path to the cars. Then she went to Jack and took his arm. He turned aside and talked to her in a low voice. She kept nodding her head. Then she was crying and nodding her head. He touched her hair with his hand. He held her hands. She nodded her head again and went back to her friend and walked away.

"Who was that?" Sarah asked.

"A nurse at the hospital." He stood up straight, took a deep breath. Sarah turned to her son, took his arm. They walked to the car. There was nothing to say.

Twenty or thirty people came to the house and stayed awhile but it was not like Eugenie's funeral. There was no conversation, nothing to say.

After the people had left, Sarah took Jimmy out onto the patio. They lit cigarettes and stood very close to each other. "Do you know I love you?" Sarah asked. "I don't think you know that, Jimmy. I would do anything in the world to have you believe it."

"I know you do. We had broken up, Mother. I told her I couldn't marry her. I told her not to have that tubal ligation. That was her idea, not mine. She was crazy. You and Uncle Jack don't know how crazy she was."

"I want you to come back to Paris with me. Can you leave for a few weeks?"

"No. I'm in summer school. If I keep on I'll be done in August. Then I'll have the damned degree and I can go to work."

"Could you come in August? There are all sorts of jobs around a film that a lawyer can do. Just for a break after you finish."

"I don't want a job in the movies, Mother. I have a job with a good firm in Lexington. I like it there. I want to live there if I can."

"Do you want to go into therapy? I think you should find someone to talk to about this. You could be feeling guilty."

"Mother. Elise is dead, okay. She was very close to me even if I had decided not to marry her. I'm pretty broken up about this. I don't want to talk about how I feel. It's Elise's funeral, all right? I think you better take care of Uncle Jack."

"I am trying to help."

"I know that but you can't, and you aren't."

"I think I'll lease the farm again. Do you mind? I'll have them send the money to you. Perhaps we had better go on and sell it. It's yours. Would you want me to go on and sell it and give the money to you?"

"I don't care. Do whatever you want to with it. I've never even been there. It doesn't matter to me."

"I couldn't work there now."

"I don't want to talk about it anymore." He meant it. She touched his arm, tried to get near him but he wouldn't let her near.

His father and stepmother were in the kitchen. In a while she saw him with them. Later they left together.

"I left the ring you gave me in Paris," she said, when she and Jack were alone with only the servants cleaning up the food. There was the housekeeper and two or three other servants. They were all stone-faced and quiet. She and Jack stood in the dining room with them moving in and out beside them.

"I noticed that. It's irrelevant. I have to go to the hospital, Sarah. I have to see Jay. I haven't seen him since this happened. It's too much. Too many bad things."

"You don't deserve this."

"I don't, do I? I hate to leave you alone in this death house. Will you be all right for a couple of hours?"

"Yes. I have calls to make." She picked up a chicken salad sandwich and ate it. Then she ate another one. Then she picked up a plate and put some food on it and sat down in a chair. She felt very old suddenly. Desperately tired. "I'm jet-lagged," she said. "What do you have for that?"

"I'll give you a sleeping pill. Go to bed early and sleep it off." He left the room and returned carrying a bottle of pills and handed it to her. "Put it on my dresser when you've taken one."

"What time is it?"

"Six-forty. I'll be back by nine. I'll understand if you're asleep."

She put down the plate and got up from the chair and went to him and took him in her arms.

"This isn't how it's supposed to be, Sarah. You were the smart one to always run away from here."

"Maybe not. Okay, go on then. I'm going to bed." He moved away from her and went out into the hall and out the front door and she stood watching after him.

She went upstairs and went into the guest room and took off her clothes and then she got into the shower and took a long hot shower and washed her hair. She got out and dried herself and put conditioner on her hair and fluffed it dry and tried not to look at her worried face in any mirrors. She went into Jack's bedroom and lay down on the bed and called her answering machine in New York

City. There were ten messages, two from Paris. One from Dean and one from Francie. There were messages from her boss at *Time* magazine and one from her agent. She called her agent back. He was the only one who would be in an office that late.

"Hello, my darling," he said. "Everyone in the world is looking for you. You heard what happened at *Time?*"

"No."

"James was fired and so was Denege. They said they quit, of course, but it's a housecleaning. I hope you weren't thinking of going back."

"No. That's far from my thoughts at the moment. I need to get back to Paris, but I'm at a terrible funeral. A young woman, a suicide. It's rough out here."

"You sound exhausted."

"I'm going back on the Concorde. They have Francie Mankowitz and Cleta Wrightsman for Cary and Bill Calder for the young man. They have Allen's cinematographer. It's a full house, Freddy. We might really make our living on this. Of course, I may have to be committed by the time they start filming. They brought in another writer to 'help out the dialogue,' without telling me, of course. I need to get back but what can I do?"

"Are you still thinking of getting married in the fall?"

"I don't think so. I can't bear it here, Freddy. I think I'm going to suffocate. I'm no good around death and suicide and dysfunctional lives. I've been away too long. Had too much therapy. I can't be polite, can't talk around it. God, I'm glad to talk to you."

"Let me know what I can do."

"I'll call tomorrow. I'm going to sleep." She got up from the bed and found the bottle of sleeping pills and took a ten-milligram Xanax and then put the bottle of them on Jack's dresser.

She found a pad of paper and wrote Jack a note and left it on his pillow and then she went into the guest room and went to sleep.

Stacia was waiting for him at the hospital and they went to the cafeteria and she held his hand and they talked for an hour. Then he went to see Jay and held his hand for a while. Then he made rounds. Then he drove home and went into his house and read the note and took one of the sleeping pills and went to sleep. He had practically forgotten Sarah was there. None of it mattered anymore, he decided. There was nothing but decay. Nothing that didn't break and decay and fall. No dreams came true. No plans were completed, no rewards posted. Just the same old fucking, boring, hard, endless grind, day after day after day.

I can, of course, do it, he decided. Just like I always have. Eugenie couldn't do it and Elise had her genes. Elise was always so weak, so weak, sometimes I wonder if she was my child. Weakness, sickness, God I'm sick of it.

CHAPTER 33

Jack left at five-thirty the next morning for the hospital. He was scheduled to operate at seven and he wanted to study the X rays. A hip replacement, something he did five or six times a week. Still, every one was different from the one before. Applied science is predicated on the idea that human beings are alike, but every surgeon knows how different they are. The temperature, the mental state, so many things can make a crucial difference.

This one went smoothly and he went to his office for two hours afterward and then back to his house to talk to Sarah. She was packed and in the living room reading a magazine. She was leaving that afternoon.

"Will you be all right?" she asked. "I could stay a few more days if it would do any good. The best thing I can do is get back to Paris and finish my work and then come here as soon as I can."

"Do you want to come here, Sarah? Look at me. Tell me the absolute truth. This is no time for kindness. The worst things have already befallen me. I can take anything but not half truths or uncertainty. Do you want to come here?"

"I don't know. So much is going on. I want to stay there for the filming. This is the biggest break I've had in my career. It's the golden ring. I don't know if I can leave it."

"Then stay. I have been seeing another woman, Sarah. I should tell you that. A young girl."

"I see."

"Will you let me take you to the plane? Will you forgive me?"

"No. It's the girl who was at the funeral, isn't it?"

"Yes."

"Do you want me to send you back the ring?" Sarah started laughing. "Did I say that? Did I just say that?"

"Please let me drive you to the plane."

"I'll let you lend me a car. I'll leave the keys at the TWA desk. Lend me Eugenie's old car."

"I'll lend you mine. It's nicer."

"No. I'd like to drive in her old car. I'd like to think about her one more time. Think of her fingerprints everywhere."

He tried to argue with her and give her the Mercedes but in the end he gave her the keys to Eugenie's old Honda and she drove off alone to the airport.

He stood in the driveway watching her until the car was out of sight.

Sarah cried most of the way to the airport. For Eugenie and for Elise and for Eugenie's parents and her own mother and father and the past and all irreconcilable loss. She wasn't crying over Jack and his girl. That seemed irrelevant, since they would die too someday. She cried for Tyler, Kentucky, and its kind inhabitants and quiet streets and the Sweet Shoppe and the swimming pool. She cried for Mr. and Mrs. Becker, who were dead now too. She cried for the *Tyler Favorite* and for Mrs. Becker's small white dogs.

She left the car in the long-term parking lot. She wrote the location of the car on the parking receipt and put the receipt and the keys into an unused bank deposit envelope she had found in the car. She lugged her suitcase inside to the TWA desk and handed her ticket to the agent. "I want to make a connection at Kennedy and go on to Paris," she said. "If it's possible. I'll take anything you have tonight."

"You can probably make flight six hundred," the agent said. "It leaves JFK at ten. That should give you time."

"I'll try it. Put me on it." The agent printed a new ticket, took her Visa card and scanned it, then handed her the new ticket and a Visa receipt to sign.

"Do you have your passport?" he asked.

"Here." She handed it to him. "Also, may I leave this envelope here for a friend? It has his car keys."

"Sure." He handed back the passport and took the envelope. Then she bought a sandwich and ate it. Then she bought five or six magazines and stuck them in her carry-on. Then she decided to go outside and smoke her second cigarette of the day. Why the hell not, she argued with herself. I'm down to two. I can have a cigarette before I fly across the ocean if I like. I'm smoking it. I'll just light it and take one or two puffs, then I'll put it out.

CHAPTER 34

Sarah arrived in Paris early in the morning. She was so glad to be there, so glad to smell the city, to feel the city. She was sometimes afraid to use her schoolgirl French but not this morning. She chatted with everyone. She went through customs, collected her suitcase, got into a taxi and was driven into town. She went inside the apartment and took a bath and then climbed into the high blue bed and started calling people on the phone."

"I'm back," she told Dean. "When's the meeting?"

"Oh, my dear, we'll have one right away. How were things?"

"I don't want to talk about it."

"Then you shan't. Let's have dinner at L'Ami Jean Paul. Have you been there?"

"No."

"It is the only place to eat. We'll come for you at six. Is six all right?"

"It's lovely." Sarah put the phone down and snuggled down into the pillows to go to sleep.

She slept until five. Then she washed her face and hands and put on a pretty rose-colored blouse and beige slacks and a sleeveless jacket. She put on platform shoes and makeup and a string of pearls. She was waiting when Dean and Stefan arrived, sitting on a velvet sofa, drinking a glass of Chardonnay, pretending she was French.

It was growing dark, an unearthly blue, as they walked along boulevard St.-Michel and past the vendors closing up their shops and past the outdoor cafés which were beginning to fill up with students. Past the great couturiers' shops and the lighted windows full of shoes and on and around to the rue Val-de-Grâce and into a café with black and white marble floors and beautiful statues and windows filled with shutters and green plants. The maître d' led them to a table and seated them and brought them glasses of water and thick white linen napkins and they ordered a bottle of Chablis and sipped it while they studied the menus. "I feel like I haven't eaten since I left Paris," Sarah said. "This restaurant is lovely, Dean. How do you find these places?"

"I have my spies. What will you have?"

"Please order for me. I don't want to have to decide."

Dean ordered Brittany oysters and sea bass and steamed carrots and broccoli. There was fresh hot bread that had just come from a stone oven and delicious salty whipped butter and more wine and a raspberry tart with whipped cream and coffee and they sat in the luxuriant air of the café and talked of the movie and the script.

"Everyone's excited," Stefan said. "There's an air about it. We can really do it with this one."

"Francie asked if you would write a précis of the script for the publicity department." Dean batted her eyes and made a funny face at Sarah. "I said I wasn't sure if you would. It's up to you. Of course, if you don't, someone will do it wrong. They always have us there."

"I'd be glad to do it. That's nothing. I'll write two or three and let them choose one."

"Oh, God, don't do that. They'll patch them together and make a mess. Give them what you want them to use."

"Jaen's gone," Stefan said. "That's the big news. He quit because Cleta and Bill Calder went to Francie and said they hated the scenes he wrote for them. Cleta said she had signed on for your script and she wouldn't stay on board if it was corrupted. He wrote a nude scene at the farm. We were glad you weren't here. That all happened two days ago." He started laughing and Sarah laughed with him, then Dean joined in. It was the polite, tremulous laughter artists reserve for members of their guild who blow it by being obvious or tacky or just plain bad at what they do. A wonderful, nasty, cocky laughter that can only be shared with your peers in any profession. Stefan and Sarah kept on laughing but Dean pretended to be serious. "Cleta said she had let that happen to her once when she was young and it would never happen again and she was leaving if Jaen touched the script again. They were yelling in front of two cameramen. Then Cleta left the set and Francie followed her and stood outside her dressing room for ten minutes talking through the door. Then Cleta let her in and we finally started work. We were filming three scenes for the trailer. They want it finished before they even start the film. Hollywood. The next day Francie paid off Jaen and he left. So, it's all yours again, Sarah. Don't leave town again. We'll start filming the first of September, maybe sooner. The cinematographer, Allen Dades, was here for three days. He loved the villa. He was out there all day looking at the light. I can't wait for you to meet him. I think you are going to get along."

"I'm sorry I missed that. Where did they film these scenes for the trailer?"

"At the Arc Studios on rue Lecourbe. It's fabulous. You've never seen a studio like this. I keep wanting to find a way to use their dressing rooms in the film. Really, the French take films more seriously than we do, don't you think? Absolutely gorgeous young technicians. I fell in love several times."

The waiter returned with a tray of petits fours and poured more coffee and they talked for another half an hour, then walked back to Sarah's apartment and left her there.

She went to her computer and pulled up the last scene she had worked on and added a few things to it and removed one line of dialogue and then she put all the parts of the script neatly in stacks on a table and dusted off the table with her sleeve and turned out the light and the computer. Good night, she said. Thanks for all the good stuff. *Merci, gracias, merci.*

She went into the bathroom and removed her makeup and put on a layer of Chanel Alpha Hydroxy cream and climbed into her high clean bed and went to sleep.

She woke at dawn and worked for half an hour, then put on her walking shoes and walked out into the still sleeping city. She found a café and had coffee and a fresh sweet croissant, then walked back to her apartment and worked until eleven o'clock. At twelve Francie Mankowitz called and wanted her to come to lunch with the actors. She dressed and went out to meet them. I haven't called home, she thought several times, then banished the thought. But I have no home, she decided. I am casting my lot with the gypsies. I adore this life. I like it here. I'm going to stay.

Francie was waiting at the restaurant with Cleta Wrightsman, the leading actress, who was playing Cary Milligan in the film. She was a beautiful woman with alabaster skin and long silky hair pulled back in a bun. She was from Minnesota originally and had received her early training at the Guthrie in Minneapolis. She was eager for the role and wanted to talk of nothing else.

"Bill's coming later," Francie explained. "Cleta insisted on having you to herself."

"I wrote the précis for the publicity people," Sarah said. "But I wouldn't want the actors to read it. It would direct your thinking too narrowly. I'd rather tell you what I know."

"I want to know anything you know about Cary," Cleta answered. "I'm still learning who she is. I was going to read the book but Francie said not to. She said it would confuse me because you'd changed it so much. She said it was the script that mattered."

"She's right. Shall I tell you how I see the film?"

"Oh, please." Cleta leaned across the table, devouring Sarah with her eyes, excited, ready, eager to learn what she knew. Sarah could not help thinking of the contrast between this accomplished, hardworking woman and Elise's insecure mania. I have worked all my life to fix it so I could be with healthy people, Sarah told herself. With people who work, people who are successful at what they do.

And I will stay with them. I will not enter into the unhealthy madness of anyone, not even my own family.

"The main thing," Sarah said, "is that her parents died when she was young, in a small plane that crashed into the ocean near Calais. Her memories are of a villa near the ocean where they were living. After their death she was raised in the United States by her grandmother.

"All her relationships are shaped by this trauma. The young man is beautiful and powerful and has worked his way through engineering school. She seduces him in every way, out of her need, but she's a good person, she knows she mustn't devour him. It's Colette, of course, and, of course, there must be a sacrifice. She knows that love is loss and her face must tell us that, Cleta. Your face is more important than my dialogue. You must know in your mind that your mother and father vanished on a sunny morning. If you can believe in love and suffer loss at the same time, if you can suffer loss and never stop believing in love, then you have her, at least the Cary I imagine." Sarah giggled, then laughed out loud. "If we could only know that in real life."

"Does she always know she must give him up?"

"I think so." Sarah was quiet. No one spoke. Cleta's face was already changing into the part she must become. "Isn't that what makes all love affairs so poignant? There will either be sacrifice, or there will be death. Only the moment remains."

"When she buys the villa for the young man to rebuild for her does she know she is seducing him further, or does she think she's helping him, giving him valuable work?"

"What do you think?"

"She knows she is seducing him."

"Trying to put off the inevitable."

"Francie said you were talking about a new ending."

"I think now he leaves, as in the book, but she does not go back into the villa and weep or be maudlin, much too strong a character for that, our Cary Milligan. I want her to get into a sports car and drive into Paris in the gathering dusk. Park it haphazardly on a street and walk to a café and pick up a beautiful mulatto actor and begin to dance with him. Cut to the skies above Calais where her parents died, the cloud formations there are amazing. I watched them for two days. Then cut to the beautiful fields of the Somme and then vineyards and white linen tablecloths drying in the sun and a stone oven somewhere making bread and all the beauties of the earth. Life is too complex to be answered by anything but acceptance. They keep on dancing. I want this to be rich, rich, rich."

"The objectivity of the camera gives you all the power you will take," Francie said. "A great cinematographer once told me that. The scenes Sarah just told us would use that power."

"Stefan began it," Sarah said. "He told me he wasn't sending a film crew to France to mess around. He said to use the country and to use Paris, to use the place. If ever a place was a player in a film, this is the one for it. The book uses the death of the parents as a small piece of background, but there's so much more that can be done with it, especially since Cary takes the young man there. She uses him as a shield to go back and confront the central trauma of her life and it works. She gives up the young man, or, at least, at the end of the movie he has gone back to the United States, but she gains a mastery over her trauma."

"We won't cheat our audience," Francie said. "They can dream he will come back to her. I've never seen a real-life romance that ended that easily, have you? Well, Cleta, what do you think? Do we have a film?"

"Are you kidding? I think it's the best role I've ever been given. I can't wait to play the scene with the dance. I was a dancer, you know. I suppose you know that?"

"A pale yellow silk dress, with panels?" Francie laughed. "Or a plaid skirt with pleats? She would dress up to go to town, don't you think, Sarah? Or would she go in what she was wearing when he left?"

"She would dress up," Sarah answered. "Since she is on her way to save her life."

"Tell me one more thing," Cleta asked. "If you know. Why does she get into the car and drive into town and go dancing instead of staying alone in the villa and being sad? Why is Cary Milligan stronger and smarter than most of us can ever be? What does she have that makes her do this, that drives her to life instead of sadness?"

"Energy," Sarah answered. "Pure libidinal energy. Given in the genes, paid for by having to always clean up the messes we make out of our lives when we ride that wild stallion some of us have inside ourselves. It's true," she added. "Some people have that fire inside themselves, that driving force, and they ride it. Almost everyone has it when they are young, it's the demon of puberty, but most of us lose it when we get older. Cary has a store of it that lasts. It's why she found and seduced a younger man to begin with, why she brought him to France and seduced him further, and why she is too healthy to harm him in the end. She sends him off for the same reason she took him when she needed him. 'The force that through the green fuse drives the flower,' Dylan Thomas called it. It's the thing that fascinates me most in life. Nothing interests me as much as that power, when it manifests itself in a man or woman. France is the place, Cary herself is the plot of this movie. A study of existence."

"I can do it," Cleta said. "I don't know if I have that in me, Sarah. But I know it when I see it and I love it as you do."

"Tomorrow we film interiors," Francie said. "You are both welcome to come and watch if you like."

CHAPTER 35

Black and white marble floors, beautiful Italian statues, shutters in the windows, white painted walls and woodwork, windows looking out onto careful flower gardens, elegant thin china, a chest of silver forks and spoons, cedar closets, silk sheets, a blue door, the brick streets, the carpeted stairs. "We will use the camera to show everything beautiful made by man," Sarah was telling Dean. "If the camera can't do that, the film will fail.

"I want film of that blue door, that china, that woodwork, those shutters. She doesn't want to ever see another office, another computer screen, another broker's office, another frantic phone call from an investor. The American century is over for Cary Milligan. She has quit. This beautiful culture is all she wants now. I don't care if we'll be slaughtered for saying that, do you?"

"Now you're getting daffy, Sarah. We're just trying to tell a story here."

"So we are. Will Denzel Washington play the beautiful stranger? I don't want to start sounding starstruck, but every time they say his name I get excited. Because he would be perfect. Foreign, and yet, just what Paris would create if it were Pygmalion. A Paris dream but not Parisian."

"He's going to try, that's the last I heard. We have to film around his schedule. Stefan told him to name his price. If we can't get him there are plenty of beautiful actors dying for the work. He doesn't have to be black, does he? Couldn't he be French or Italian?"

"Not Italian for Cary. Denzel's smile would carry the scene. See, Dean, I'm going to kill myself if I start calling actors I've never met by their first names." Sarah held her fingers out in the air in the sign of a cross, as if to ward off devils.

Dean laughed. "Don't worry, Sarah. I'll tell you if you start going Hollywood. As for the smile. A beautiful stranger's smile, someone the audience had never seen, might be even more effective, more dreamlike, and we wouldn't have to shoot around any star's neuroses."

"Now I'd rather have a stranger. God, it really is a complicated process, isn't it? So many possible moves, like chess. Some days I understand why people get caught up in it."

They were drinking café au lait at a café on the boulevard St.-Michel. It was a gorgeous, cool day. A front had moved down from the north and east and Paris was having three days of seventy-degree weather. "Let's walk," Dean said. "I want to walk down by the Cluny and see the Roman ruins. Francie wants to film there on a cloudy day but I think the sunshine coming in skylights would be more effective." They paid the bill and left the café and walked along the boulevard St.-Michel to the boulevard St.-Germain and along its broad sidewalks to the Musée de Cluny and walked around the exterior before going inside. It took up most of a square city block with a public park behind it down Place P. Painlevé. At the ticket desk in the entrance to the Musée they ran into Maurice Demoillere, the cinematographer's first assistant. He had been sent by Allen Dades to make an assessment of the light in the room with the canopies. "It will never work and they won't let us film here with lights," Dean told him. "Tell Allen he's wasting his time on that. We can reproduce this in a studio."

"Very expensive." He moved nearer to Sarah and began to flirt with her. "What does the writer say?"

"I'm Alice in wonderland. I'm just here for the ride." She found herself flirting back and allowed it to happen.

"I was on my way to Sacré-Coeur when I leave here," he said.

"Come with me. We want to film on rue St.-Rustique so I want to see it in different lights. Will you come along?"

"Of course."

They decided to take a cab to save their feet for the narrow cobbled rue St.-Rustique.

"I was in this quarter many times with Simon Levarve," Dean said. "The love of my life. I will probably cry."

"We would love to have you cry," Maurice said. "Ah, the beauty of this day, never to be repeated or replaced. We will cry with you."

They climbed into the cab and were driven off to spend the rest of the morning at Sacré-Coeur. When they parted Maurice asked Sarah if she would have dinner with him that evening and she said yes.

"He's adorable," Dean said, when he was gone. "I sense life is returning to you, Sarah, after your rash of funeral-going. Go out and meet it, that's my advice."

"I don't seem to be able to evade it," she answered. "Even if I am trailing lives behind me like a Portuguese man-of-war."

"They may not all be thinking of you, Sarah. Your son may be quite content in some fantasy of his own. Nature hates a vacuum as today will attest. They usually get filled."

"I'm so vain I forget that. Maurice is adorable, isn't he? So passionate about his work. And he's right here, in this circle of my life."

CHAPTER 36

The director wanted Sarah to rewrite the scenes where Cary Milligan goes to Calais to see where her parents' plane went down into the sea.

"I can't improve on what I've done," Sarah complained to Dean. "I gave her the best I had."

"Then make it worse. Maybe it's too fine for her. What did she say she wanted?"

"A flashback to a funeral, only it couldn't have been the parents' funeral because they don't find bodies lost at sea. Talk to her, Dean. Tell her the scenes are all right as they are."

"Just write her something and she'll realize the difference. She's just getting nervous."

"I don't want to write a funeral. All I've been doing is going to them. They are all alike. It's a dumb ploy. Life is where the drama is. At my father's funeral they had him in the dining room with the casket open. Now that was a funeral. As soon as they started closing the caskets all the drama left the funerals."

"You looked at him?"

"I went into the room four times. Once with my mother, who removed the rings from his fingers and put them in her pockets. A couple of times by myself, out of something resembling curiosity. And once with the minister to pray. Then I went out in the yard and got my shoes dusty in the driveway. We had polished them that morning with that liquid white polish people used to use on shoes. Then I went inside and sat in the kitchen with the ladies and they fed me cherry pie. They made cherry pies in Tyler, Kentucky, that could rival any tart in Paris."

"I would like to have tasted them," Dean said.

"I have one other memory of my father's death," Sarah added. They were on the gold sofas of the apartment Dean and Stefan had rented on the Place Alphonse Laveran, next to the Val-de-Grâce, one of the most beautiful churches in all of France. They were drinking coffee from small ivory cups. On the table was a plate of tarts Stefan had brought in an hour before from the bakery on the corner. "I remember going to the cemetery in the rain and Momma beside me crying and my grandparents standing beside the burial site until all the dirt had been shoveled in on top of the coffin. I stayed with them. I thought it was the right thing to do. I still don't understand when people leave burials unfinished. If we must have a funeral in this movie, we will have the mourners stay until the mound is filled and finished."

"This film ends with dancing, remember?" Stefan came and sat on a chair at the end of the sofa and put his hand on Sarah's stockinged foot. "The common theme is the death of fathers, as Shakespeare knew. If we get the footage of the chalk cliffs of Dover in the beginning of the film and then run the end credits out over the dance and the café and Cary moving on into the vast awareness and possibility of the rest of her life, I will be content and I will guarantee you an audience, if not an Academy Award. The first rushes are in an hour. I wish you ladies would get ready to leave. We now have apartments on both banks of the Seine and people scattered all over this city. I keep feeling like we are going to lose someone."

"Maurice is taking me," Sarah said. "He's coming in half an hour. He shot it, did you know that? They got it in four takes. He's already been cutting it. This is the beginning."

The doorbell was ringing. Maurice was there, wearing a beautiful white shirt with a blue sweater tied around his shoulders, so

French, so perfected. His thinning hair was cut very short and his long elegant hands reached out for Sarah's arm. If I fall in love again this soon it proves I am a whore, she decided. A French cinematographer who will have ten more women before the year is out. A ladies' man, an artist, with no more scruples than I have.

Sarah started laughing and pulled him into the foyer and kept him waiting five minutes while she went into Dean's bedroom and freshened up her makeup and put on Dean's Chanel Number Nineteen and rolled up the sleeves of her shirt and combed her hair back into a neat bun. "He is so invariably chic," she said to Dean, who was watching all this and smiling. "I should have changed clothes."

"Here. Wear these." Dean opened a box and took out a pair of beautiful little amethyst earrings. They were small, pale amethysts set in plain gold and Sarah took out the pearls she was wearing and put them into her ears. Dean reached over and pulled out two pieces of Sarah's hair and let them dangle over her eyes. The ladies smiled and held hands and went to join the men.

The group assembled to see the rushes at the Arc Studio was festive. These were the early rushes of sites and qualities of light and costumes and details, the craft and fun of cinematography. It was a tradition with Allen Dades to have the cast and crew and director and producers come to these early screenings to get the feel for where they would be, to see the world he was trying to create with his camera. There was twenty minutes of film at the villa and in the countryside, then twenty more of sites in Paris, then ten minutes of costumes.

They had used Sarah's notes to the cinematographer for a voice-over at the end. "Blue skies, perfect weather. That night, a new moon coming up behind the Eiffel Tower. We drove through the fog and the rain to La Coste. The lavender hills of the Lubéron. Lavender and sunflowers."

"It's gorgeous," Dean announced when it was over. "More than I could have hoped for."

"We're pleased." Maurice squeezed Sarah's hand. "It's going to be the best movie experience any of us has had. Thanks to Sarah's divine script. Inspired!"

"I didn't have anything to do with the beautiful things we've just seen. It's too good to be true."

"Don't anyone start getting superstitious," Stefan put in. "A good beginning is good luck. All will go smoothly now. I promise that."

"How long before we really begin work?" Sarah asked.

"Two more weeks."

"Then I'm going home and see about my apartment and have these skin things burned off my arms. Also, see my dentist and have my hair cut. Then I'll be back for the fall." She held out her arm and showed them two small scaly places on her wrist. "English skin. The price we pay for playing tennis. Anyway, I'll get everything done there and be back. Freddy and Camille want their apartment in September so I have to find another place to live."

"We'll find you one," Dean promised. "Go on. I'll have things for you to see when you return."

The next morning Sarah made a reservation to fly to New York on July twelfth, with a return flight for the seventeenth.

"Take the French Concorde," Francie kept insisting. "We will pay for it. It's invaluable to have you here. Please change your reservation."

"No, I don't like the cabin. Too confining. I'm happy with TWA."

July twelfth was a Friday. Sarah arrived in New York at dark and went straight to her apartment and began to open mail. The housekeeper had been there that morning and aired out the rooms and turned on the air conditioner. There was food in the refrigerator, frozen dinners in the freezer, super-homogenized milk and cream, mass-produced bread, toaster waffles. Sarah stood in the door to the refrigerator musing on how much she appreciated food of any kind, frozen American junk food or the haute cuisine of Paris.

She was carrying a letter from Robert and one from Jimmy,

wondering if opening them would ruin her day. She opened Jimmy's first.

Dear Mother,

I am going to be married in a month's time. Also, we are going to have a baby. We are thrilled. I am in holy awe at the thought. She's a girl I knew in high school. The new job is great. I'm making fifty-three thousand dollars a year which is like a million to me. Dad's pretty happy about all this. I don't know if you want to come to the wedding or not. You know Uncle Jack is marrying a nurse, don't you? They'll be there. Please call me when you get back to New York and I'll give you the details.

Love, Jimmy

Sarah held the letter against her breast. She took the letter into the bedroom and lay down upon the bed holding it. Somewhere in the world her DNA was helping make a child, a whole new set of teeth, hair, bone, skin, ideas, brain, fingers, toes, smiles, dreams, possibilities, appetites, a voice to speak and sing, legs to run and dance, hands to create and hold.

She tried to call Jimmy but the line was busy. Might as well push my luck, she decided, and opened the letter from Robert. It was four pages thick. A dried rose fell out from the pages. She giggled and started reading.

Dear Sarah,

Here are all the drafts of the letter. You can read them in the order they were written or you can read this one first and be lulled into thinking I'm no longer mad at you. First, you know where I am anytime you get tired of what you're doing, call me and I'll come to Paris. I'm taking French lessons from a couple who are voice coaches for Disney. They say I have a gift for it. I think you'll be surprised at how I can open doors for you when you finally call and tell me to come watch the filming and remind you that it's possible to have a good time IN THE ONLY WORLD THERE IS.

I am making a lot of money. By the time you get this, if it has to be forwarded six times, as I am assuming it will be (where are you by the way?). By the time you get it I'll be able to support you in a style to which you will find it easy to get accustomed. I know you think I came out here to get my heart broken and I know you didn't want it that way but *Going the Limit* is IN PRODUCTION. Also, I have a two-film contract with Disney. I am going to write a film set in India about a group of young people planning an assault on K-2. Tentatively, the second will be a romantic comedy set in New York in the year 2000.

Thank you for believing in me, Sarah. I carry that around with me like an amulet. I'll be in Paris at Christmas whether you're there or not. If you're in New York I'll be there. You can't get rid of me. There's too much left that you know that I want to learn. And I want to fuck you before I GET ANY OLDER.

Love and I mean that,
Robert

P.S. Are you going to marry that guy? Have you talked to your psychiatrist about this? Do you know about the proverbial snowball in hell? That is how long a marriage lasts between a writer and any sort of normal human being. You are the one who told me that. I'll be waiting.

Why don't you go exhume your father while you're at it?

"Dear Sarah," the second page began.
I am waiting to find out if the script has been accepted. Long, boring days. Not that anyone has to be bored out here a moment if they don't want to be. You can sit on the streets and watch the new world struggle to be born. It isn't pretty, these kids are crazy. I feel like an old man watching them. I've about decided all you have to do to be successful anymore is stay sober and drug free. You were right about that too. Are you always right or did you just get those ideas from that shrink you used to see and bring them home? Everyone out here talks from the couch. You can see their eyes light up when they start passing on the insights.

Sarah folded the letter back together, picked the rose up from the floor and put it back into the folds and put the whole thing back into the envelope. She called Jimmy's telephone again and this time he answered the phone.

"You've met her," he said. "Stella Conner. She went to Country Day with me."

"That's wonderful, Jimmy. I'm so thrilled. And of course I want to come to the wedding."

"Well, it's in five days. We've changed it. It's at Stella's church and a reception at the country club. You know the Conners, Mother. Michael Conner, William Conner, the law firm. They're Dad's friends."

"I'm supposed to go back to Paris on the seventeenth. I can change it."

"You won't need to. The wedding's at ten in the morning. You could leave that afternoon. We'll be gone to Mexico."

"Then I'll be there. Is there a rehearsal dinner?"

"Tuesday night. It's at the club too. We didn't have time to get too fancy."

"Then I'll be there Tuesday. I can't tell you how happy it makes me, Jimmy. How really thrilled and excited I am."

"Then come on. Stella and I will meet your plane. She's crazy about your books, Momma. She's dying to meet you again, and talk to you."

"I love you. I'll see you on Tuesday."

Sarah hung up the phone and called Paris and talked to Dean and then went downtown to see if she could find something to wear to be the mother of the groom. She went to Armani's and bought an evening suit for the rehearsal dinner. Then she went to Valentino's and found a beautiful blue dress on sale and left it to be altered to wear to the wedding. I can leave right after the ceremony and still make the evening flight to Paris, she decided.

Things turn out all right. My son is going to be a happy man. I will go to Nashville and be the best mother in the world and give them ten thousand dollars for the down payment for a house. Then I will get on a plane and fly back to Paris and get ready to watch my fortune being made. For now, I will call my newly fired old boss, James, and ask him to have dinner with me. But first I will walk around this city for two hours to see the feast that is the world. I don't have to be distracted or haunted by the past. I don't even have to be unhappy and I sure as hell don't have to care if Jack is going to marry that pretty nurse.

She walked from Valentino's back to her apartment (in her good shoes) and went up and put on walking shoes and walked the city for three hours. She went to Central Park and walked among the bicycle riders and skateboarders and dog walkers. Then she walked to Bloomingdale's and bought a layette of beautiful baby clothes and mailed them to Jimmy's address. Then she stopped at a pay phone and called the dermatologist and told his secretary she had changed her mind about having the lesions on her wrist removed. Then she caught a cab to Tiffany's and bought a gold bracelet for the bride. Then she went home and called James and listened to all the gossip about the merger between Time Warner and Turner.

Then she fell asleep and slept for fourteen hours. She fell deeper and deeper into her dreams. In the last dream, the one she dreamed just before she woke, she was walking with Jimmy's little boy along the banks of a river. Many people were watching them. They were there to solve a mystery the people wanted solved. The little boy was only three years old but he had magical powers and spoke in many tongues. The people watched them as they walked along holding hands. They knew the answer, the little freckled, redheaded boy and his grandmother knew what the people needed to know to keep on having their village on the banks of this river. Finally they turned together toward the people and told them the answer to the puzzle, the words they must remember to solve the mysteries they must solve.

CHAPTER 37

Knowing full well that it could be an emotional mine field, a real full-blown disaster, and knowing she had to go anyway and to stay even if it turned into war, Sarah got on the plane and went to Jimmy's wedding. As soon as the plane was aloft she began to think of Elise. Her death hangs over this wedding like a cloud of fire, Sarah knew. Will we speak of it? Or will it hover near, my guilt, Jack's guilt, Jimmy's guilt, our failure to love and heal her? But she wasn't to be healed and that is also true. Two possibilities existed. In one of them the three of us gave Elise our lives and let her feed on us. She always fed on anyone she could find since Eugenie wasn't there when she needed her. She ended what was between Jack and me. If it's ended. If it can ever be. She spoiled it then. And she almost captured Jimmy with her sadness, but he escaped. Thank God. I'm glad he's marrying anyone. It doesn't matter if it seems too soon. Who knows what went on between him and Elise. I think most of it happened in Elise's mind. He never agreed to it. I say that because I am his mother but I am also a fierce objective reporter of my own life. I am for Jimmy. I am for the living. I will not bring Elise to this wedding.

Jack will take her there. He can't escape, but I'll escape and maybe Jimmy will too. No one is thrown on your pyre, Elise. Sorry about that. Maybe you can come back as a fierce and powerful creature with a good mother and know how to find the power within yourself. Enough of this.

Timothy's wife had called Sarah to ask her to stay in their guest cottage while she was in Nashville. Sarah had accepted and in return had insisted on being allowed to pay for half of the rehearsal dinner. "We will have a good time," Jennifer had said.

"And a united front for Jimmy," Sarah answered.

Sarah arrived at two in the afternoon and was met at the plane by Jimmy and the bride, a sweet girl she remembered meeting one summer when Jimmy's class came to New York on a field trip. The girl resembled Jimmy's stepmother so completely it was terrifying. As it turned out, the two women were distant cousins.

Sarah dressed for the rehearsal dinner as she would dress to appear before a Senate investigating committee. Jack had called and said he had an emergency and couldn't come to the dinner so she was going to be saved that.

The dinner was at seven. They were to be at the church for the rehearsal at five-thirty. Sarah put on the Armani, knowing the presence it gave her was worth every extravagant penny. She waited in the living room of the guest house, reading the boring magazines, trying not to look at what was on the bookshelves. Then Timothy and his wife appeared at the door and the three of them went to the church and then the country club. Sarah was surprised at the warmth she felt from everyone who spoke to her. She had spent so many hours thinking these people hated her for writing the truth about their world that she had forgotten many of them had lived very interesting lives and had forgotten all about her and anything she did.

She was home by twelve and in bed with the last of the sleeping pills Jack had given her earlier in the summer. It's okay, she kept saying. I'm here. We did it. I like Timothy and I like his wife. Tomorrow I'll have to see Jack, but I'll make it through that too. I'll be kind to his girlfriend. The reception won't last long. I'll go to the airport. I'll get on the plane. I'll be at JFK. I'll board the plane to

Paris. Maurice will be waiting for me. We will make a movie. It might even be beautiful. It will be beautiful. It might even be good.

But anything can happen around a wedding. During the night one of the bridesmaids got drunk and ran away from the groomsman she was trying to get to propose to her. She wasn't found until nine-thirty, and the wedding was delayed for an hour hoping she could be sobered up and dressed.

At last, at eleven, the organ played the wedding march and the ceremony began, minus one bridesmaid. Sarah was privy to all the drama and was so amused by it that it took the edge off of Jack sitting one pew away with the young girl by his side. I will not think about Jack, Sarah swore to herself, or Elise hovering above the altar. I will think about Jimmy and his bride. I will not write this. I will not get tickled and start laughing. I will never use this in a novel. I swear I won't use it. No, I won't swear that. I'll write it if I goddamn well want to write it. If they do, if *we* do, things this hilarious, then it's like oxygen. Available to anyone with the lungs to use it.

Jimmy and his father took their place by the altar. The bride came down the aisle. The ceremony went on and on. The bride had decided at the last minute to have Communion after the ceremony. It was twelve o'clock when the guests wandered out the doors of the cathedral. It was almost one by the time everyone was back at the country club at the reception.

"My plane leaves at three," Sarah told Timothy's wife. "And I have to go back and get my things from your place."

"Don't worry," she answered. "Timothy knows when you have to leave. We have to stay in the receiving line until they've all come through, however. You don't mind, do you?"

"No," Sarah said. "Of course not. I'd forgotten all about the receiving line."

Jack came through the receiving line alone. The girl was on the other side of the room talking to people her own age. "I would like to see you before you leave," he said. "Let me take you to the airport." He was very serious. Timothy and Jennifer pretended not to hear.

"All right," Sarah answered. "What will you do with the girl?"

"I'll take her home. I'll be back in half an hour."

"My flight's at three."

"I'll get you there." Then he was gone and Timothy and Jennifer looked at her and all their faces went blank. Then Sarah started laughing. The bishop was next in line, her new friend from all the recent funerals.

"A better way to meet," he said, and held Sarah's hand for a long time, holding up the rest of the line. "Where have you been? I was hoping you were staying in Nashville."

"I've been in Paris, worshiping at Sainte-Chapelle." She smiled into his eyes. She could not stop flirting with this bishop no matter how hard she tried.

"Let's have a talk when you're finished here." He relinquished her hand and moved on to the mother of the bride, still looking over his shoulder at Sarah.

Jack's gone to take that girl home. The bishop is moving in on me. I'm in Nashville at my son's wedding. There are no clocks and I'm going to miss my plane. Didn't France teach me anything? Couldn't I just calm down and enjoy this celebration, Jimmy in his morning coat, so fine and full of hope, the bride a clone of his stepmother, there's a switch, and all these thousands of dollars' worth of white roses and tuberoses and lilies and ferns? Not to mention the hairdos and dresses and Italian shoes. In the heart of the heart of the oldest society west of the Appalachians. Not to mention the elegant cakes. The best thing about weddings is still the cakes. No, the best thing is Jack's taking that girl home.

Jennifer came and stood beside her. Sarah took her arm and cradled it. "This is the nicest day of my life, Jennifer. We went through all of the confusions of Jimmy's life to come to this and I give you credit for it. You were the deciding factor. You really were."

Jennifer turned to her with real pleasure at being praised. "Well, the bride is my cousin. I guess I'll take credit for that. I'll admit I pushed it."

*   *   *

"Have champagne with us, Mother," Jimmy held out a glass to her. She had never seen him so happy. He had achieved at last the thing he truly longed for. Status in the community where his father lived. He had married a pretty girl with a fortune. He had his law degree. He had a job. He had a future that could not be challenged.

"I love you, darling," she said, and took the glass he offered her and leaned into the caress of his hand on her arm. In that moment Sarah doubted everything she believed. If Jimmy could love her, all would be well. Maybe that movie will embarrass him, she thought, and her happiness went away. Maybe not, maybe he'll be proud of me. If it wins an Academy Award he will be proud.

The bride came to her side. Sarah was in between her son and his bride, with her genetic future somewhere underneath that lace bridal dress. Someone handed her another glass of champagne. She drank it. She drank six or seven glasses of champagne. She reverted twenty-five or thirty years. She started having fun. She danced with several men. She danced with her son. She drank more champagne. The bride disappeared and reappeared wearing a traveling suit. The bride and groom left the party in a shower of rice and good wishes.

"What time is it?" Sarah asked a groomsman.

"Two forty-five," he said.

"Oh, damn," Sarah said. "I guess I've missed the plane."

Jack came into the room and found her. He took her arm. He had made a mental list. One, two, three. He knew what he was going to do and now he did it.

"Can you leave now?"

"I've missed my plane."

"Good. Then I won't have to get on it with you. Let's go."

"I need to tell Jennifer I'm leaving."

"She'll know you're gone." He led her out of the reception room and down the carpeted hall to the front door of the country club and they went out in the parking lot and got into his car.

"Are you staying at Tim's?"

"In the guest house."

"Let's go get your things."

"Okay. I think I'm drunk, Jack. I'm very near if not fairly drunk."

"We're going to be together, Sarah. I won't spend the rest of my life like I've spent the past."

"Where are we going?"

"I don't know. Let's go get your things."

They collected her bag from the guest house and then they drove to a hotel in downtown Nashville and checked in and went up on an elevator and got into bed and made love and went to sleep.

At nine they woke and brushed their teeth with Sarah's toothbrush and dressed in hotel robes and ordered dinner from the room service menu. Sarah ordered a bacon, lettuce and tomato sandwich and a Coke and Jack ordered a steak and baked potato and a salad. They got back into the bed and turned off the lights.

"How do you feel?" he asked.

"Terrible, wonderful, I have a headache. What do you have for that?"

"Nothing with me. I'll go down and get you something."

"We could order it."

"No, it's faster if I go." He was already out of bed and pulling on his clothes. He took the room key from the bedside table and went out the door.

Sarah sat up and decided not to think. Then she went into the bathroom and washed all the makeup off her face and brushed her teeth again. Then she opened her cosmetic kit and put on some new makeup, not much, just enough to make herself feel better. Then she combed her hair and curled several pieces with the comb. Won't think, she decided. Nothing to think about.

There was a knock on the door. Sarah tied a robe around her waist and let the room service waiter in. The young man rolled a table into the room. "Where do you want this?" he asked.

"By the window will be fine."

Jack came in the half-open door. The waiter finished his work and moved toward the door. Jack gave him five dollars and he left. Then Jack went to the table and poured a glass of water and handed Sarah three aspirins. "Here, take these. I'll give you a Fiorinal in the morning if you still feel bad. These will cure the headache." She took the pills and swallowed them. They moved to the table and ate dinner.

When they had finished eating they got back into the bed and turned off the lights and the television set and lay in the bed with their bodies wrapped around each other. "We'll have a grandchild," Jack said. "That's all I can think about. The endless DNA, the future, the fate of it, Sarah. Too much mystery, too hard to understand. Nothing to fight. If you fight it, it comes back like the ocean. The first time I saw the Pacific I thought of that. How we think we are in charge. We aren't in charge. Maybe it's God."

"So, now you have decided Jimmy is your son?" She moved nearer to him. "At least we know he's mine. God, he's snotty and sure of himself. I never knew he would be. It's hard when they are skinny little boys to imagine they will ever turn into men."

"I know you won't come live here, Sarah. I've accepted that. I just don't want to let you go. I'm not comfortable with other women. You and Eugenie have had me for too long. Whatever the four of us made together, there hasn't been anything else to equal that. And I'm tired of looking. I won't replace it. I don't want to replace it. I want whatever part of you I can have. I don't say I'll be satisfied with it, but at least I know I want it."

"I hope you didn't hurt that girl. What did you say to her?"

"I told her it was a mistake. I told her I loved you and that I was putting fifteen thousand dollars into a bank account so she would be able to pay off her student loans. She said thank you. Then she said I was a goddamn son of a bitch and she should turn me in for sexual abuse but she wouldn't because she was too nice."

"Do we need to talk about anything?"

"No. I just need you here when I wake up in the morning."

CHAPTER 38

Sarah stayed in Nashville for ten days before she flew back to Paris. She went to lunch with the bride's mother. She went to lunch with the woman engineer she had known at Vanderbilt. She drove up to the farm and made a list of furniture to buy. She called the shop in Paris and told them to save the blue sofa.

"I have to go back to the film," she said, finally, on the eighth day. She and Jack were in his living room. It was late afternoon. It was time to talk. Not that they had ignored the future. Just that they had never finished a conversation about it.

"I know. I wish I could go with you. I can come next month, not for long, but for a week at least."

"Then I have to be in New York for a while. You could come on the weekends."

"I'll try. I know you have to go on with your life. I know that, Sarah. I've told myself that every day. I won't pretend I like it, but I won't complain about it either." He got up and went to the bookshelves and began to read the titles. "We'll figure it out. We'll see what happens." He took down a book.

"What did you find?"

"Sartre. I never could get into that. Gobbledygook."

"You're in it now."

"In what?"

"An existentialist gamble. Seize the day. Still the best philosophy for the short haul. The French use it as an excuse to drink, however."

"I'll use it as an excuse to go out to dinner. I'm starving. Get your jacket. Let's get out of here."

"But not out of the conversation. We have to talk about where we will be. I don't want to come back and find you shacked up with another nurse."

"If it made you jealous it was worth it."

"It made me jealous. It still could." She got up and went to him and began to move her hands across his shoulders. She caressed and claimed him. Cynicism, intellect, space and time dissolved. "Thank God," she said. "Thank God I love you."

"Next year I'll be here for a long time," Sarah promised, later, when they were seated in the restaurant and had ordered drinks. "I'll stay at the farm and write a book and see you in the evenings."

"You could stay at my house. It's quiet there. Tell me what you want, Sarah. What you expect of me."

"I know I can't have both worlds. I can't have my career as I have had it and also be fair to you. I know that. It's what we have to talk about. You can't change your life and I can't abandon mine and we can't keep each other around like insurance for our old age. I don't know. I think about it constantly and all I can come up with is that we can live in the present. In tonight. Next month when you come to Paris. Holidays together. It will take a huge fierce trust, but we have that. We have always had that together." She stopped, looked for a long time into the reflection of a candle in a spoon. "We'll do what we can and we'll get mad at each other and we'll misunderstand and be misunderstood. Sounds like a marriage, doesn't it?" She laughed then and he joined her and they kept on laughing.

Before she left Nashville Sarah went alone to the cemetery and stood for a while beside Eugenie's grave and Elise's grave. She decided there was nothing new to be learned from their deaths. Maybe human existence was all luck after all, some fortunate turning of the earth's magnetic core. Fortune, the blind goddess, whimsical, uncaring, although, she, Sarah, was still allowed to be lucky.

On the day Sarah visited the graves, Jack was attending a different death. The bedside of an eighty-eight-year-old family friend. The man had died of congestive heart failure. The room was filled with his sons and grandsons. His widow was in an adjoining room surrounded by the women in the family. The dead man had been a Vanderbilt baseball player in Jack's father's time. His wide, strong shoulders and arms seemed untouched by age or death. The wide, strong forehead, the handsome, freckled face, the high cheekbones, the wide, elegant hands on the white bedspread. Two weeks before, Jack had signed a release so the man could leave the hospital and go home to die. Now he was dead. This is how we end, Jack knew, as he sat beside the deathbed with the family. This is it. If I gave up Sarah I would give up every hope of having part of my life be pure and clear, would never have real understanding with a woman. You cannot manufacture that at any age. Cannot find it in a trophy wife or young woman no matter how smart they seem or how much they adore you. They can't know you. Only a woman who has shared your world *in your time* can know what is being said behind the words. But it isn't age. It's Sarah herself at any age. She knows the world is funny. It is funny. It's hilarious. Death is hilarious. Take it all away from us, you say? Every single thing, our memory, beauty, heartbeat? Take every single thing? Never lie beside a woman holding her rib cage in our hands? Never breathe?

"He was a beautiful man," Jack said to the oldest son, who was sitting beside him. "He died as he wished, with all of you around him."

"Without a whimper," the son said and began to weep. "We won't see his like again."

"I have to leave now." Jack took the man's hand and held it. "His courage has helped me, Peter. It made me see the worth of something I almost let get away from me. I have to go now and act on that." Jack told the family goodbye and left the house. On his way out he met the men coming to take the body to the mortuary.

Driving back into town he wanted to stop at a jeweler's and buy Sarah something made of jewels. But in the end he couldn't decide which exit led to stores. I'll do that when I get back to Paris, he decided. I'll go back to that place in that building where they had the ties. The thought satisfied him and he imagined himself on the boulevard St.-Germain buying a jeweled bracelet from a Frenchman.

Before Sarah left, Jimmy and his bride returned from Acapulco and spent a night in Nashville. Sarah went to dinner with them alone, as Jack was on call. They were very silly and in love. As Sarah listened to their honeymoon stories, she relinquished Jimmy as she had never done before, to this well-mannered girl he dreamed would help him mend his past. They must take back their childhoods and remake them into what they wish they had been, Sarah knew. The girl needs excitement, which she lacks, and Jimmy needs a confining order and a woman who will not change. Fate be kind to them, she prayed. Fate shine down on them and keep them safe.

On the day she left, Jack took off early and drove her to the airport. This time their parting was not sad. "I know it's going to be complicated," he said. "As soon as I go home and you aren't there, I'll start thinking both of us are crazy."

"Do you want me to call you from the plane?"

"No. I want you to get finished with the movie. I'll be there in three or four weeks. Be waiting for me." He took her hand. She was wearing the ring he had given her. It was the first time she had worn it since she had been in Nashville. He took it as a sign. "I'm going to buy you some more rings," he said and laughed. "I started to buy you one the other day."

"Oh, God, don't buy me jewels," she said, but she was completely enchanted by the idea, standing by the security check where she must leave him. "Or buy me some. Go ahead. Get me some emeralds and sapphires and rubies. Don't forget the rubies." She kissed him and threw her bag on the security X-ray machine and kissed him again and left. He stood watching her until she was out of sight.

*   *   *

On the plane flying back to Paris Sarah decided to stop making decisions about her life. I do not have to know the future, she decided. I am an observer. A girl from Tyler, Kentucky, who dreamed of going out into the world and knowing poets and writers and people at *Time* magazine. Whatever a child dreams they will end up doing, if they can. If the dream is big enough and they dream it long and hard. So what if the dreamscape seldom resembles the place they dreamed of going. I didn't even know about Paris and I wouldn't have wanted to miss that. I would have wanted to know Paris in any age.

So I am on my way there again but no longer under the illusion that I'm free. I'm held to the past by tentacles as strong as mountains. Held forever where Jimmy is and his baby, held by Jack, not bound but held. I can't let go of that. I can't pretend I can leave a thing behind.

So I'll pretend I'm going to have it all. Every sweet drop I can squeeze out of the world and why the hell not? I'm not doing any harm. Trying to amuse people with a film. Maybe actually try to write a book that's clean and true, that passes on some things I've learned. Downside, now I have to add Jack to the list of people who will be embarrassed by what I write.

The stewardess came by offering drinks. Sarah ordered a Virgin Mary and sipped it while she fell asleep.

CHAPTER 39

October. Sarah was standing on the Pont St.-Michel, looking down the boulevard St.-Michel, watching the life on the street. The film was dragging on into November and the rains had come to Paris. Twice she had been forced to buy umbrellas on the street to escape being drenched. If she stayed on the bridge much longer she was going to have to buy umbrella number three. The skies were clouding up to the west.

Sarah watched the clouds. She was counting things. Nine days until Jack came to Paris. Twenty-four days until the blue sofa arrived in Tennessee. God knows how many days until the filming was over. It had lost interest for her. Too many hands in the pot. She had rewritten scenes so many times she had forgotten what they were about. Francie would ask her to rewrite a scene and she would go back to her apartment and type up something. Fifteen thousand dollars a week to be a whore, she counted. It doesn't even bother me that it's a waste. The modern world is mostly about waste for a lucky citizen of the United States of America.

Sarah walked down off of the bridge and down onto one of the beautiful cobbled streets. A thousand years since those stones were laid. Four months until the baby would be born. Nine days until Jack was coming. Ten more years to be pretty. Twenty more years to write. Five blocks to the umbrella shop on the boulevard St.-

Michel where she could buy umbrella number three. I will have an umbrella collection when I am old, she decided. I will be an old matron with a marble stand full of really nice umbrellas.

She kept walking faster as the first fat soft drops of rain began to fall. One fell on her nose and another on her hand and she moved into the shelter of the buildings and began to race the rain to the umbrella shop.

F
GILCHRIS
T

Gilchrist, Ellen,
1935-

Sarah Conley.

DATE			